THUNDER ON THE BATTLEFIELD

VOLUME ONE: SWORD

Thunder on the Battlefield

Volume One: Sword

Edited by James R. Tuck

Copyright © 2013 by James R. Tuck
All rights reserved. No portion of this book may be copied or transmitted in any form, electronic or otherwise, without express written consent of the publisher or author.

Cover art and design: Enggar Adirasa
Cover art in this book copyright © 2013 Enggar Adirasa & Seventh Star Press, LLC.

Editor: James R. Tuck

Published by Seventh Star Press, LLC.

ISBN Number: 978-1-937929-24-4

Seventh Star Press
www.seventhstarpress.com
info@seventhstarpress.com

Publisher's Note:
Thunder on the Battlefield: Sword is a work of fiction. All names, characters, and places are the product of the author's imagination, used in fictitious manner. Any resemblances to actual persons, places, locales, events, etc. are purely coincidental.

Printed in the United States of America

First Edition

Copyright Acknowledgements

G. Jerome Henson: "THE HORDE" (c)2013 by author. Printed with permission of the author

Jay Requard: "PAPER DEMONS" (c)2013 by author. Printed with permission of the author

D.T. Neal: "THE WOLF & THE CROW" (c)2013 by author. Printed with permission of the author

John F. Allen: "FOREST OF SHADOWS" (c)2013 by author. Printed with permission of the author

Marcella Burnard "EMISSARY" (c)2013 by author. Printed with permission of the author

David J. West: "THE DOGS OF WAR" (c)2013 by author. Printed with permission of the author

Alexis A. Hunter: "THE RED HAND" (c)2013 by author. Printed with permission of the author

James R. Tuck "WHERE THE RED BLOSSOMS WEEP" (c)2013 by author. Printed with permission of the author

Loriane Parker: "THIEF OF SOULS" (c)2013 by author. Printed with permission of the author

W. E. Wertenberger: "THE GNAWED BONE" (c)2013 by author. Printed with permission of the author

Stephen Zimmer "ALL THE LANDS, NOWHERE A HOME" (c)2013 by author. Printed with permission of the author

J.S. Veter "THE WITCH OF RYMAL PASS" (c)2013 by author. Printed with permission of the author

DEDICATION:

As are all things I endeavor to accomplish this work is dedicated, first and foremost, to The Missus.
She inspires me to strive across battlefields.

This one is also dedicated to the legacy of Robert E. Howard. A giant among writers, without his blaze of glory would would not be able to find our way in this genre.
Gone, but never forgotten.
You left too soon.
R.I.P.

LIST OF WORKS IN THIS VOLUME AND THE CULPRITS RESPONSIBLE

A WORD FROM THE EDITOR, James R. Tuck..........................1

THE HORDE, G. Jerome Henson...7

PAPER DEMONS, Jay Requard...35

THE WOLF AND THE CROW, D. T. Neal................................83

FOREST OF SHADOWS, John F. Allen..................................109

EMISSARY, Marcella Burnard...139

THE DOGS OF WAR, David J. West....................................189

THE RED HAND, Alexis A. Hunter.....................................213

WHERE THE RED BLOSSOMS WEEP, James R. Tuck.................233

THIEF OF SOULS, Loriane Parker......................................251

THE GNAWED BONE, W. E. Wertenberger...........................283

ALL THE LANDS, NOWHERE A HOME, Stephen Zimmer...323

THE WITCH OF RYMAL PASS, J. S. Veter............................381

A WORD FROM THE EDITOR
(IN TWO PARTS, THIS BEING THE FIRST)

JAMES R. TUCK

It's Frank Frazetta's fault.

This book you hold in your greedy little hands and it's companion (THUNDER ON THE BATTLEFIELD Volume 2: SORCERY which I know you're going to buy also if for no other reason than the completely kickass, two-piece, cover art by Enggar and your OCD, completist nature) are totally Frazetta's fault because he is the reason I discovered Robert E. Howard, Conan, and Sword And Sorcery as a genre.

Bear with me as I explain.

I have always drawn.

Since the early mists of my memory I've been drawing monsters and robots and guys with swords, so when I discovered a book of Frank Frazetta's artwork in my Junior High School library you're damn straight I checked it out immediately and then proceeded to keep it checked out for the rest of the school year.

The book was a revelation, a throatpunch to my preteen brainpan. Inside those pages I found everything I was ever looking for. Monsters unlike anything I'd ever seen, heroes with blood dripping from their swords, eyes glinting with bloodlust and confidence, and women painted lush and lovingly and with very little clothing.

I was never the same.

The images sparked a lightning storm inside my mind and I was fascinated.

Within weeks of discovering Frazetta and the power of his artwork I happened to be at the used bookstore with my mother. I'd gotten my love of reading from her and we didn't have much money, so to indulge both our voracious appetites for books she would take me to the local used bookstore where for five dollars you could buy ten to twenty books. My mom went in search of King, Koontz, or Saul while I headed to the science fiction and fantasy section.

There, sitting on a shelf as if it were any other book to be bought, I found CONAN: THE ADVENTURER by Robert E. Howard.

From the 4x6 square surrounded by white a barbarian stared into my young heart with lazer-beam eyes. He stood on a mountain of slain enemies, massive sword thrust into the bodies at his feet just so he could rest his battle-calloused hand on it's hilt. At his booted feet lay a woman, safe in his shadow.

He stared at my soul with sullen eyes brimming with confidence in the strength of his own prowess, challenging me to either man up and fight him or man up and become him.

Oh shit.

It was a Frazetta painting on the front of a book!

I snatched that book so fast I am sure I left behind a skidmark of young James fingerflesh on the dusty, raw-wood shelf that held it. I had no idea what the book was about but if it had Frazetta's artwork on the cover then in my young mind it must be the most totally awesome book ever written ever.

And, by God, twelve-year-old James just might have been right.

(Continued in: THUNDER ON THE BATTLEFIELD Volume 2: SORCERY)

SWORD

THE HORDE

G. JEROME HENSON

The singing of my axe through the flesh of my enemies trembled up my arms, ringing in my bones and shaking my heart. The earth would shake the world would remember, and remnants of the fallen would pave our roads to glory. All men must die, but only the few of us in moments like these could truly live.

"Blood Eagles!" I called to my brothers. The men beside me raised shields and pressed in at the wall of Pale soldiers before us. We redoubled our efforts in a frenzy of blows and savage cries that the enemy expected from those of our race.

And feared.

They hacked and stabbed with spears, but our defense was strong, our wills stronger. Behind us, on the twelfth count after my call, the third rank crouched low as practiced, and the fifth rank of men surged forward as perfected. Their feet hit the shields. The brothers lifted in an explosion of effort, and three score warriors sailed over the front line.

The Blood Eagles' talons tore and warded. Serrated greaves and hooks blunted spear thrusts, ripping blue eyes from sockets. The Blood Eagles' wings were sharp feathers of steel. Bladed bucklers at their arms turned away swords and slashed through the throats of heads upturned in surprise.

We were thunder roaring in the still of the night. We were lightning scouring through the green of leaves.

We were the Horde.

* * *

I remember the march of Fate. The long road to war.

Perhaps twenty years ago, as the Pale measure it, a man walked into the circle of Karuta, my village, my clan. He called out in strange words to us, plunged his sword into the earth, and waited. The great blade was taller than I was in that time. Its razor edge was twice the width of a man's fist, etched with strange runes, and the pommel was crowned with a bright blue gem the color of the sky, the color of the man's eyes.

A small one, Uisa, I think, was frightened by the spectacle of the man and ran away to summon the warriors from their lodge. The youths like myself were curious and unafraid and gathered laughing since there was only one stranger among us and our warriors were many.

I remember that the mighty and wise Majok Twosticks was there, our champion and chief. Wind-That-Kills could be felt watching from the shadows though he could not be seen. He was legend because he could never been seen.

The stranger's fair skin, white like the clouds, we took as a weakness since we of the People have skin that only pales to such a hue when touched by sickness or at a great loss of blood. His armor, too, was bleached, a shining beacon in the morning sun. It was strange and bulky, not the supple leather and cured folds of hide that protected our warriors and scouts. It was more like layers of pottery, the baked and polished clay that Nassaga still uses to store his powders, except white and unmarked by rune or design.

The stranger called out again and though I did not understand his words, Majok did. He called again and again, pointing to the warriors and to Majok, gibbering away with his nonsense. I listened closely and watched, finally his thick-tongued half words took meaning in my mind.

"Doomed!" he yelled. "Bring me your doomed!"

As he called to us, he tapped the blade of his sword and smiled as if it were some child's game to trespass our lands and make taunts at our warriors. Muro, I remember his name only because of this day, asked that he be allowed to take the madman's challenge and silence the fool forever. Majok nodded after the stranger spat onto the ground near Muro, obviously understanding the young warrior's desire, if not his words.

Muro took-up his long axe and rushed the man, throwing a mighty blow, chopping down toward his head with a great whoosh of air. The stranger's blade came up swiftly, deflecting the axe high, but slipped free in a smooth turn to cleave through Muro's hide armor in passing as if it wasn't there at all. Muro collapsed, and though I had seen many men die before, his death I remember well. His legs twitched behind him, his bladder loosed, the gash high across his back peeled open, and he coughed bright red blood onto the ground. He had not the strength to reach his blade, spine severed and bleeding to death before our eyes. The stranger pushed the axe into Muro's hand, and they made eye contact then, one warrior to the next. Then the great sword pierced Muro's back and freed him from the agony.

Muro First-to-Fall is known in our legends.

The stranger turned back to the warriors and the champion and simply spoke the word again: "Doomed." A

THE HORDE

gesture of his hand challenged them all.

* * *

The Blood Eagles broke the enemy spirit as easily as we broke their lines.

A full garrison of soldiers had been sent to halt half a garrison of us savages. They didn't wait for our forces at the river crossing as their war strategies preached, but came to us at a place of our choosing. They, the learned men of steel and houses of stone, came at us unbridled, in mindless fury and proud of their winnings in the last war of the Pale against the Pale. What they forgot was that so many of the People had served in that war. Many of our blood had earned the victories of their Sapphire King.

"Allow them to flee!" I commanded my troops.

My main line was strong, an unbreakable wall, and the Blood Eagles had turned the slow advance of my more skillful and disciplined force into a sudden rout. Chaos erupted among the enemy, their leaders in the rear slain easily as these men of rank had more practice at sand tables and fantasies of war than they had with sword in hand and life hanging on every stroke. My leaping, whirling, brutal shock troopers slaughtered them swiftly like lambs caught within a pen.

I didn't bother to call upon my archers left unused, hidden, flanking the enemy to the right and left. I did not allow the second of my small armies to advance into the fray, keeping their numbers hidden as well as the color of their skins.

"Allow them to flee, those few," I continued. "They carry word of a savage horde of brutish outlanders ready and eager to die. They speak of men flying like birds with spells and sorcery!"

My men chuckled, knowing the many weeks of training that went into the magic of the Blood Eagle's flight.

"Their leaders will be furious. They will disbelieve every word and think that poor leadership led their men to defeat and doom. In part they are right. But they will be equally as foolish when they try to crush our advance swiftly, recklessly, lest we few savages appear to give them pause."

Once the many men would have roared their defiance. The forest would have shook with savage glee and the voices of my thousand men.

But not this day. Our discipline was steel. Fists and blades were held up to the heart, but their battle cries echoed only in the souls of the ancestors watching us with pride.

The enemy would not know our true numbers and true

THE HORDE

strength until it was much, much too late.

* * *

A dozen warriors had charged that single stranger invading our circle. In an instant, three of them were defeated by one stroke of his blade. Blood flew through the air along with sundered weapons, bits of flesh and whole limbs. He battled and hacked and slashed and dodged through the churning mass of blades that sought him out.

Yes, our warriors wounded him, cut him countless times, but the man continued to move and turn and twist and parry. He left no still moment for a blade to deeply score his flesh. The blows that rained against him with sharp and cleaving blades, blades that veterans used to slay foes and sever heads, were dulled against the might of his armor coming as staves and threshers of wheat against him. Whenever a space opened, he charged through to bash another man from his feet like a bull smashing through milkmaids, and dashed again into the fray, scattering the warriors there who were poised to pursue him.

The clamor of the battle rang out over the settlement and into the woods, the hills passing the sound back and forth between them like children tossing a gourd. The sound steel clashing with steel. His armor was not in plates of hardened earth, but of metal painted white. At the noise, our scouts came from their lookouts and joined the circle of warriors waiting to do battle. Many warriors were wounded, grievous enough to take them from the fight but well enough to someday heal and make war again. Seven who fell would never rise again.

The stranger swung his sword in an arc, clearing a path around him. He spun and spun and suddenly charged through the ring of men fighting him. He stopped with his back to a tree, breathing hard and bleeding but reveling in the glow of battle lust. He called out in our tongue again. He remembered a learned phrase, a trained phrase, and the time had come for him to mouth the words.

"You are brave and strong but doomed. We can make you mighty!"

A dozen armored men marched from the woods behind him. If one man could not be killed by our warriors, how could we face a dozen of them? This thought filled the minds of each man there, and each child.

Majok laughed then and walked over to grasp the man's arm in the bond of brothers. He spoke for us all to hear. "You are the best of your men, and these others could not stand as you stood." Majok pulled his arm, causing the breathless man to stagger. "*I* am the best of our warriors, and you could not stand so against my sword. My blade *does not* touch steel when flesh is its target."

The blue-eyed man grinned blankly, a bloody lip coloring his large teeth pink as the sunset.

A smaller man holding aloft a light gray banner with a blue star-burst stepped up. He spoke to the strange warrior, translating Majok's words.

The warrior spoke to the banner man who gave those words to Majok in our tongue. "Your strength is known to us. We come to you with the gifts of brotherhood, new blades, and the skin of steel."

Majok conferred with them long, and many words passed between the three. By the time of sunset upon the circle of Karuta, we had a feast in full roar to celebrate the joining of our warriors to the banner of the Sapphire Keep.

* * *

My army crossed the bridge into the expanded realm of the Sapphire King. This land had once been the place of freemen, farmers who worked the soil and waged no war. Their way was strange to us, and we avoided them, but their way was not without honor.

The land between the rivers was fertile, a region called the Fording. The rivers were too small for great stores of fish as near the ocean shore, and the flat, almost treeless land was too sparse to provide for great hunting. Especially considering the numbers of the pale folk who lived there. But the earth itself gave to them. They farmed a great abundance of crops and labored enough to sometimes grow wealthy in the ways of the Pale, trading or selling their excess in markets for other goods.

Beyond the bridge was no longer the Fording, but the realm of the mountain lords. The former Stone Kings. I had walked this very road, joining it from the south, when the young men of Karuta were sent forth to train with their new Pale lord in the Sapphire Keep. Sent as tribute, as fodder for the turning wheel of their war machine.

I could not see it yet, but after the next day's march, the gray walls would become clear.

I remembered my first sight of stones piled high enough to look down upon the trees. Stone perfectly flat, smooth, unclimbable. Beyond the great walls were towers that seemed to reach into the clouds.

These pale people with eyes the color of gems, I had thought. They have magic beyond any we could fathom.

Today I laugh at such thoughts, but then there was

THE HORDE

only awe.

* * *

I don't know the age, but I was less than fifteen when I walked within the walls of the Sapphire Keep. Up close, the smooth wall of stone was revealed to be carved brick set upon brick. I knew not how to accomplish this feat, but it was only a matter of trial. A wise one could master the task, if there could ever be a reason to attempt it at all. The Keep, with its gleaming cap of shining blue, was not a thing built as high as a mountain, just a grand tower indeed, but set high upon the rising slope of the ridge.

All thought of magic was lost.

I knew the Pale had wizards who could hold glass in hand to light fire in brush or wood without word or gesture. They had rods that moved toward the finest steel, ignoring bronze and lesser alloys of metal. They had talismans enspelled to always know the way home, and black sand that burned ten times as bright and swift as lamp oil. The Pale had many feats of wonder, but their magic was not a thing of spirits and knowing, instead of tricks and clever hands. Only our shamans, like Nassaga, knew the ancestors and the living spirit of the land.

The Pale knew stone. We lived within their walls of stone and flowing water with their men and women and beasts. We ate among them, slept among them, and trained as they trained.

In a wide yard of packed earth, young men gathered to practice their craft at war like our women's circles at weaving. I watched as the men stood in neat lines, sword and shield, right and left. They hacked at each other and danced on clumsy feet while their Master of Swords looked on with approval in his eye.

"Don't lower your shield Lariat," he warned one of his men. "The shield is survival; the last man standing wins the war."

I could not help but laugh.

"You, boy!" the master pointed at me. "You find something funny?"

I wiped the smile from my face. I was a boy by the ways of the People, and he was a man of the folk my chief swore to serve. He could kill me where I stood, sword-less and naked but for a tunic and rough leather upon my feet. He could not catch me if I chose to run, but to run would bring me a hunted death so I stared hate at him. But even if I had the strength in my young body, to fell this man would bring a different kind of wrath down upon my people. The bauble-eyed men were many, and in their numbers was might.

"Answer!"

"I... fight to kill, not to live," I said in their milky foreign tongue. "No battle wins without swords, even with a thousand shields."

The master spat upon the ground and stepped close to me, wrinkling his narrow nose.

I sniffed and only smelled flowers. And oil. His hair was covered in grease that plastered it up and to the side, almost covering his bald place. I spat at the stink of it; too easy for hounds to follow.

He grew angry when I spat as he did. "I am Master Kedric; refer to me as such," he said, poking me in the chest. "Sword in your right hand, shield in your left. That's how we train our soldiers and how I'll train you left-handed savages."

"Two swords better," I said. I did not like his tone and it shone clearly in my eye despite the language barrier.

"Lariat!" he called to the young man standing in the first position. "Teach him the basics."

I ran over to a barrel and pulled out two practice swords. They were more like wooden clubs, but clubs are tools of war and there was no dishonor in that.

Lariat was a head taller than I at the time, and broader through the chest and shoulders from hefting shields and hammering at them with swords. Their way might be poor for battle, but it was good for strengthening arms.

"The rules!" Chakta called from where he watched. This was wise for Chakta was wise, and he was our leader here. Setting the rules made a game of the match, nothing serious, and would tell us when to end it.

"A kill touch, like combat," the master quickly said. "Full speed."

A blunt sword at full battle speed could still break bones or kill, especially when unarmored as I was. But I have always been quick.

I waited for his signal to begin, and I _moved_.

Lariat's sword speared toward my chest. I gently guided it away with my right blade and circled past on the left. I jabbed my free blade underneath his arm, angled to slide through the ribs.

"Kill," I said with little satisfaction.

"No kill!" Lariat denied.

"Lung wound," the master agreed.

The swordsman kept his blade close to home and the shield ready, but I simply advanced as before. I closed, bashing my swords high against his shield while he eagerly blocked. He never saw the foot I pushed into his groin, but he felt it, leaning forward in reflexive surprise rather than

THE HORDE

pain.

As he did I passed left, double slashing my swords against the back of his neck for twin kills. I spun to strike the back of his knees for a maiming of both legs, and managed to shove my left sword up beneath his mail armor, simulating a blade under the ribs and into the heart, for a third kill strike. At the same time I shouldered into his spine to toss him onto his face instead of his knees.

His helmet flopped off his head and I touched a blade to the back of his skull.

"Four ghosts," I said. He was a dead man four times over.

And I was just a boy.

The master spoke swift wet words that I did not understand, but they shamed Lariat. The lesson ended.

When night came, I found myself patrolling the outskirts of their walled city. The Pale men were allowed to walk the walls and the streets to protect the dwellers within from other dwellers within, but we of the People were not trusted to behave properly among such civilized folk.

We do not steal from our neighbors. We do not rob or rape in the dark of night as these men with eyes of gemstones.

I heard noise in the wood around me, but it came from the direction of the gates. Moving into the shadows, I stalked closer to its source. I found four men from the sword class crouching and waiting. They talked amongst themselves with angry words and often their soft sentences ended with a phrase I knew well. "That savage!"

I did not sound my horn for aid, but I did not approach them either. I watched as they stumbled about like toddlers crawling through a tinker's pans. They could not see me in the dark or hear me for their own noise. If they chased, they could not catch me for they knew nothing of the forest surrounding their own homes.

"Karuta," a voiced called from behind. He had used the name of my clan, not knowing my own, but did not call me "savage."

I turned swiftly. I had not noticed a person approach from my rear. A fool I was to watch these other fools so closely! Not far away, protected by the trunk of a tree, was Lariat. His hands were open and pressed to the tree as if in a loose embrace of friendship. Weaponless.

I narrowed my eyes and moved to place the many enemies and this one on the same side of my shield. We were forced to drag shields along on patrol just as the Pale ones.

"Master Kedric sent us here," Lariat said in a whisper. "He suggested you be taught a lesson for shaming me. *Him,* actually." He grimaced in anger as I tried to fathom his words, half a sentence behind. "I *hate* Kedric. He should be whipped for teaching us something so useless. I wish Chakta or one of your fighters was instructing us. You are obviously the better warriors."

"Kedric is of your people. He teaches your way."

"My people are *farmers*." He stared me in the eye as he said it, pride shining. "We sweat over the land and draw life from it to feed ourselves, our wives, our children. We don't make wars and then steal men from their family fields to die in battles we can't win. He is from over these mountains," Lariat gestured beyond the walled city. "I come from the low lands between the rivers."

"You are not one people?" I asked, confused. "One people warring against a different one people?"

"Kedric Bron," he said. "Lariat Melithandre. All foreign names to you, but to me, they speak of very different lines. Like Smiths and Leighs, craftsmen and lords. Hillfolk and Fordlanders."

"Earth workers are strong. Farmers," I said. "From the earth comes everything; all strength. The hunter eats of the hunted, who eat of the green things that eat of the sun and earth. And in death, even the greatest hunter feeds the earth with his blood and bones. This, all men know."

"I'm happy to hear that. But Kedric's teaching is…"

"*Different.*" I held up a hand for him to wait while I stitched together the words. "My people lost in battle against . . . the Pale army. When we first came to this land. Chakta told me so today, when the lesson was over and my brothers slapped my back with joy. We lost because we are strong *men*, great *warriors*. We lost because we are not. . . *soldiers*."

"And you will never be!" Brown eyes moved from the thick undergrowth beside me. Gray eyes, blue, and another pair of brown moved in from their places almost surrounding us.

"Shields together!" Lariat commanded me.

I thought of running away, but pride would not let me. Instead, I drew the short metal blade given to each sentry, allowing the spear to fall to the side. Instantly Lariat's shield pressed close to my left to block a spear thrusting at my side as I prepared for the brown-eyed man rushing in at my right.

In that one instant of battle as Lariat's shield saved my life, I knew the truth and value of the soldier's way of war. I promised to master it.

And I would.

The end of the battle saw two of the four men go down with light wounds, one without use of an arm, and the last fleeing without injury.

At the end of the battle, Lariat and I were bonded

THE HORDE

brothers at arms.

* * *

"Commander!"

I recognized the voice of my Second. The emerald-eyed man led a mixed band of the Pale and warriors of the People, but he was of the People now, as my brother and my friend.

"Lariat, how tastes our dust?"

Lariat laughed heartily as I echoed the complaints of my Third.

Janjin of the Logna Wolves was a great horse lord commanding our cavalry and an accompaniment of swift light infantry. His spearmen could lope for hours keeping pace with the strongest horse. Janjin thought it an insult to follow behind another warrior. In his lands, the leader rode first and never tasted the dusty trail of another man. Even scouts rode on side trails while the leader forged paths anew.

He saw differently now. He first learned to ride second when I beat his best cohort of cavalry with a company raised from among the Pale farmers his Logna Wolves were raiding. After the battle, discussions went long and hard, but it was settled. He would join my banner as Third, but command his own, and I would have it no other way.

"If sheep can be taught to stand against wolf," Janjin had said. "Then the Wolf Star might one day eclipse the Moon."

I smiled at the memory.

"Your dust has the taste of victory in it, my brother." Lariat gave me the salute of his empty fist to heart, then grasped my arm in the brothers' embrace. "All the river lands are free this day, and nothing keeps our army from sweeping through to the Stone Kings' mountain realm but this Sapphire King."

"The Sapphire Keep," I corrected. "The Stone Kings are no more, and I promise that soon the King of Azure Eyes will follow. Only the white *walls* delay us."

"It has been a long journey," he said. "I remember when I stood taller than you, and stronger of arm."

"I remember when magic held up the walls we will soon overrun." I was a finger or two above Lariat in height, now, but with his fold of blonde hair, he looked the taller and much sillier. I learned the ways of the Pale in making war, but I never learned to love their queer faces, and never made the slightest pretense of understanding their fashion. I dealt with them by their custom, but only because their rigidity of mind left them little freedom to understand a different way.

Besides, there were too many of them. To be unbending

and act only in the way of the People would mean teaching so many of the Pale how to deal with us. It was a waste when I could simply learn their customs, their tongue, and communicate in such terms.

And I had done so.

"I only wish Chakta could be here to see this day," I confessed.

"His spirit watches, no?"

"He died without sons or daughters, so his ghost waits in the earth to be born again," I said. "Born again wise and mighty."

"I am glad Kedric did not live to see this day. He would try to claim his *teachings* led us to greatness if the traitor had managed to flee overseas." Lariat spat on the dirt as Kedric was fond of. "The Sapphire King did one thing well in stretching that bastard's neck. Him and those pirate spies."

"Now the King waits, just beyond sight, for the march of Fate to cast him from his high place." I gestured for Lariat to follow me back toward the tent my attendants were erecting. "The king dreamt large, but in the end, he did not dream large enough."

* * *

When these decorated men with colored jewels for eyes first came, they believed us low beasts for their use and tools for their war. But they knew nothing of the old ways, and could thus, truly know nothing of war. We marched through their lands with them as one great clan of sparkling men did battle with another. They hid behind walls of stone as grand as mountains and burned fields beyond to end all forage for food. They thought it clever to starve themselves hoping to starve the enemy. They thought it clever to work a field through long days and seasons, happy that an extra hour of work might bring an extra sheaf of wheat. One less hour of sleep could perhaps become a pumpkin.

I once thought it folly to enslave strong men to dirt and watch them weaken while other men raised arms for war, and leeched away at the efforts of the field slaves and women. I came to see that this was not an error of the farmer, however, but of the men among them who did not sow and did not hunt.

They could not know what they unleashed by showing us the strength of a single man in skin of steel. They could not know the folly of showing great warriors the ways of war in the wider world. A farmer tends his fields all day, but a hunter takes what he needs and stops, for to take too much is to kill the life of the forest and leave only bones for the feasts of tomorrow. The hunter takes what he needs spending a tenth of a day, and has nine tenths left for other things. For training. Forging and becoming weapons of war. A hunter's son hunts in the land of his father, using the knowledge of his grandfather, and the ancestors before him. A farmer's son, to stand as his father, must find new lands to make his own, traveling far, wide, thinning the blood and loyalty. He forgets the face of his grandfathers, losing his place in time and the blessings of the ancestors.

Majok Twosticks saw the strength of their Pale way, with the weakness excised. He saw the future of the People with our vulnerabilities armored over. He gave me, his son, to that dream and sent me out into the coming world in the care of his younger brother.

Senta Shadetaker was sire of Uisenta of Nine, sire of Kupra Longhair, who was sire of Majoc Twosticks and Chakta the Wise: I come from a strong line.

We learned the way of war and steel from them as we served, at my father's command, and brought it home with our injured or the elderly. We birthed new warrior sons at unprecedented levels, swelling our ranks in the homeland while grain and produce from the Fordlanders kept us fed and our traditions of hunting yet unchanged.

I journeyed among the many clans of the People and

forged a strength unrivalled in the known lands of men. For twenty years we grew stronger.

For twenty years we prepared for these very next days.

* * *

At dusk I watched as Lariat galloped toward the walls of the Sapphire Keep with a small band of his Pale men. Close on his tail were warriors of the People, riding poorly and feigning ignorance of horsemanship. Some of the horses were wounded by arrow, and a few of the men were selected from scouts injured on duty or the few Pale men who had stood the line and fought in our recent skirmishes. They dressed so that the wounds appeared recent, the blood fresh, and even new gashes were hacked into the flesh of Pale men who fought among themselves for the honor of the mission.

Arrows streamed down from the high walls, missing Lariat and his men, and coming far too close for comfort of those pursuing. A man spurred his horse to unleash a javelin. The weapon sank into the flank of a horse which immediately tumbled to the ground. The warrior gave a cry of victory as the rider and horse vanished in a cloud of tumbling dust.

It was great acting.

THE HORDE

Then an arrow took him in the throat, silencing his taunts and selling the story of a desperate escape with a sacrificed life.

The pursuers were not of Lariat's band, so none of his men would be seen to mourn that unknown hero. Thomas Wavetoucher was his name, half of the People's blood, and half of Seafolk.

We honor him in legend.

Lariat's men posed as mercenaries, men from the region who sold their skill at arms to merchants and city-states far to the east. On hearing of troubles at home, they journeyed swiftly to be of aid, for no price but honor, and braved the lines of the enemy losing many in the attempt.

Their story was good. And hidden in their gear were flasks of seaflame, a wizardly solution worth its weight in spice.

Two hours before dawn I watched as silver fire bloomed beneath the edge of their main gate. Slingers hidden on close approach rushed forward to hurl their own flasks of seaflame over the wall, onto the battlements, it mattered not where. The substance was said to burn hot enough that would eat away at the salt in sea water or burn away the ashes of a long dead hearth.

That it disabled the gate was one goal, but the sun-bright silver fire blazing beyond the wall stole the night sight of every defender. My men swarmed the walls in disciplined silence, none of the catcalls and battle cries that haunted the dreams of the Pale folk within the walls as we had done on each night and in each battle before.

It was a thing of beauty to see two decades of work come to fulfillment. First the Sapphire Keep, then the baronies of the Hillfolk beyond the mountains would fall. It was glorious to know that the pale folk's way of expanding war and ruin would not be long upon this land.

The great wood and iron gate fell to a sparking storm of fiery motes as dawn shed its light over the scene. My warriors owned the walls as the blinded defenders fell with little effort. The archers within were now firing east, into the light of dawn, making distance and the motion of their targets hard to judge.

I saw Lariat there, on the wall, and he bellowed like a demon. "For the Fording! For the People! For freedom to reap and sow!"

I hefted my axe and strode through the gateway, first of many bringing promise of a new tomorrow. We were a mountain top tumbling into the valley below. We were warriors forged by Fate and flame.

We were the Horde.

THE HORDE

G. Jerome Henson has been a technician for twenty years, an amateur philosopher, and a last generation soldier of the Cold War. He has always enjoyed telling tales, none of them true, and decided to start writing them down. He is a husband, a father of two, and the family are happily living tales of their own.

Contact: gjhenson717@gmail.com

PAPER DEMONS

JAY REQUARD

Lightning ripped through the storm clouds, setting the pouring rain alight in a thousand crystalline shards. Jishnu the Srijati raised his spear and shield, teeth gritted together as he dug both feet into the mud of the narrow rice paddy.

"Get ready!" he commanded his men.

The Grinders lowered their spears atop their bronze shields. Another bolt of lightning creased the sky. At the other end of the rice paddy the two hundred cultists charged. Jishnu sneered at the oncoming enemy, his green eyes wide as the rain passed by the brow of his iron helm, mixing with the sweat on his face, dripping into his vision. The two hundred men smashed into the line of sellswords, battering their shields with clubs and bamboo spears.

"Now," Jishnu shouted.

The Grinders thrust as one. Jishnu yanked his spear back. His victim, a young boy no older than fifteen, fell to his knees with both hands over his pierced chest.

Jishnu stepped atop the body. "Push!"

The thunderous sky drummed as the Grinders lurched forward. The front line of cultists slid back, trying to keep them from advancing. Leaning into his shield to absorb the blows of the attackers, Jishnu checked behind him. Only three of his men had been slain in the initial charge, their bodies half-submerged in the muddy water.

The Grinder next to him tripped over a corpse but quickly regained his balance. "How far, Thumbs?"

Jishnu hid behind his shield as the archers on the far bank loosed a small volley of arrows. "A few more feet, Marl."

"Have we gone that far already?" Marl's handsome white features twisted in bemusement. The arrows tapped on the wall of shields, creating a chaotic beat that wove itself into the chorus of dying men. "Well, at least we'll be back in time for breakfast."

"Old Boy will have some of those chicken eggs we stole from that farm yesterday." Jishnu caught a charging cultist in the face. Blood spurted in an arc as the old man fell back in the mass of men pressing against the sellswords, disappearing under their trampling feet and sloshing water. "And a drink as well, I hope. This fighting has drawn a grand thirst out of me."

Marl stabbed down, making sure Jishnu's kill did not

rise again. "A drink would be nice."

Jishnu's knees burned, but the thrill of violence stayed the pain, driving him onto the glory waiting on the other side of the battlefield. "Aye."

Marl peeked over the battered rim of his shield. "You see the sorcerer?"

More cultists pressed in an attempt to reclaim the few inches of ground they had lost. They offered little threat with the crude clubs and bamboo spears they carried, yet their numbers were enough to force the Grinders into a long slog through the gore-colored broth. "Thank Asdra, no," said Jishnu. "Magic is the last thing we need tonight."

"If he's not here then why are they still charging?" asked Frog the Anjpuri, his squat body hidden behind Jishnu's tall frame.

"Fools never know that they're fools." Jishnu thrust in, laughing as he claimed another life. "Keep on, men!"

Another step turned into two, two into three, and on the fourth push the cultists broke in retreat.

"First one to bring me an intact head gets an extra ration tonight," Marl shouted. The Grinders cheered at the challenge, their steps quickening in hopes of winning the prize. Letting his men rush by him, Jishnu halted near the rise of the enemy embankment, body aflame in exhaustion.

"You coming, Thumbs?" Frog called.

"No. I'm done supping on death for today." Jishnu slumped to both knees, holding his body up by his spear alone. The rain sputtered into a light drizzle. He hooked a brown battle-scarred arm around the shaft of his weapon and tore off his helm to free long black hair, letting it fall down to his muscled shoulders. Folding his hands together, he shut his eyes.

"Aum," he intoned, invoking in his mind the image of Asdra. The four-armed deity of warriors and kings, Jishnu hoped his prowess pleased his homeland's king-god.

"Thank you, Asdra," he whispered. "Thank you."

* * *

Marl picked his dirty teeth with a twig. "Look at these idiots."

The wagon rumbled over the rocks of the valley's lone road, shaking its three passengers as they tried to keep from bouncing out of the straw-covered bed.

"You'd think the Shen would know their own roads better," added Snatchbreath, another white soldier from the western nations. Thick patches of healed burns scarred his cheeks, the result of a childhood accident. He dragged a whetstone down the bitten edge of his curved sword, focusing on the wagon's occupants. The rest of the Grinders spread out on the bank of the rice paddy, sleeping off the tremors of last night's battle.

Jishnu raised his head off the grass. He squinted to keep out the bright sunshine beaming from behind the puffy clouds. "Quiet," he barked. "The Captain's here."

A man dressed in an iron cuirass, helm, and greaves hopped off the wagon and landed lightly on his feet. He looked toward the rice paddy. On a far bank a massive pyre burned, black smoke reaching into the blue sky as the pile of cultists smoldered upon it. The three Grinders who had died in the battle remained off to the side, away from the fire, their bodies wrapped in their bedrolls.

The Captain called in his booming voice. "Thumbs."

"Oh, gods preserve us," griped Marl. "You know that's not good."

"Go get the men ready. He's here to move us." Jishnu took up his spear and marched to the Captain. His left knee popped, sending a jolt of pain up his hip. He stopped before his superior. "Captain," he greeted with a slight wince, banging his fist against his chest.

"Morning, Thumbs. Hope your knees aren't bothering you." An older man, the officer's greying hair spilled out from under the confines of his helm, forming a dingy collar around his neck. A pair of bright blue eyes flashed with envy at the battlefield. "Wish I could've been here last night. Looks like you had a grand run of it."

"Most of the cultists were farmers. I doubt the Golden Dragon has many soldiers among his ranks."

"Did you get a look at him?"

Jishnu rested his spear against his shoulder. "No sir."

The Captain's brow furrowed. "No?"

"In all honesty, Captain, I don't think he was ever here."

The Captain's face reddened. "Qui Lin," he shouted. "Qui Lin, get over here!"

One of the two passengers in the wagon scurried off the bed, nearly tripping over the hem of his bright azure robe. He laughed at his stumble, waving off any offers of help. "No, no," he said.

"Has he been smoking those damned seeds on the way here?" asked Jishnu, his voice low.

"Like a chimney," The Captain whispered. "Qui Lin, why did you send us here?" he questioned when the official made it into earshot.

A scholar in his late thirties, the thin-faced man with high cheekbones and stern eyes gave the pair of foreigners a quizzical expression. He tugged on the ends of his long mustache. "Whatever do you mean, good captain?"

"Tell him, Thumbs."

"Thumbs?" Qui Lin asked, even more puzzled. "Why do they call you such a name?" His reddened eyes roamed over the Jishnu's form until they settled on his right hand. At the first knuckle on the Srijati's thumb grew another hooked finger, thinner and more twisted than his natural digit.

"It is not a name you have permission to speak," Jishnu warned, his dry lips parting in a snarl. He balled his right hand into a tight fist. "The Golden Dragon wasn't here like you said he would be."

"Really?" Qui Lin raised his thin eyebrows. "Oh, well."

"Oh, well?" The Captain's hand fell on the pommel of his sword. "I lost three men over this, you idiot."

"I do not know what to say, honored captain," replied Qui Lin, his annoyance clear on his pinched face. "The Jade Emperor's spymasters only told me so much."

"You better get them to tell you more. Or else."

"Or else what? We have a contract," the official reminded.

"And we have a clause to leave that contract," The Captain retorted loudly for all to hear. He smirked to Jishnu. "We are more than happy to march back west—taking whatever we want along the way as payment for our broken deal."

A few of the Grinders snickered, an ominous sound the official understood immediately. "You westerners would ruin the world over the smallest things."

"And don't you forget it," The Captain said, eliciting loud laughter from his men.

Qui Lin slid his hands into the voluminous sleeves of his blue robe. Putting on an insincere smile, he bowed. "Allow me a moment." He puttered back to the wagon where the third man still waited.

"Who is that?" Jishnu asked.

"He wouldn't say." The Captain adjusted his helm, making the red plume shake in the gentle wind blowing through the green valley. "But I'm now guessing that he is one of the Jade Emperor's incompetent spymasters."

After a few minutes of quiet conversation and whispering, Qui Lin returned from the wagon with three pieces of parchment. "Here," he said, his bitterness unhidden. "This is the latest intelligence. Wei-Tzu should be at one of these locations."

The Captain unfolded the three maps. "How long have you had these?"

"That is the Jade Emperor's business."

"Of course it is," The Captain said dismissively. "You

can leave."

Qui Lin scuttled back to the wagon, muttering curses along the way.

"New orders?" asked Jishnu, offering a hand to The Captain.

"Yes," he said, handing him the maps. "Look these over quickly and then get the men ready."

"We're splitting up?"

"Aye. Let me go talk to these damned bureaucrats and see if I can get any more from them."

"Yes sir." Jishnu walked back to the embankment.

Marl met him, dressed and ready to move. "Are we leaving?"

"We are." Jishnu studied the map in his hands, taking time to translate the delicate calligraphy etched at the borders of the small rectangle of paper. "The Captain's trying to get us more information."

"All the good that did here." Marl motioned at the rice paddy. Pools of blood collected around the shoots of rice growing out of the water.

"It's the job." Jishnu let his tired star linger on the battlefield. "Get the men lined up."

"What do you want done with our dead?"

Jishnu hung his head in exhaustion. "Who fell?"

Marl soured at the question. "Um, I think it was Fats, Curry, and One-Tooth."

"Curry?" Jishnu glanced to the bodies on the ridge, trying to figure out which one was his friend, now wrapped up in his brown woolen blanket. "He was from Srijan."

"You two were from the same kingdom in Sutia? I didn't know that."

"Aye," said Jishnu, his sullen eyes glazed in sadness. "His father hunted tigers with mine."

"I told him not to buy one of those stupid paper talismans at that temple. All the good that did." Marl shut his eyes and swallowed his grief. "Sorry, Thumbs."

"It's the job," he whispered. "Just make sure they're buried before we leave."

The Grinders dragged themselves to their feet. Rubbing their eyes as they put on their wet leather armor and black helms, the thirty-seven survivors formed a single line, roughhousing with each other to wake from their restless sleep.

Jishnu strode down the line. "To me! Shed the blood, save my brothers."

"Shed the blood, save my brothers," they repeated, rousing into wakefulness.

The Captain arrived moments later, his mouth set in a grim line. "All right, Grinders," he barked, "We are still hunting the fugitive sorcerer known as Wei-Tzu, known to his followers as the 'Golden Dragon' or whatever silly Shen title he has given himself. As you all know, our target was not at the battle last night."

"No shit," grumbled Frog from his place in the line.

A few of the others laughed, and even their grim Captain found it hard to contain his mirth. "Either way our good employer, Ator save him, has sent us three new targets where the bastard might be. I'm sending out three units of five to capture Wei-Tzu. The Emperor wants him alive for a demonstration, so no bringing back just the head. There are three towns along the Qua River, one for each team. Thumbs will take one, Wood will take another, and Lucky will take the last unit. The rest of you are coming with me to make sure these Shen don't get to thinking they do not need us."

"We will find him, Captain." Jishnu snapped his fist to his chest. The Grinders mimicked his salute.

"Shed the blood, save my brothers," The Captain said, reciting his company's time-honored motto.

"Shed the blood, save my brothers," they repeated before breaking off into their units.

* * *

Five cranes flew to the southeast, wings flapping in steady synchronicity. As they ascended to meet the low-hanging clouds, two of the flyers dove into the valley's misty trench, vanishing in the forests of bamboo and grey-barked pines. Jishnu waited for them to rise, yet they did not, leaving him wondering what had befallen those birds.

"Anything ahead, Thumbs?" asked Marl.

Jishnu glanced back at his unit as he rounded the goat path. Marl took up rear of the five-man column, behind Frog the Anjpuri, who followed Behnam the Dager, a humorless man whose past stayed hidden behind a dark brown mask of cold emotion. Snatchbreath marched behind Jishnu, watching the same birds disappear off in the distance.

"If the map is right, we are not far from this town." Jishnu pointed off to his right at the valley's opposite slope. "Lucky and his boys should be over that way, still a day from their target. Wood shouldn't be far behind."

"If he isn't giving that girl we saw back in the last town another run of 'wood'," Frog said with a crass chuckle.

They made their way down the trench, entering the dense woods. Hacking a path through the overgrowth of tall bamboo with their swords, the Qua River came into view, a long vein of blue cutting its way to the northeast. Jishnu knew if he followed the river, past the towns and past the jungles, he would find the glittering cities known as the Five Divine Lords, where the Jade Emperor ruled from his majestic fortress on the coast.

Frog spoke. "Jishnu, look."

Across the shallow waters a group of ten men dressed in rags and bits of armor walked on a trail above the river, their spears and bows rested on their shoulders.

Jishnu raised a closed fist, silently ordering his men to halt. They crouched in the reeds.

Marl crawled beside him. "There's too many of them for a simple hunting party."

"They're heading back to the village." Jishnu opened his hand, signaling the Grinders onward. Trailing the cultists for many miles, they followed the valley as it sloped deeper with the Qua River, ending at a sprawling lake which mirrored the overcast sky. On the north bank sat a small village surrounded by tents, making it seem more like the headquarters for an army than a tranquil settlement of fishermen and farmers.

Frog whistled a sharp note. "What does that look like to you, Marl?"

"It looks like a base, my ugly little toad," Marl replied. "Think we've found our 'Golden Dragon', Thumbs?"

Jishnu rubbed his aching knee, not taking his eyes off

the town. "We need to do this carefully. Behnam."

Behnam the Dager looked him right in the eyes, his face devoid of emotion.

"I want the entire town scouted, understand?" Jishnu pointed at a small hill overlooking the village from the northwest. "We'll be there. Meet us at midnight."

"I understand," Behnam said in his whispery voice. He left behind his spear and shield as he slipped into the river, swimming until he broke the surface many yards down from the Grinders' position. The remaining four removed themselves from the riverbank, disappearing into the forest like malevolent ghosts, hungry for the night's work.

* * *

Jishnu lay on his back in the grass and studied the starry sky. He wrapped his fingers around his deformed thumb, an anxious habit, as he and the rest of the unit waited for Behnam to return. Posted on the hill above of the cultists encampment, hundreds of lanterns danced below, a moving carpet of warm red lights against the cold purity of the heavens above.

"Think he's dead?" asked Marl. He lay next to Jishnu, his battered helm on his stomach.

"He's not dead."

"Oh, he could be," said Frog, who lay next to Marl. "Remember when Behnam wrecked that house full of insurrectionists back in Dageria? He didn't come out for a good long time."

"He was in there butchering them." Jishnu pursed his lips into a grim frown and scratched his bearded cheek. "He really hates his own people."

"He hates everyone." Snatchbreath sat at the apex of the hill, searching the darkness for their fifth member. "And you two always think everyone is dead," he told Marl and Frog.

"It's the job," both said in unison.

"Any sign of him?" Jishnu asked Snatchbreath.

A cool voice spoke from the darkness. "I'm right here." Behnam materialized from the shadows.

Jishnu offered Behnam his spear and shield. "Report."

"There are five hundred men, a hundred or more women and handfuls of children. They are moderately armed, better than what we dealt with a few days ago, and they have enough food for this to be a permanent base. There are enough shrines and decorations around for me to think the Golden Dragon is here."

"The Shen do love their shrines." Marl pulled on the

ties of his armor, tightening the cuirass to his body. "Did you see him? Did you see Wei-Tzu?"

"I think so." Behnam put on his helm. "There is a large house in the middle of the town which is heaped with treasure and offerings. Only one person is in it, dressed very well for a villager."

"That's him. Leave your spears." Jishnu started down the hill, his sword drawn. "Take point, Behnam."

The five snuck to the western edge of the town. Behnam led them into a narrow alley between two small homes.

Halting at the mouth of the alley, Behnam motioned for Jishnu. "There." Across the path stood a grand house, its carved lintel depicting a sinuous dragon wreathed in fire, accented in flares of gold flakes and cinnabar paint. Two men with short spears and wicker shields guarded the black door, straw hats obscuring their faces as they dozed on stools. Clouds drifted in, bringing with them a rolling thunder followed by a rain shower, a constant occurrence in Shen's balmy summers.

"Perfect timing." Jishnu patted Behnam on the shoulder. "Are those the only guards?"

"No others. The rest of the soldiers are in their tents, and the streets remain clear most of the day. Only the villagers live in these houses."

Jishnu paused when a soft wind blew through the alley, raising the hair on the back of his neck. "Are you sure?"

Behnam's constant scowl deepened. "I know what I have seen."

Marl crept up from behind. "Are we going?"

Jishnu glared back at him. "Hold on. Behnam, are you sure there's no one else guarding this house?"

"I checked the entire village," Behnam repeated. "You're in charge, Jishnu. You make the call."

Jishnu thumbed the edge of his sword, lost in a moment of thoughtful planning. "Behnam, you wait here with Snatchbreath. Marl, Frog, and I will go around the back and sneak in. Count to ninety and take care of those guards. First one to grab Wei-Tzu should head back to the hill immediately. Anyone who gets separated should meet at the mouth of the Qua River at sunrise, understood?"

The other four nodded, the points of their crested helms bobbing in agreement. "Shed the blood, save my brothers," they whispered.

"Shed the blood, save my brothers," Jishnu repeated.

The Grinders parted. Jishnu and his two cohorts broke right, then right again, ending up on the road between their original position and the house. They let the booming thunder cover their squelching steps, nearly crawling in the flooded patches of grass and dirt. They reached the rear of the house, found it unguarded, and climbed through one of the open windows.

The rain pounded the shingled roof, vibrating the paneled walls in the peaceful silence of the dark room. A pallet surrounded by thirty small oil laps rested in the center of the polished wooden floor. There slept a woman wrapped in a white silk robe embroidered with swirls of gold, tied shut by a wide sash of blue cotton wound in strands of dark green jade. Long unkempt hair gathered in a glossy black pool upon her pillow.

"That is Wei-Tzu?" asked Marl, his uncertainty visible even behind the high cheek guards of his helm.

"The Golden Dragon is a girl," Frog whispered in surprise.

Jishnu stepped over the ring of lamps, his finger on his lips. He scanned the room, mentally counting until he reached ninety, and right on cue Behnam and Snatchbreath entered, their bloody swords glinting in the dim lamplight. The Grinders edged toward their prey.

A sudden light flashed, and when their vision cleared the paneled walls had fallen, revealing men swaddled in black clothing surrounding the house. Their long spears lowered as another group burst through the front door with

PAPER DEMONS

bows drawn.

"Circle," Jishnu shouted. His men fell into a tight perimeter around Wei-Tzu. With his shield forward and sword up to attack, the Srijati growled like a tiger, coiled in anticipation for the fight. He did not hear Marl's body thump on the ground near his feet until a small prick of pain blossomed on the back of his thigh. He turned to find his four brothers sprawled in the ring of lamps.

Wei-Tzu had awoken, her bare shoulders slipped out of the confines of her luxurious raiment. Her seductive smile mocked Jishnu. She wiggled pale fingers in a small wave.

He blinked once before collapsing.

* * *

Jishnu awoke to the sound of laughter. The sun burned above him in the sky, cloudless save for a few wisps on the edge of his sight. Lurching into a sitting position, he covered his eyes as an ache pounded his skull.

"Oh good, one is awake," said a female voice. The armed cultists surrounding the five Grinders roared in laughter.

Jishnu removed his hands and found Behnam beside him, face down in the drying earth before the steps leading up to the grand house. He slapped him hard on the back, eliciting a small groan. The other three Grinders awoke as well. Their swords stood in the mud next to them.

"Look, they're all up now," mocked Wei-Tzu, skipping around the five men. "The big bad westerners have come to get me!" The folds of her white robe swayed with her movement, revealing a peek of her bare legs, smooth like ivory. The sorceress stopped in front of Jishnu, lips puckered in a small kiss. "You're all so cute when angered, you foreigners. We could all laugh at this, but no, you are too busy worrying about what I will do next."

Jishnu bared a dangerous smile. "Who says I'm not laughing?"

Wei-Tzu tilted her head to the side and lowered to his eye level, bird-like in her movement. "Depends on what you find so funny about this situation."

"I'm laughing at you," said Jishnu.

"Why?"

Frog sat up, pawing at his balding head for wounds. "Because we're going to kill all of you one day."

"Oh, is that so, little one?" she tip-toed over to him. "And how are you going to do that?"

"You haven't killed us yet," Jishnu answered. "That was your first and last mistake."

"Was it now? You're all so unimaginative." Wei-Tzu

pranced around them in a circle. "There's no fun in just slitting your throats. Not for me and definitely not for my men. They want to savor your deaths for the brothers you dirty foreigners took in battle."

The five Grinders stood in unison and retrieved their swords.

"Come on then," goaded Snatchbreath. He waved the cultists in with his hand. "Send me up to Ator's mead hall. I need a drink for this headache."

"But there's no fun in that!" Wei-Tzu threw her hands up in the air. "You need to suffer."

"If you are going to kill us, kill us," Jishnu demanded. "Don't play games."

From her calm expression emerged a sinister smile. "But that's exactly what we're going to do, my dear brown beast."

"What do you mean?" Jishnu asked.

Wei-Tzu raised her hands to the morning sky, arching back to bask in the light. "The Emperor is a cowardly man, the last vestige of abusive lords who have raped Shen for nearly a thousand years. It doesn't matter if it is I or the masters of Heaven who rips him off his throne, it will happen. But why not find joy out of this sorrow, some entertainment out of the endless gray of it all? A transcendent such as I has a sense of fair play."

"You are far from a goddess," Marl snarled.

"So says a fallen man." Wei-Tzu dashed forward, hands held out to Jishnu. "Take me in, if you are so bold."

Jishnu stepped back. "What?"

"I won't run." She pressed her hands against his armored chest. "Take me to the Jade Emperor. I dare you."

"You must be joking," he said.

"No joke at all." Wei-Tzu batted her eyes at him. "My men will let us go. They have no fear for my safety. Why should they? I am the chosen of Heaven."

"I'd take this game," Frog commented with a broken smile. "I'll never turn away an insane fool's foolishness."

Jishnu stared into Wei-Tzu's bright brown pools, finding insanity and hints of a child-like playfulness, disturbed yet steadied by something beyond a sane man's understanding. He slid his blade into its scabbard and took her by both wrists. "We accept."

Wei-Tzu's gentle laughter melted into the amused roar of her men.

* * *

Jishnu shoved the sorceress ahead of him, hand clutched

PAPER DEMONS

on her shoulder. "Get going." He looked back at the cultist encampment. Wei-Tzu's rebels stood at the edge of their patch of civilization, wide smiles on their faces as they leaned upon sharpened bamboo spears, completely at ease with the Grinders carrying off their leader.

Frog put on his recovered helm. "Is this actually happening?"

"I actually think it is," Marl said with a disbelieving smile. "I'm telling The Captain when we get back that we need to kidnap more like her in the future."

Wei-Tzu giggled as she marched, hands neatly folded behind her back.

"What are you on about now?" Jishnu asked.

"One of you will die by the time you can get me over the next hill."

Her pronouncement stopped the five sellswords in their tracks. Jishnu turned back and saw the cultists had not yet followed to reclaim their leader. He prodded her with the wide point of his short sword. "Did you send men ahead?"

"No men," she said, her ever-present confidence mocking him. "Just paper and demons."

Frog dismissed her with a wave. "The little girl is mad, Thumbs. Ignore her."

Jishnu glanced to Marl, who replied with a silent shrug.

"Either way, keep your eyes out. Snatchbreath will take point. Behnam will cover our backs. Frog, you and Marl keep watch on our flanks. I don't want any surprises."

They forced their captive up the gentle incline of a shadowed green knoll, behind which lay the shore of the lake they would follow back to the mouth of the Qua River. Ascending the climb, Jishnu kept his eyes on the tops of the pine trees, expecting hidden enemies to fall from the twisted branches in a shower of green needles and weapons. Once they passed the crest he relaxed.

"See?" said Frog, his hands held out in a triumphant pose, "No more demons here than there are blushing maidens, and there's definitely no damned paper to worry over. She's just crazy."

"Perhaps," Jishnu whispered, his gaze now fixed on Wei-Tzu. He had just reached the conclusion that she was simply a madwoman when Snatchbreath stopped in front of the group.

"Something up there, Snatch?" Marl called.

Snatchbreath slowly spun about to face them. His curved sword fell from his hands and he stared down at his open palms. "Can't you smell it?"

"Smell what?"

"The burning flesh... I..." He screamed, tossing his

arms up as his cry echoed through the valley. Snatchbreath threw himself on the ground and rolled in the dirt.

Jishnu slung Wei-Tzu into Frog's open arms. "Hold her!"

"I'm burning! I'm burning," Snatchbreath wailed as he slapped his body.

"Hold still," begged Jishnu.

"My face." Snatchbreath pushed Jishnu away, sprung to his feet and ran for the lake at a desperate speed, quickly disappearing into the thickets. "I'm burning!"

"Follow him," Jishnu yelled as he gave chase. Charging through the brush, he followed Snatchbreath's cries until they were silenced by a loud splash. He reached the edge of the water. "Rolf," he shouted, using Snatchbreath's true name. "Rolf!"

Bubbles pocked the lake's surface, and a shadow rose, growing until it formed into the shape of a man. The rest of the Grinders came up behind Jishnu, dragging their prisoner along. The corpse broke the water.

Frog gasped. "Look!"

Floating above Snatchbreath's drowned body, a white demon danced in the air, its hands clutched to a small transparent image of a man in armor. The warrior, scarred at the cheeks, opened his mouth in silent terror as the horned demon spun him around. On and on they danced until they faded into the sky.

Jishnu fell to his knees, sinking into the mud of the shore. "Asdra save us."

Wei-Tzu freed herself from Frog's grasp and walked around Jishnu, bending over so they were face to face. "Think me a fool now?" Caressing his bearded cheek, she kissed him on the corner of his mouth.

"How?" he asked in a mixture of awe and horror.

"I never play, foreigner," she whispered into his ear. "And you're about to learn that."

* * *

Jishnu slammed Wei-Tzu into a tree and laid the edge of his iron sword against her pale cheek. "How did you do it?"

"Slam me again." Her head lolled as she licked her pink lips and lifted her right leg up to his hip. "That felt good."

"She's a devil," whispered Frog. He knelt beside the water-logged body of Snatchbreath, hands shaking as he laid the dead Grinder's sword on his chest, a brother-in-arm's final affection to the fallen. "Better gut her now or we all die."

PAPER DEMONS

"Get a hold of yourself, toady," Marl whispered.

Jishnu scraped his sword blade against Wei-Tzu cheek. "I will mar that pretty face if you don't tell me what you did to him," he warned. "How did you summon that demon?"

"Paper." The sorceress blew him a kiss.

"Paper?"

"You really are quite handsome, you know. Perhaps I will tell the demons to spare you so you will be my concubine."

He pulled on his sword. A small line of blood trickled down Wei-Tzu's cheek. A pleasurable moan escaped her lips. "Deeper," she requested in a husky tone.

Jishnu slapped her hard in the face, sending her to the ground. "How did you kill him?" He grabbed her arm and yanked her back to her feet. "Tell me!"

"It isn't a game if I just tell you everything," she yelled back at him. "And killing me won't end them. The demons will only stop when you finish the game. Take me to the Qua River and they'll leave—if you make it."

Marl placed his arm between Jishnu and the sorceress. "There's more money on her alive than dead."

"Look what she did to Snatchbreath," Frog retorted. "What about us, Marl?"

"Quiet," snapped Jishnu, scowling at Wei-Tzu. Bloodied yet defiant, she bit her bruised lip seductively, slightly opening her naked legs to draw his eyes. "Behnam, what do you think?"

"It's the job," Behnam replied. He stared at Snatchbreath coldly, not showing any sign of regret. "We are to do as The Captain ordered."

Jishnu stuck his sword in its scabbard. "Hold the right flank, Behnam. Marl, Frog, lead on. I got her."

Frog patted Snatchbreath's chest. "Aye."

The sun cut shadows out of the tree branches as they resumed their march. The hillsides were quiet, ruled by an eerie calm that did nothing to assuage the sellswords' fears. Around every tree, in every glade, they no longer watched for cultists to arrive to rescue their leader—instead they searched for weirder shapes, horns and claws, the infernal faces of demons in the peaceful climbs of the valley.

"Anything ahead?" Jishnu called to the two Grinders running point. Wei-Tzu bounced on his shoulder, squealing in delight with each footfall.

Marl answered first. "Nothing. Frog?"

Silence.

"Halt!" Jishnu flung Wei-Tzu on the ground and drew his sword, clutching both hands around its short hilt. She rolled to her knees like a cat and started to brush the dirt off the silk skirt of her robe.

Marl stood off ahead between two trees. "He was to the left of me, near the water."

"You stay here," Jishnu growled at Wei-Tzu.

It was not a minute later when Behnam called first, his fist raised high. "Over here."

Frog curled on his side in the weeds, his sword lost. In his hand he held his dagger, which he thrust out at Behnam and Jishnu as they approached while using his other hand to press down his helm. "Stay back! I won't let you take me like you took him! Damned tigers."

Jishnu knelt beside him. "It's me, Frog. We're just going to get up and—"

"Keep off of me." He jabbed his knife at Jishnu. "You won't get me, you damned tiger. You may have gotten my father but you won't get me."

"What is he going on about?" Behnam asked.

Jishnu fell back on his knees. "Tigers."

"What about them?"

"His father was killed by a tiger." Jishnu's eyes widened. "That's how she's doing it."

Marl walked over. "Doing what?"

"Marl, Snatchbreath was burnt as a child, yes?"

"Aye, he was. So?"

"The demons are slaying us with our fears," Behnam

concluded.

Jishnu shut his green eyes and sighed sadly. "Snatchbreath drowned trying to put the flames out on his face."

"And we're next," said Marl. All three turned toward Wei-Tzu. She waved at them, batting her eyes as they watched her, looking as sweet and innocent as a young maiden at high court.

"What do we do, Thumbs?" Marl asked.

Jishnu hated the Golden Dragon. Her pompous smile, her endless confidence, her beauty all hid the fact that she was nothing more than a demon herself, set into the world to spin chaos and strife. Yet Jishnu was a man of blood and will, a fighting man destined from birth to walk the earth in pursuit of victories and hard-won glories, be they gods-given or taken from the hands of the slain.

He turned back to Frog, who shivered in the presence of his imagined beasts. "Grab him when I say so, Behnam."

Behnam lowered his stance.

"Now!" Jishnu thrust his hand forward. He slipped by Frog's frightened stab and grabbed his wrist, wringing it until the dagger fell to the ground. Behnam held Frog down, grunting as the maddened warrior kicked his feet and screamed.

"Tie him up. You're carrying him," Jishnu told Marl,

handing him the knife.

"But what about us?" Marl asked. "The demons will come for us next."

"We are Grinders," Jishnu rebuked loudly, hoping Wei-Tzu heard him. "We will march until we fall."

* * *

They ran along the shore, heads down and grunting under the weight of fear and the burdens they carried. Jishnu led this time, eyes always set on the ground in front of them, not to the hills or the shadows where he might see his death waiting to embrace him.

"You won't make it," Wei-Tzu said, tittering in his ears.

"I hear the fear in your voice, girl. Where are demons and paper to save you, loon?"

"On your back, foreigner. Always on your back."

The miles melted into a timeless haze until there was only Jishnu, his breath, and the weight of the girl's slight body hung over his shoulder. The sound of his brothers' steps had faded in the blur when he tripped on a hidden root. Falling to the ground, they tumbled onto the lake's shore. Jishnu pushed his face out of the sand and flopped over on his back.

"Look at that. You fell down." Wei-Tzu mounted Jishnu in an instant. The fall had reopened the tiny cut on her cheek, smearing her alabaster skin with a red stain. "Why are you running? There is no escape."

He growled at her. "Get off me."

"You would do better to just let the demons get you," she cooed. She rubbed her hands down his scarred arms. "Unless you want mercy."

He laughed at her. "Mercy? Who am I but another foreigner?"

"You're strong," she said, hissing the second word. "I like strong men. I like breaking them."

"I'm not broken yet." He shoved her to the side. "We're going to that river whether you like it or not."

"We? Look around you. They're already gone."

The other three Grinders were nowhere in sight. "Oh, no," lamented Jishnu, his bravado sapped in an instant.

"Leave them to their fates. They are already dead men, food for the servants of heaven and earth. Just tell me I won and you won't have to be one of them."

Jishnu grabbed his sword's handle to make sure he still had his weapon. "That's where you are going to lose."

"Oh?"

"Victors do not make concessions." He left Wei-Tzu

PAPER DEMONS

behind, knowing instinctively that she would not attempt an escape, and went back the way he had come hoping to find signs of his three lost friends.

In the middle of a clearing he found two sets of tracks leading off into the hills. Following the second, he slipped through the gaps in the forest, hiking to a small stream that branched off from the lake.

"Stay away," a voice in the brush whispered. Frog huddled underneath a fallen log. "Stay back, tiger. You don't want to eat me."

Jishnu arranged the branches to keep his friend's hiding place covered. Wandering away, he slashed the trunks of the trees to leave a trail back to Frog, and headed further into the forest to find his other two companions.

* * *

The sun sank in the sky, transforming the woods before him into a dense canopy of shadow. Jishnu stood in the quiet, trapped between his own fears of what may come to claim him in the night and what may happen to his brothers if he could not find them. Each spot of darkness seemed alive in his eyes, twisting into evil shapes that seemed ready to spring off the floor and attack.

He chopped branches off dead trees and built a small fire. The pleasant warmth soothed his roiling emotions, allowing him a brief moment of peace among the chaos Wei-Tzu had wreaked upon his men. Exhaustion, frustration—they fused into a heavy weight in the pit of his stomach, eliciting a growl of hunger. He lay back on the cool ground and spied the stars through the roof of the forest.

Jishnu's eyes fluttered and when they reopened he was no longer in the valley, but a roofed structure of stone and timber. Oil lamps lined the window spaces, revealing a mountain scape peaked with diamond summits. The blue moon sat in a purple sky beside a red sun, and below miles upon miles of the earth went on, populated with vermillion trees that bore green fruit. Constellations he had never seen in the sky swirled in complex patterns, forming into singing dragons that summoned torrents of rain to nourish the earth.

Searching the small room, Jishnu froze before a familiar thing—upon a great dais stood a statue cast in bronze, four-armed and glittering with gold and jewels. Asdra gazed at the warrior in cold judgment.

Jishnu knelt, hands pressed together to pray before the god of war when the great storm roared. Outside the thunder boomed as the sinuous dragons, their scales plated in bright gold, twined themselves between the green clouds.

PAPER DEMONS

Their song rose to a deafening volume. Asdra moved, his four limbs swaying in a delicate war-dance. He stepped off the dais.

Jishnu stood, startled by his god's sudden manifestation. "This is a dream."

"Is it?" Asdra asked. He paced forward on the matted floor, tongue darting in and out of his mouth to lick his sharp fangs. "You failed me, Jishnu of Srijan. You are no warrior Ksharti, just a murderous pretender."

Jishnu blanched in horror. "No! I have fought in your name, Lord Asdra. I have fought bravely."

"You have fought for vice and gold, not for dharma. You are as much a demon as the ones who hunt you."

The Srijati dropped to his knees, hands clasped together to beg. "Please, Asdra. I only tried to do as my father did, and his father! I did not mean to shame you."

The god towered over him. "Yet you did." Asdra dropped his weapons and laid his hands laid upon Jishnu's scarred shoulders. "I shall rip you limb from limb in punishment."

Tears wetted Jishnu's eyes. "Please."

"Begging will not save you, for it did not save your father, or his father, or your barbaric brothers-in-arms, who died coward's deaths."

"Cowards?" That word struck an odd chord within

Jishnu's mind, breaking his terror.

Asdra's grip tightened. "You failed to protect them, warrior, as you failed to protect yourself from your own sin. Now they will die because you did not adhere to the teaching of the holy ones."

"They were Grinders," said Jishnu. The remembrance cleared his mind. "My brothers died bravely in battle. Asdra blesses those in battle for their courage, fallen or victorious, good or evil."

Asdra paused at the statement. "You are a murderer and nothing more."

"I am a Grinder."

"You are a nothing."

"I am a Grinder." Jishnu knocked the four hands off of him. "And you are not Asdra."

A flash filled the room, and when Jishnu's vision cleared a horned demon with white skin stood in the bronze god's place, hungry for violence. Asdra's bronze statue reappeared back on the dais, a smile on its face as he blew into a flute he held in his two lower hands. The two upper hands held a sword in the right, and in the left a familiar domed shield painted with a charging bull on a red field.

"I will eviscerate you," the demon promised in a guttural tone. He lashed out with his claws, forcing Jishnu to duck and roll past in a single movement.

The Srijati rushed to the statue to collect his weapons. Secured by the heft of the shield and the intimacy of a sword, he turned to face the enemy. Raising his shield in front of his body, he laid the blade upon the top rim, pointing it at the demon. "Shed the blood, save my brothers," he shouted.

Both combatants clashed in the center of the mountain shrine, claws upon shield, sword upon otherworldly flesh. The demon scraped past the wide wall of protection, tearing lines of blood into Jishnu's brown arms.

Jishnu struck back, chopping and thrusting past the flailing limbs to pierce the demon's hardened flesh. He hacked, driving the beast backward, until they reached the small entryway of Asdra's shrine. The rain showered upon them in drops of red, painting a gory scene.

Jishnu's fought with a furor, focused on destroying his infernal enemy. Behind the demon's tortured screams he heard the mocking laugh of Wei-Tzu. The sorceress' disdain pushed him into frenzy. He whipped his sword out in a wild slash.

The demon fell. He grasped at his wounded neck, trying to stymie the rainbow blood spraying from the severed artery. His voice faded. "As long as the talismans are whole, I will find you again."

Jishnu gazed down in confusion. "What talismans?"

"Thumbs!"

* * *

Jishnu bolted up beside his small fire, his sword drawn. Marl sat next to the meager flames, rocking back and forth as he chewed on his thumbnail. His blue eyes, reddened after hours of sleeplessness, darted around the woods in search of danger.

"Marl?" Jishnu whispered, his voice dry and raspy. The dawn's light flooded the world, raising the darkness into a grey-hued day of mist and dew. The green foliage glistened around them as if made of polished jade.

"My pa's here, Thumbs," Marl whispered. "He's coming to get me."

"Your father?"

Marl nodded, head bobbing up and down. "I thought I killed the old man. He used to beat my ma and I stabbed him right in the throat. But he's here!"

Jishnu scooted around the fire to sit next to his friend. He put an arm around Marl's shoulders. "He's not here."

"I saw him."

"Marl, I need you to concentrate. You remember that

temple we stopped at on the southern border of Shen?"

"What?"

Jishnu jostled him. "The temple! Do you remember what those priests were doing? You know more about their ways than I do."

Marl covered his face with his hands. "They were painting on little slips of paper to make talismans. Curry bought one on a lark. He stuck it on the back of his shield."

Jishnu laughed loudly. "Paper! That clever little shrew."

"Quiet. My pa might hear you."

"To the underworld with your pa." Jishnu unbuckled the straps of his cuirass. Inside the back plate was a large strip of rectangular paper inscribed with Shen pictographs written in black ink. He scraped it off and showed it to Marl. "Paper and demons," he said triumphantly. "Take your armor off."

Marl did as instructed, and much to his surprise found a matching talisman on the chest piece of his cuirass. "What do we do?"

Jishnu crumpled up the talisman and threw it into the fire. It sparked as the small flames consumed it, sending up a plume of red smoke. "Throw yours in."

Marl's talisman reacted the same way and a change came over him. The fear left his eyes, and he sat straighter, unburdened by the ghost of his past. "He's not out there, is he?" he asked in sheepish tone.

Jishnu patted him on the shoulder. "No. Now get up. We have to go help Frog."

Following the trail of marked trees Jishnu had left the day before, they found Frog still hiding underneath the log covered with the branches Jishnu had left over him. Dragging him out from underneath his cover, Marl held him down while Jishnu removed his cuirass.

Jishnu tossed away the armor. "It's not there."

Marl struggled to keep hold of Frog, who kicked at him, gibbering on and on about the dreaded cats and their stripes. "Well, figure something out!"

Jishnu focused on the broken red crest of Frog's helm. He yanked it off his friend's head and looked underneath. "Smart." He pulled out the talisman and ripped it into pieces. Each tear shed a bit of red dust.

Frog stopped kicking his feet. "Marl?"

"Yes, it's me, you damned little idiot."

"I thought you were a tiger," Frog said in a bewildered tone.

"We know," said Jishnu. He offered a hand to his confused brother-in-arms. "Come, we need to leave now."

"Where's the girl?" Marl inquired as they helped Frog

to his feet and dusted him off. "Did you leave her behind?"

"She will still be by the river where I left her, thinking her demons are slaying us. She is confident that she is going to conquer us." Jishnu grinned at the thought of meeting her again now that he had done away with her fell magic. "Let's go show her better."

Frog put his helm back on his balding head. "What about Behnam?"

Jishnu's smile dampened into a nervous line, tight as he pressed his lips together. "If Behnam's the man we think he is, he'll come to us. If not, gods save us from what terrifies that man."

* * *

The walk back to the shore where Jishnu left Wei-Tzu appeared through the natural tunnel created by the leaning trees and bamboo stalks. She had remained where they parted, bathing in the morning rays of the sun. She greeted Jishnu with a serene smile. "You made it. Perhaps you are stronger than I thought."

"The talismans were clever." Jishnu jerked her to her feet. "And yet you are not fearful of what comes next."

"The game isn't over." Wei-Tzu took his hand in hers

and bobbed on her toes. "You still have to get me to the river, my strong man." Tossing her hand away, Jishnu went to shove her onward when she stepped back. "Help me, Behnam," she wailed.

Marl furrowed his brow. "Behnam?"

A form leapt out of a gingko tree near the water, landing atop of Frog and Marl. Behnam shouted curses as he thrashed them with his fists. "You damned bastards," he roared. "I'll kill you for what you did to her! I'll kill you all!" He ripped his sword from its scabbard.

Jishnu tackled him to the ground, hands clutched around the wrist of the Behnam's sword arm. They rolled into the lake. The two parted, dodging away to avoid the other's attacks.

"Behnam, it's me." Jishnu held his hands out in a non-threatening gesture. "It's Thumbs."

Behnam's face contorted in a twisted mask of hatred. "I'll kill you," he screamed, stalking forward.

"Wei-Tzu has ensorcelled you with a talisman that is letting her demons control you. Listen to me," Jishnu pleaded, stepping back to keep the distance between them.

Behnam paused, lowering his sword for a moment, and tried to steady his trembling limbs. "But… you're him. You're the horse-loving bastard who raped her."

"It is him," Wei-Tzu cried. "That's the man who raped me, husband. The others held me down, but he did the deed!"

"No," Jishnu said. "Don't listen to her—she's not your wife."

"You didn't save me, Behnam. You let them rape and murder me," Wei-Tzu moaned, a twisted smile hidden behind her pained expression. She reached out to him. "You didn't save me."

Behnam fell to his knees. Hunched over in the water, a muffled gurgle vibrated out of his body, followed by a sad whimper of despair. He held his sword with both hands and rocked back and forth, mumbling incoherent words as spittle frothed from his mouth.

Frog and Marl crept forward, looking to Jishnu for a signal to charge. He held his hand up to stop them and shook his head. "Behnam." He inched forward, taking careful steps in the muddy river bed. "Behnam, look at me. I'm trying to help you."

"You ruined her." Behnam raised his head, his brown face reddened in such rage he ceased to be a man, transforming into a desperate beast, vengeful and thirsting. He rose to his feet in a staggered manner, each leg popping as they extended. Behnam pointed his sword at Jishnu. "You ruined me." With a cry he charged.

Jishnu ducked the slash and drew his sword, driving the bronze pommel into Behnam's armored stomach. Knocking the wind from his attacker's body, he pressed forward with a fierce assault, battering Behnam's sword with many unanswered swings. "Grab her and get her to the river," Jishnu ordered Frog and Marl. They ran after Wei-Tzu, who for the first time since her capture broke for an escape.

Behnam stabbed at Jishnu's face, snarling every time the Srijati parried against his blade.

Jishnu bashed him in the temple with the pommel of his sword, opening a small cut that seeped blood. The strike sent Behnam stumbled backward, momentarily dazed.

"Stop, Behnam," Jishnu said. "I don't want to kill you. I order you to stop."

Behnam shook his head, whipping smatters of blood off his dark face. "You raped her. . ." He stalked forward again, his sword waving in front of him.

Jishnu hesitated, tormented by the choice before him. He parried another blow, but failing to react with the proper counter, howled as Behnam's blade cut a shallow wound into his arm. Spurred by the pain Jishnu thrust his hand out, grabbing his fellow Grinder by the collar of his black cuirass. He sliced Behnam on the wrist, causing him to drop his sword. Kicking him hard in the shin, Jishnu drove him down to both knees.

Jishnu pressed his sword's point into the hollow of Behnam's throat. "Stop, Behnam. Stop," he begged. Tears rimmed his eyes. "Please."

"You have shamed me for the last time!" Behnam grabbed Jishnu's sword hand and pulled, skewering himself on the short blade. Blood leaked from his mouth as he choked, eyes filled with a sudden clarity of knowing where he was and what was happening. There was acceptance in those brown eyes—simple, sad acceptance.

One more wheeze and he was gone.

* * *

Jishnu caught up to the two remaining Grinders on the way to the Qua River's wide mouth. They stopped when they saw their gore-smattered leader, but knew well enough not to inquire about the fate of Behnam the Dager. Frog and Marl carried the writhing Wei-Tzu by her arms and legs. She screamed profanities at them, promising them their demise when she was finally freed in her glorious revolution. The worst of her threats she directed at Jishnu.

"Was it worth it?" The Golden Dragon asked in her

mocking tone. "Was it worth the lives of your two friends?"

"I'm not the one who lost."

"Oh, you lost foreigner," she retorted. "You're just a pawn for the corrupt. The Jade Emperor may imprison me, even execute me for my righteous war against him, but you will forever march in misery until some good soul finally claims you for your evil. What will you do when that day comes?"

At that moment three cranes flew overhead, off in the direction of where the sellswords were headed, back to present their hostage before their Captain. Jishnu knew that he and his men would be given their payment for their deed; their fallen brothers would be written in the company annals of the Grinders, yet watching those birds go he recalled his battle with the demon in his dreams.

"I'm a Grinder," he told her with a wry smile. "It's the job."

Jay Requard is a sword and sorcery warlord living in Charlotte, North Carolina. When he is not driving his enemies before him and hearing the lamentations of their women, he is either brewing mead or sharpening his next story for publication.

PAPER DEMONS

He has a fluffy cat named Mona. You can find out more about Jay at his blog: sitwritebleed.blogspot.com

THE WOLF AND THE CROW

D. T. NEAL

Farys rode slowly through Barrow while snow fell in fat flurries, past the withered trees that carried countless corpses, hanging at the ends of ropes, handbills tacked to their chests with Manticore writs, a single iron spike through the chest, written in words no one dared or cared to read.

This was the price of peace in the Land of the Manticore.

Barrow had no walls, only earthwork ramparts now, and stories of restless dead to keep the curious at bay. For Farys, the dead meant little, and the undead, even less—but he needed to go west, and in winter that meant passing through Barrow.

A mining town, drawing blackrock from rounded mountains, Barrow clung to life with a miser's thin-fingered grip, and order had to be maintained.

Once there had been walls, but no longer. The Manticore had torn them down when he razed this place and laid claim to it, as he did to everywhere he turned his eyes. The conqueror and his endless appetite would not be satisfied until all bent the knee.

The horse snuffled at the dead-scented air, maybe at the swinging bodies, or the caw from murders of crows, or possibly the crowd up ahead and the holy man speaking with the gold standard of his master: a brooch at his breast. He was the good shepherd in robes of cloth-of-gold, his weak chin churning milky words to butter while gazing out with glittery eye at his assembled flock.

He wore the office of his station, the high hat, the Manticore standard at his brow, for any bold enough to look him in the eye. It marked him as a man who mattered, a Patriarch, and his voice careened across the clearing, over the creak of rope and the cries of crows.

The crowd was small but held rapt by the man's words, not bothering to shake the snow from their heads, or, more likely, not daring to. Beside the priest stood a burly Unhuman, one of the Manticore's favored stock, a monster man, a half-head taller than most, gray-skinned arms, corded with muscle, promising death to any who faced them.

The half-man saw Farys approach, hard features creasing to a toothy grin, jagged teeth marking him as an eater of men. His hand flexed at the saber he held, a great, curved,

THE WOLF AND THE CROW

Unhuman blade. Those curved sabers had helped carve out a kingdom that moved faster than men would have thought possible. Rain or snow, day or night, the Unhuman reavers carried the fight.

The priest didn't notice Farys, kept speaking from his scroll.

"By the Law of the Land, this woman is to be tried for witchcraft, she who will hang upon this rope," the priest said. Farys looked past to the woman who stood snow-covered and weary, a rope around her neck, and a trap in the platform beneath her feet.

Her red and black, diamond-patterned gown marked her as a soothsayer, her head bare, shaved, blue eyes tearing. The drops traveled down her cheek and soaked the gray-brown rope around her pale neck. Her breath clouded the air as she quietly cried. She looked young, but it could have been magic that kept her so. She could have been ageless—a strong nose, a tapered chin, and those big eyes full of worldly wildness, but lost in themselves, at least until seeing him ride up. A glance passed from her to him.

". . . this witch, this sorceress, who would even now flout the will of our lord, the Almighty Manticore," the priest said. "Who would seek to enrapture you with just a look, to take good money from the hands of honest men, would seduce with her red-painted smile, to tell false fortunes to the witless. You all know her to be the bane of Barrow—look about you, gaze upon her, Brethren, and know that this town is riven with her kind."

The townsfolk did not look, did not need to, for, as was customary in a town taken by the Manticore, there was an inevitable house-cleaning that would occur, undesirables were rooted from the ranks, leaving only the meek and the weak to tend to the will of their monstrous master.

Farys had seen this play out in so many forms in his travels. In any place upon which the gold and pink banner of the Manticore flew, there were these show trials, and though he had no stake in them, he had paid close enough attention to understand how they would play out.

". . .but do not gaze too closely, my children," the priest said. "For to meet those sapphire eyes of hers is to be at the mercy of her magic. You know her, you suffered her to live in Barrow. I absolve you of any responsibility for this, my children. I know you lived in fear of her: we have witnesses to speak to it, duly notarized in the Hall of Records."

The woman was lost in her thoughts, hands tied behind her back, her mouth gagged. She would die this day, but, to her credit, she stood her ground, had not collapsed in a heap.

THE WOLF AND THE CROW

Nearby, the crows cawed.

The priest pointed. "You see, my children? Even now, her servants call for her, they beg her release."

This made the Barrow-dwellers turn and look, for there were hundreds of crows on the branches, watching, cawing, almost threatening to drown out the priest's words.

"But we are not accountable to crows," the priest said. "Who travel in the wake of armies and feast on the dead. Scavengers and rascal rogues. It is telling, is it not, that *these* are her defenders? How like a witch they are, are they not? You know what comes next, my children: if there be any among you who would defend this witch, let them come forth and do so by trial at arms against my champion."

The priest held out his arm to the Unhuman, who stood proud and tall in armor of black leather set with discs of gray, a great quilted coat, and a black leather neck guard, studded with the same gray discs of steel. He wore his pointed helmet back on his head a bit, revealing some of his jet black hair.

"You see, Witch?" the priest said. "Your hour of reckoning is at hand. There are none among your kinsfolk at Barrow who would dare to stand against Lord Rohr."

"I will," Farys said. Everyone - the witch included - turned their eyes to him.

"You?" the priest said, squinting at Farys, at the standard on his shield. The priests knew their heraldry, and he could see him going through the standards in his head, trying to identify him. "Who are you, Ser?"

"I'm Farys," he said. "I will take your Master's challenge and defend this woman."

"The Wandering Wolf," the priest said, fixing his eyes upon the black wolf standard on the field of white that was Farys's by right of arms, that many had tried to take from him, only to meet a ready death.

"You have that right, although I would urge you to reconsider, Brave Ser. This woman is a witch, accused by the good people of Barrow. You would risk the wrath of the Manticore to defend this woman, whom you do not even know?"

The priest knew of Farys by reputation as a sellsword and a duelist in the wake of the Manticore's War that had laid low all of the lands within reach of his great, golden paws.

"I would," Farys said. "It's cold, and a duel with your champion would be just the thing to warm my bones. That, and some food at whatever taverns Barrow cares to offer me."

"Lord Rohr is Barrow's champion," the priest said. "He has ridden with Juguthra himself in thousand campaigns, and has slain many, many knights. Food for thought, Ser."

"Then he'll be worth my time," Farys said. "I would expect nothing less of the Manticore. He knows how to choose his flesh wisely."

The priest considered Farys's words, for no one made light of his Master.

"A knight errant," the priest said. "This free-lancer is what rises to defend your honor, Witch. This reckless mercenary man would be all that stands between you and the gallows. Behold, my children, the power of the witch lingers even as her neck sits in the noose. This man, who does not know her, would fight for the honor she does not, by definition, possess. This man, himself a relic of another time, for has not our Master shown the value of a knight on a battlefield? That you would even serve in this capacity shows how far you have fallen, Ser. This is not one of your duels-for-hire. There is nothing to be gained here but this woman's life."

The witch seemed emboldened by the willingness of Farys to risk his own life for hers. She met his gaze evenly, now, with what could have been silent satisfaction.

"Are we going to settle these accounts, then?" Farys asked. "As much as I enjoy your speeches, Priest, I would get on with it."

"Of course, Ser Wolf," the priest said. "I only wanted to give you the time to consider the gravity of your situation, and of hers, that you may have the opportunity to step away and move on, with honor. If you would wish to throw away your life in this place, in this manner, Lord Rohr would happily be your executioner as surely as the rope will be hers."

The witch's eyes traveled from Farys, to the priest, to the Unhuman, and then back to Farys once more, and she strained at her bonds, just a little.

"I do have one request," Farys said. "What is her name?"

"Sibyl," the priest said. "Her name is Sibyl."

Sibyl's eyes again met those of the mercenary knight's, and the crows cawed from the trees, as if in answer.

The Barrowsfolk stared in wonder at Farys, unwilling to believe that a complete stranger would stand in defense of an accused witch. He could see it in their gaping mouths and stunned expressions, could feel their fear and confusion. Who was he to stand in the way of the Manticore's justice?

Rohr, for his part, spoke up, voice deep and resonant. "I accept your challenge, Vagabond."

The priest looked at Rohr, nodding, and back at

Farys. "So it goes. You and Rohr, here and now. Watch, my children, and learn."

Farys dismounted, handed the reins to one of the shocked townsfolk. Farys was a big man, fit and strong, although Rohr was taller and broader, the Unhumans bred for battle over generations.

Farys took off his winter hat, placed it in one of the saddlebags, drew out his helmet, which was a silvery metal, with a wolf motif inlaid across it, lacked a visor, but had a nose guard. He put it on.

The Wolf Knight took up his shield, hung it from one of the nearby tree branches not yet encumbered by a body, while the priest shooed the townsfolk into a ring around Farys and Rohr.

"The condemned are permitted this last defense of their honor," the priest said. "Should the knight prevail, you, the accused, may go free, having earned a temporary reprieve from judgment, until your wickedness ensares you again. But should the knight fall, your beloved crows will dine on you, my dear. On my mark, let the battle begin."

Farys stretched a bit, having been cold and tired in the saddle, while Rohr practiced cuts with his saber. He bore no shield, as was typical of the Unhumans, who scorned shields as unworthy of them, which was why Farys would not don his shield. He would fight the Unhuman sword to sword, a proper duel. Farys looked over his adversary, watched him move.

Rohr noticed his look, nodded. "Yes, Vagabond. I have seen many battles in my day. Are you sure you have not overstepped yourself?"

The Unhuman tested his saber again, a couple of quick cuts. From the pommel, dangling from a braided maroon tassle, was a platinum coin punched through the center. That was the coin for their Lord of War, the price they paid to enter into the Halls of Hereafter, where the Unhuman dead would go.

Why they had to pay to enter that hall was something only the Unhumans knew - Farys thought that honorable battle should be enough to appease any god, but for the Unhumans, that coin was always present, whether it was bronze, copper, silver, gold, electrum, or platinum. The higher the price, the greater the warrior to hold Hell to ransom that way. That Rohr carried platinum on the hilt of his saber meant he was quite the champion for such a faraway place as Barrow.

"I was thinking that saber—it would make a fine souvenir," Farys said, securing his helmet. "And the coin it

THE WOLF AND THE CROW

carries, better still."

It got Farys to thinking, even as he removed his own sword belt, a blade with the basket hilt of a maiden monster, a mermaid who wound herself around his hand, held a great black pearl at the pommel in silvery hands. The blade was long and straight, two thumbs across, and tapered tip.

"Rapier," Rohr said. "A fallen knight with a rapier. No broadsword for you?"

Farys smiled at the Unhuman, who loomed perhaps half a head taller than he did. "This rapier is not for you, my friend. But you are welcome to it if you kill me."

He stowed that rapier on his horse's saddlebag, and drew out, instead, another blade, wrapped in a maroon and gold blanket. Farys unsheathed it, draped the blanket on his horse's saddle, and produced a Wildland saber.

"This is for you," Farys said. From the pommel was a braid of black and white, and dangling from it, a dozen coins.

The sight of it did not fail to impress Lord Rohr.

"You are fortunate to still breathe, bearing a blade like that," Rohr said. "Are you sure the weight of all that coinage won't slow you down?"

Farys smiled at Rohr, shrugged. "If anything, I'm counting on it to, so we can make this a fair fight."

His cocksure manner rankled Rohr, who could only look on in wonder at how this man could have possibly prevailed in battle against a dozen of his brethren.

"Begin," the priest said, clapping his hands together. "And may justice prevail in this, as in all things."

At the signal of the priest, Rohr dropped into a crouch, holding up his saber, while Farys assumed a streetfighter's stance, holding his own saber in his left hand.

"I'll take that pretty blade of yours as *my* souvenir," Rohr said. "Along with your head."

"Fair enough," Farys said, dodging as the Unhuman went for him with a series of sweeping saber cuts that sliced holes in the air, sending flurries chasing in its whistling wake.

The ground was treacherous, wet with the fallen snow and footprints. Farys wore his winter boots, had been dressed for the weather, so he was not unprepared. And the Unhuman was bred for hardship, could hardly be said to feel something as mundane as discomfort.

Farys countered Lord Rohr's strike with a turn of his wrist, making cuts at him, exploratory forays into the Unhuman's defense. The big Unhuman blocked each of his cuts, offered sweeping ripostes that were carefully, not recklessly, delivered. Rohr knew his business, Farys could tell.

THE WOLF AND THE CROW

"What are you doing so far from your Master's court, Rohr?" Farys asked as he blocked and parried blows from the Unhuman. Each cut made the sabers sing in turn, a keening between them. Both blades were well-forged and worthy weapons, neither seeming able to overmatch the other.

"My business is my own," Rohr said, cutting at Farys's forearm. Farys parried it and threw a cut at Rohr's other arm, forcing the Unhuman to pivot to dodge it.

"You are disgraced," Farys said. "It's so clear to me. You have fallen out of your Master's favor, and are consigned to the farthest reaches of his domain, far, far from his golden gaze."

The Wildland saber sliced at his throat, but Farys brought up his own saber and stopped it, the blades ringing out again. He riposted with a flick of his wrist, finding flesh along the unguarded inside of Rohr's arm. The blade bit and drew blood, and Rohr threw a lateral cut of his saber at Farys's head, but the knight had already disengaged, moving out of reach, and suffered only a slash on his cheek.

Rohr looked at his wounded sword arm, blood dripping on the snow, while Farys bled beneath his helmet.

Lord Rohr switched his grip, moving his weapon to his left hand. It was one of their gifts: their ability to fight equally well with either hand, along with speed, strength, and constitution.

The Barrow folk murmured among themselves, unaccustomed, Farys was sure, to seeing Unhuman blood spilled in the wake of the Manticore's invasion, and not used to seeing someone actually challenge one of the Manticore's minions so openly.

"I know of your reputation," Rohr said.

Farys pressed the attack, a series of lunges and thrusts in the direction of the champion of Barrow. He put himself at risk with each lunge, trusting in his speed to evade Rohr's counters. The brazenness of his attack actually angered the Unhuman, for it betrayed some measure of contempt for Rohr's ability to retaliate.

"I am not such easy prey," Rohr said. "I will not fall so readily."

Rohr used his saber to distract Farys and then threw a kick at the knight, catching him squarely in his armored chest. Despite his armor, Farys staggered back, had momentarily lost his footing, a dent in his quilted metal breastplate. If he had not been wearing armor, his chest might have been caved in by the force of the kick.

Sensing his advantage, Rohr cut at Farys, the saber catching air and steel as they crossed the circle of combat, the man driven back by the force and speed of the Unhuman warrior's attack.

"You are already fallen," Farys said. "Fallen far afield, that this Barrow is your field of honor."

The Unhuman refused to be distracted by the Wolf Knight's taunts, and only pushed harder, trying to break through his defense. Farys had absolutely dueled with his people before, Rohr could see. He knew his strokes and parries, understood the whirling dance of death that was the signature of the saber in the hands of his people. This experience made the difference between life and death.

Farys was breathing heavily now, and Rohr was breathing harder, himself, for even as well-skilled warriors, they knew how quickly the duelist's dance drew breath from one's lungs.

"Are you warmed up, yet, Vagabond?" Rohr asked, managing a strike that skinned the knight's thigh, the steel of the saber shearing off a bit of armor there, hacking off ~~flensing~~ some meat, in turn.

Farys grunted at the impact, turned aside to throw Rohr off-balance, and swung quickly with his own saber, a slice that Rohr moved to block and catch with the gauntlet on his bloodied hand, banking that the steel would protect him from the sword's stroke.

Rohr was half-right, managing to catch the blade, but

at a cost, as it had bit deep into his hand, severing tendons, preventing him from gripping tight on the blade, which Farys quickly drew out of the bloodied hand of the Unhuman, taking three of his fingers with it as it passed.

Lord Rohr howled at the loss of the fingers of his favored hand, seeing them tumble in the snow. But he was not beaten. He struck hard at Farys with his saber hand, smashing the human in the face with the hilt of his weapon, pleased by the crunch of the steel and the momentary distraction it brought, as he wound up and struck hard down on him with the blade, only to have that infernal saber up again and deflecting the blow from its brother blade.

The Unhuman smashed his wounded hand into Farys's face, blinding him with his blood, striking hard for him yet again, only to have the knight dodge under the cut, forcing him to overshoot. Rohr's saber struck the ground, smashed the snow, lodged a moment in the mud.

Farys struck, another cut, this time at Rohr's right leg, behind the knee. The blade cut into flesh, and Rohr's leg burst into agony. He stumbled and fell in the snow.

The onlookers at Barrow gasped and spoke louder now, and the priest looked on with evident dismay. This was not at all how he had expected things to turn out. No one had dared to challenge Lord Rohr before, no one had challenged

THE WOLF AND THE CROW

any of the past hangings. To see the challenge answered and so strenuously fought gave them pause.

Farys actually let Rohr get back up, took the moment to step back and take a breather, while Rohr fought his way to his feet, bloodying the snow as he did so.

"Had enough, yet?" Farys asked, spitting some of the Unhuman's blood from his lips, wiping his face with the back of his gauntleted hand.

Rohr looked at his ruined right hand, and his wounded right leg, and compensated, held his saber up, using his good leg for support. He had never faced a swordsman like this, who fought like a Wildlander, though he dressed like a beggar knight, this wanderer.

It did not matter; he would fall.

"Not yet," Rohr said.

Farys took that with a nod. From where he stood, he could see the witch on the platform, a hint of hope in her eyes, while the priest looked on the duel with increasing worry. The leaden gaze of the townsfolk was animated at the spectacle of spilled blood that was not their own. Either way, they'd have some entertainment, and something to speak about.

Rohr held himself at the ready, blade up and out, braced for Farys's attack. It would be like this, for having been hobbled in the moment, Rohr had wisely determined it would be foolhardy to charge forward into an attack, risking losing his balance on his wounded leg, utterly at his opponent's mercy.

No fool, Rohr left it to Farys to besiege him, to venture in and match him blade for blade, trusting in his superior strength to carry the day against the knight's speed. It was a sensible tactic, a worthy gamble.

Farys took a few moments to circle Rohr, giving him time to regain his breath in the cold mountain air, while the snow fell around them, between them. Rohr looked on, his red eyes ablaze, without a trace of fear. Whatever fate had led him to this forlorn and faraway place, this was what Rohr had been born to do, and there was no cowardice, no fear—there was simply his determination to win, no matter what befell him.

The Wolf made three circles around Rohr, changing his direction during one of them, while Rohr reversed his pivot. Both sought the others' weak points, coldly assessed each other in the snow-filled sky, the crows peering down from the trees, the townsfolk looking on, the priest seeing all, and, always, the witch watching.

Farys made a feinted attack, and saber met saber as he disengaged, out of reach once more, while Rohr bled down his leg and arm, staining the snow, a red slush beneath his feet. He was not mortally wounded. He would heal. His people always healed when wounded, which was why it was always a point of honor between them that a fight should be to the death, without the possibility of surrender, for as long as a breath was in their lungs, they would fight. It was all they knew, all they had ever known.

"What if your champion yields, Priest?" Farys asked.

"I will not yield," Rohr said, more to himself than the priest. He understood what the knight was doing, insulting him that way, trying to throw him off, to anger and unsettle him, to distract him from the necessary focus of the duel. It was one of the many tricks of the duelist, to maintain that keen dispassion while enraging their adversary. But Rohr would not fall for such tricks, though his pride suffered for them, just a little.

"In these matters, the Law is the Law," the priest said. "With a life in the balance, a life must be taken."

"Of course," Farys said, and struck again at the Unhuman, who turned aside his cut and countered with a blow that sparked across Farys's breastplate, missing his gorget by only a couple of blade widths, making his steel breastplate ring like a gong that made the Barrow-folk exclaim and gesture.

Farys held up his saber, let the coins jingle, let the braid dangle. Rohr understood what this meant: those stolen coins, taken from the weapons of dead Wildlanders, meant that he had consigned their souls to perdition, had denied them passage to the Halls of Hereafter, had forced them to walk the world as wraiths and specters, beyond honor and hope of redemption. It was a cruel fate, and the Unhuman bristled at it. Another of his tricks, but to see that Soul Stealer standing there, mocking him, it was almost more than he could bear.

"Enough of your games, Vagabond," Rohr said. "You may have banished my brothers, but you will not do that to me."

"Are you sure?" Farys asked, almost conversationally. He was mocking Rohr, this death-dealing duelist, contemptible creature, this fallen knight who had not the valor to have died on the battlefield with his brothers, but who now plied his deadly trade from town to town, avenging his fallen brothers in this way.

Farys swung at Rohr, another feint, which had Rohr countering a cut that did not come, for Farys had reversed his swing, saber arcing back the way it had come, catching the braid that hung from the Unhuman's pommel. The steel sliced it free, sent the coin and braid tumbling, which

THE WOLF AND THE CROW

Farys caught in his free hand, and as Rohr reacted to it with outrage, his focus split a moment, Farys reversed his swing yet again, slicing Rohr across the throat, just below his jawline, catching him above his quilted armor of black leather and gray iron, finding gray flesh, instead.

A sharp blade, it was a clean cut, and Rohr gasped, dropping his own saber into the snow, falling forward, pitching himself at his enemy with a strangled cry.

Farys stepped aside, and knelt into the reddening snow, drawing the platinum coin into his palm as his lips went to Rohr's ears.

"No Lord of War for you, Champion," Farys whispered to his dying foe. "No Halls of Hereafter. Only death here, in Barrow. Here you will walk these dusty reaches for all time, damned to share the fate of all the victims hanging from those trees."

Then, while Rohr breathed his last, Farys pried off his helmet, revealing that great mane of braided hair, no doubt fashioned by his slave women, and Farys took the saber and sliced off the braid, pulling it up and holding it aloft for all to see, to see the great length of the braid, the coins bound up in it. Farys wound it around his fist five times, held the end of it in his hand, brandished it.

Farys stood up, pointed the bloody blade at the priest.

"Your Champion's beaten," Farys said. "Release the witch."

The priest looked at Farys with curdled contempt and loathing, but he nodded and his acolytes came forth, drew the noose from the neck of the witch.

"You have won this woman's life, Wolf Knight," the priest said. "But I will tell the Manticore everything I have seen. I will tell Juguthra about Rohr's passing, and you will know their vengeance. They will hunt you down."

Farys walked up to the priest, who blanched at the bloody blade, which Farys cleaned with a cloth, having placed the braid in a satchel at his belt. He tossed the bloody cloth at the priest, who yelped, dodging it.

"Please do," Farys said. "I want him to know. I want them all to know."

Sibyl removed the gag, glared at the priest, tossed the gag in the snow near the priest.

"You have good fortune, Witch," the priest said. "But I will spread word of this, and you will yet hang. The knight has bought you time, but only so much time, a pinch of sand from an almost-empty hourglass. We will find you, wherever you go, and we will hang you yet. We have watchers everywhere. And when your knight protector has, himself,

THE WOLF AND THE CROW

fallen, you will know my Master's justice."

The witch was led down the steps, and she looked up at Farys with wonder and worry. Her wounded beauty was all the more apparent in her baldness, the delicacy of her features.

"My Lord," she said.

"I'm no lord," Farys said. "But let's move on before the priest finds another champion to avenge his champion, or, worse, before an archer finds me, instead."

Farys took his horse back, and wrapped up the saber again, putting that bloody coin in with it. Having stowed that, he put on his rapier again, pried his dented helm from his head, mopped the blood from his face, and donned his winter hat, pulling the ear flaps down to take the wind from his neck.

He walked the horse up to the witch, helped her upon it, and then drew a fur from another of his saddlebags, handed it to her so that she could wrap herself with it.

And then they walked their way into Barrow, through the town, past the gray and dismal dwellings that clustered in beneath the gay gold and pink banner of the Manticore, their lord and sworn protector.

"I'm no witch," Sibyl said, as they cleared the far side

of Barrow, between the rounded mountains. If they made haste, they'd reach the passes before the winter snow sealed them up until springtime. The key was knowing when to go, and when to stop. At best, they'd make it through; at worst, they'd lose themselves in the wilderness. But the Wolf Knight knew how to survive in winter.

The crows cawed and flew from Barrow, overhead, fleeing the trees in a great, black cloud. Farys gazed up at them, and then at the witch, and grinned.

"Of course you are," Farys said. "You would be no good to me if you weren't, for I have need of a witch, where I'm going."

"And where is that?" Sibyl asked, her blue eyes on his.

"Anyplace but here," Farys said, climbing aboard his horse. They rode out of Barrow together, up the mountain pass, accompanied by chorusing crows, into the very heart of winter.

D. T. Neal is a writer and editor who lives in Chicago. He's been published in Ireland's premier speculative fiction magazine, "Albedo 1," and won one of their Aeon Awards in 2008 for his short story, "Aegis." He has also published several books, including his werewolf novel, "Saamaanthaa" (2011), the horror thriller, "Chosen" (2012), the vampire novel, "Suckage" (2013), and the novella, "Relict" (2013).

He's very fond of history, loves swords, art, music, masks, Westerns, and ancient ruins. He also enjoys cooking, photography, and making plants grow, and is working on several new horror, fantasy, and science fiction stories, although not necessarily in that order. His author blog is dtneal.com

FOREST OF SHADOWS

JOHN F. ALLEN

The sun of the new day began to rise above the snow covered hillocks. He huddled in his makeshift tent as the wind threatened to douse his campfire. Jaziri, son of Xiambu, the King of Kimbogo Province, was wrapped in the hide of the giant grizzly bear he had killed the day before. Its flesh had provided him with sustenance that staved off starvation as he planned his travels to the East.

It was a dangerous time in the Forest of Shadows, even more so than usual. Spring had awakened its sleeping denizens, who were focused on satiating their hunger. Just as he sought to survive, the great beasts of the forest had pledged the same goal.

He had been forced to live here all winter, the only place where the King's men feared to follow him. King Arturian of Arsuria was nothing if not superstitious and to Jaziri's good fortune, a trait his men also shared. Many of the King's men feared the forest due to the legend of a sorceress Heolstor who they believed lived there. According to legend, she was a powerful practitioner of the Black Arts, and nearly as old as time itself. She was known around the entire continent—even as far as his native lands in Kagiso—as a powerful witch and the only one who refused to submit to the King.

Jaziri found it fortuitous that in his time in the forest he hadn't crossed paths with the sorceress whose name was spoken only in hushed tones by the villagers in the inn where he had stayed. Shortly after he arrived in the King's village, the innkeeper's daughter—Rasheeda—had been even more forthcoming about the witch and the other evils of the forest after he had serviced her quite well one night.

He attempted to deflect her inquiries into his reasons for seeking this information by pleasuring her more, but he eventually relented. He told her of his heritage and his mission. She had been so fascinated at the prospect of bedding a Subani warrior that she'd have likely slit her own father's throat in the night, provided him the deed to the inn, and handed over all of her father's gold had he asked for it. It was rare for his tribesmen to venture so far north into the outer realms, and the sight of a tall, mahogany skinned warrior enthralled most amorous wenches he'd encountered here.

FOREST OF SHADOWS

Making his way to the Eastern edge of the forest, he saw an odd glimmer in the horizon. Ahead, a small clearing housed a large rock formation. The rocks which formed the mound ranged from the size of Jaziri's fist to huge boulders more than half his height.

He drew his long saber and moved cautiously around the stone edifice. The muscles in his neck tensed like spring steel in anticipation of battle.

The ground began to vibrate with a thunderous sound and the highest rocks rolled down the pile. A tall emaciated figure emerged from the center of the mass, as the smell of brimstone and rotten flesh filled the air. The skeletal face glared at him and its eye sockets held an uncanny glow. Its gnarled hand gripped a large broadsword.

Jaziri backed as far as the trees allowed him and watched as the creature slid down the rock pile towards him. It was followed by two more battle ready corpses.

The animated carcasses moved with the dexterity of living foes. One held a large battleax and the last to emerge from the mound wielded a long spear.

Jaziri backed into a tree so they couldn't surround him and waited for their attack. The one with the battleax attacked first, with an overhead swing of its weapon. Jaziri's panther-like reflexes saved his head from being hewn from his shoulders.

He rolled to the side and struck out with almost inhuman savagery, at the monster with the spear. The skeletal warrior dodged, but not before its spear was severed in two.

Jaziri leapt at the figure with a bloodthirsty cry and ran it through with his saber. He pulled his weapon free from the corpse and spun to meet the figure with the broadsword with a clang of steel.

His muscles strained under the might of the undead creature. Jaziri found himself pinned against the boulders, with his own blade nearly pressed alongside his throat. He struggled to gain ground with the monster's inhuman strength, but to no avail.

The other creatures closed in on him from the sides of the one he faced. He had a split second to act lest he was doomed.

He crouched to the ground, and with his free hand, grabbed a hand sized rock. With all of his might, he smashed the rock into the monster's skull.

It slackened with the impact so that it toppled one of the others behind it. With a agile twist and shift of his body, Jaziri attacked.

The monster with the battleax lost its head in one deft stroke. Its body continued to swing the weapon with no determinable aim. Jaziri ducked beneath its powerful arc and split it in two at its waist.

He wheeled to find the creature with the broken spear had lunged at him. Jaziri dove under it, rolled to the side and made a backhand slash. His saber severed the monster's leg, and it fell forward into a tree.

With an overhead arc, Jaziri hacked off the creature's head and limbs. He turned and was met with a blow that sent him into a nearby tree. Stunned, he groggily sat up against the tree. The remaining monster climbed the mound of boulders and stood atop it.

The clouds overhead swirled in a giant vortex and the ominous din of thunder boomed. The creature raised its broadsword to the open sky. A large bolt of lightning struck the sword and enveloped the creature in an aura of energy.

The ground shook and the monster glowed. The bones of the other creatures pulled to the top of the mound and fused with it. It grew in height and girth to form a leviathan.

Jaziri glared in awe at the sight of this behemoth which stood before him. The monster leaped down from the mound and struck at him, but Jaziri had recovered enough by then to avoid its lumbering attack.

He surmised that the only way to fell the creature was to somehow deal it a mighty blow, something he would be unable to do in direct combat.

With simian agility, Jaziri leapt to the side of the creature, grabbed the battleax of the other and scaled the mound of stones. Behind it he threw himself at the monster, landing on its back. It struggled to shake him off, but couldn't. Jaziri held on with every bit of strength he had.

The monster thrashed about and slammed itself into nearby trees in an effort to dislodge Jaziri from his perch. He spotted a cliff about a hundred paces northwest of their location.

Jaziri struck and tugged the creature in an effort to guide it towards the cliff. When they made it to the crag, he raised the battleax and slammed it into the monster's skull, pushing off its back with his feet.

The creature fell forward.

Over the cliff.

Jaziri peered over the crag and watched as it hit the rocks in the water filled chasm below. It shattered into pieces from the impact and swept away in the raging current of the river.

Jaziri returned to the mound, grabbed his weapons and hurried eastward. As he continued his journey, he thought back on all of his encounters with the strange creatures and demonic monsters in these haunted woods. He had

FOREST OF SHADOWS

destroyed them all and never took a day for granted, but he often wondered if he'd been better off had he faced down the King's men and died in a blaze of glory rather than live with the enchanted horrors that roamed within this forest.

* * *

Jaziri passed through the kingdom from the south, on his way to the far eastern lands of Hoda and Lapenia. He wanted a change in scenery from the dry lands of the Cardenac Region with its devastating sandstorms and tyrannical lieges, although he did miss the broad bottomed wenches who serviced him while he fought in Shah Rojah-Shadu's army.

It was said that the women of the Far East were even more beautiful than those in the lands he'd just left. It was something he was bound and determined to experience for himself. In his heart of hearts he knew of none fairer than those of his village.

Then he remembered he was the last of his village.

He'd been in need of gold, and hired himself out to King Arturian as a palace guard in exchange for it. His detail had been to protect the King's daughter Laila from any threats made by a rivaling kingdom. Laila was the fairest maiden in the land and the King's enemies coveted her hand in marriage, some willing to kidnap her and force the King into merging his kingdom with theirs. King Arturian believed that Laila was the key to some great prophecy that would unite the kingdom under his rule, and for that divination to take place, she had to remain a virgin until her twentieth winter.

It had come to the warrior's attention that the ritual surrounding the prophecy involved the sacrifice of Laila on her twentieth winter. Then the Arsurian gods would be pleased and rain down great fortune upon King Arturian. Jaziri saw the King's motivations as despicable and craven. And he was also not a man to turn down the opportunity to bed a beautiful woman, especially when the deed would save her life. So when Laila became infatuated with him and pursued him for carnal pleasures, it had been his honor bound duty to oblige her.

He could still smell the honeysuckle and coconut oils in her fire-red hair, mixed with the scent of her jasmine infused flesh as he pounded her from behind, her moans stifled only by the goose feather pillows afforded her royalty.

She'd been a good lay and the satisfaction of taking her maiden-head was particularly satisfying as her father had crossed him on numerous occasions by shorting his pay.

FOREST OF SHADOWS

When King Arturian caught him while Laila was servicing his phallic region with kisses in her private chamber, he looked as though he'd likely drop dead on the spot. He had clutched his chest and flailed about, moaning his dead wife's name repeatedly, while vowing to join her in the afterlife. He barely managed to call out to his guards, but it was far too late as Jaziri had made his escape through the chamber window. Despite the twenty cubit drop into the moat below, he managed to not only survive, but also steal a horse and make his way to the Forest of Shadows.

Now that spring had dawned, he would be free to continue his travels through the forest towards the East. He'd waited to travel in the lighter weather as his journey over the Metrophian Mountains would prove perilous enough in fair weather, let alone in the heart of winter. He had very little to carry save his sabers, bow and quiver. The horse he had ridden into the forest now served as the fabric for his tent and food for his first few weeks. He survived by hunting small winter creatures. As they were few and far in-between, he'd lost quite a bit of strength over the last month or so. The bear had provided him with much needed energy to begin the hazardous journey ahead.

After a day's journey, he made his way to the eastern edge of the forest. He came upon a clearing and in the distance stood a large hut. Smoke from a fire billowed from its roof, giving it a serene and majestic appearance. A moderate sized stable stood to the side of it, from which he could hear the faint neighing of horses inside. He started to pass it by and make his way out of the forest when he saw a woman exit the front of the hut.

Wrapped in a fur cloak with her head uncovered, she stood in the doorway and looked out into the woods where Jaziri stood watching. Despite the fact that he was over 300 paces away and partially hidden by a large tree, her gaze seemed to focus on him. She dropped the woolen cloak to reveal her naked body.

It was the color of a harvest moon and unblemished, as far as he could tell. Raven hued hair cascaded down along her shoulders and backside. He became mesmerized, and though he fought to turn and continue on his journey, he was beckoned.

She turned to walk back into the hut and left the door open. An invitation if Jaziri had ever seen one. Given the way in which she had delivered it and how long it had been since he'd felt the warmth of a woman's flesh, he was unwilling not to accept it. Besides, the sky was growing dark and he'd have to find shelter somewhere. Stealthily, he made his way to the hut, observing the ground and surrounding areas. Jaziri had found it strange for a beautiful young woman to live on the edge of a haunted forest alone and suspected there was more to this alluring female than what met his eyes.

He stood cautiously at the entrance to the hut. She lay on the floor by a hearth, body again wrapped in furs. The fire blazed, providing heat like which he had been unaccustomed to for more than a season. Her almond shaped eyes were like that of a doe, innocent and furtive. She also radiated a quiet strength and energy he couldn't quite fathom.

"Shut the door, warrior, else the warmth of my womb will surely dissipate," she said.

Jaziri complied and continued to watch her from across the room. The interior of the hut was decorated in various animal hides stretched out and affixed to the walls. Odd symbols had been painted into the fur. Shelves housed an assortment of candles, scrolls and small animal skulls. The floor was covered in fur rugs in various tones of brown and gray.

This woman practiced the Dark Arts, and most likely was the sorceress Heolstor. She'd somehow used her magicks to make herself appear youthful and tempting.

Jaziri had never bedded a witch before. Although there were plenty to be had in the village where he grew up, they had always made him feel wary. His grandmother—Mpho, the village shaman—had placed protection spells on him since birth. She also gave him an amulet to protect him from evil spirits. Even though he'd witnessed some odd happenstances, he placed little stock in the superstitions of his people.

She claimed that one day he'd carry out a great historic act and rid the world of an ancient evil. He had seen the power his foremother had wielded with his own eyes, but was hesitant to believe that his destiny would be so great. He lived in the present and carved his own destiny with his wits and the steel he wore at his side.

"Who are you, woman?" Jaziri asked, his hand resting on the hilt of his large curved saber. As she stood and dropped her fur covers, he narrowed his gaze. The flickering light from the fire danced across her flawless skin. Her comely appearance belied a virtuousness that certainly didn't apply to her true nature. The carnal expression in her eyes alone spoke volumes of her intent.

"What is it that you seek, warrior?" She stepped slowly towards him.

"I am on a journey to the East. What is it that you offer, witch?"

She looked at him with an intent gaze. A sly grin slid across her face as the catch-light in her ebon eyes swayed in unison to the hearth's flames.

"I would think that to be apparent, as it is your desire as well. Does that which you see please you, warrior?"

She reached out to him and began to undress him of his bear fur cloak and woolen pantaloons. He stood before her as she savored his physique. Her gaze lingered on his broad shoulders, barrel chest, and thick arms. His skin was the color of birch bark as was the case for most of his tribesmen.

The witch slid to her knees and covered his manhood with warm, wet kisses. It awakened quickly as she pleasured him. After a while he backed away from her, scooped her up in his arms and carried her to the pallet of fur near the hearth.

He removed his pants and boots before kneeling over her prone frame. She slid onto her knees, turned her head, looked over her shoulder and smiled. He entered her with a savage abandon and vigorously engaged his hips to her own robust cadence.

* * *

After an hour of animalistic pleasuring, she lay next to him purring like a satiated cat. Her leg was draped over him as she nuzzled her face into his shoulder. Her hands stirred his manhood as though tempting it to life. As her hand made its way to his chest, her fingers lingered on the amulet beneath his tunic.

Her body tightened as she ripped at his blouse with taloned fingers to reveal the amulet his grandmother had given him decades ago.

"You are no longer welcomed here, warrior! Leave immediately," she spat, and leapt to her feet.

Jaziri smiled. "So my amulet frightens you does it witch? Why is that?"

"You belong to the Tribe of Atumba, my sworn enemies," she said.

"Yes, that's true, but I am not here seeking to destroy you."

She glared at him with a venomous stare, her face already distorted into a nearly demonic visage. "Why did you spend all winter in my forest warrior if not to slay me?"

Jaziri laughed in a bellowing manner. As he clothed himself leisurely, he shook his head at her. "As I told you witch, I am on a journey to the East. Need I remind you it was you who offered the warmth of your fire and the pleasures of your flesh to me?"

"That was before I knew you to be a son of Atumba."

"What is it that you sought from me, witch?"

FOREST OF SHADOWS

"I was merely lonely and you appeared to have a strong back."

"That might have been true, but there is more to this than you are speaking of. The legends throughout the kingdom say that any foolish enough to venture into these woods are seldom ever heard from again, and those who do survive speak of great horrors. It was on my way to this area that I encountered demons and monsters, much like those described by the villagers who fear this place."

"You are tenacious warrior, I will give you that. You have had your pleasure; now leave this place while you still can."

The witch gestured in a manic manner. Jaziri drew his saber in a swift motion and struck at her. She dissolved into vapor and disappeared. A high-pitched shriek filled the room. He warily turned and made his way to the nearest wall. At least with his back to it, he could see whatever was coming, if it was to be seen at all.

While he was astonished by her transformation, he knew that now was not the time to let it deter him from leaving this place. The amulet he wore would only protect him so much, as he was aware that he would have to fight his way out in order to survive.

He reached down with one hand to retrieve his cloak,

bow and quiver. The door of the hut blew open and he was sucked outside into the cold dark night. He landed hard in the thick snow. The sting of the bitter-cold powder kept him from losing consciousness. He shook his head to clear his thoughts and regain his focus.

The silvery moon hung in the sky like a judging eye, watching him as he struggled for survival. The wind howled and shrieked in the same manner as the witch had. He got to his feet with saber in hand. The trees which lined the clearing formed a dark and foreboding wall to this wicked arena.

The snow blanketed the ground for as far as he could see and appeared undisturbed save for his own foot impressions. He crouched, prepared to attack whatever made its way to him. In an instant the wind stopped howling and the only sound he heard was his heart thumping in his chest.

In the rush of the moment he hadn't noticed until then that the amulet had heated and now glowed. Close to burning his flesh, his first thought was to rip it off, but he thought better of it, as that might be precisely what the witch wanted.

Jaziri turned in a tight circle and observed the eerie landscape before him. There was a tinge to the sky which he found difficult to recognize. In an explosion of snow, three

FOREST OF SHADOWS

forms erupted from the ground and sprang towards him. He made them out as Dire wolves, a species long believed to have died out, yet here they stood, snarling at him as plain as the nose on his face.

A wicked laugh pierced the air and alerted his senses even more. He focused on the six glowing amber eyes that surveyed him. The great beasts' fangs dripped with saliva, and gray and white fur lay thick on their bodies. The fur around their necks reminded him of the giant cats from his native, land and from the distance which they stood, appeared to be the same size.

They circled him, slowly moving closer with each pass. He knew the grim odds of destroying all three, but if he must, he would go out of this world in the same manner he'd arrived, fighting.

He drew the short saber with his left hand and stared the deathly trio in their eyes, prepared for battle.

One of the beasts lunged covered the distance in one leap. Jaziri thrust his saber with the full might of his dark, broad shoulders. The blade sunk into the flesh of the dire wolf and tore through muscle and sinew with astounding veracity.

The creature's blood rained down upon him and covered him in its sticky warmth; a pile of steaming entrails rested at his feet. He turned and stood crouched like a lithe jungle cat. Another wolf leapt upon him and knocked him to the ground.

The long saber flew from his hand, and the massive paws of the beast pinned Jaziri' arms. As amber eyes bored into him, warm spittle dripped from its gaping maw.

The other wolf circled them and growled savagely.

As Jaziri prepared to meet Atumba in the afterlife, the creature which had him pinned stiffened and froze in place before Jaziri even heard the sharp sound of the arrow which penetrated the wolf's skull.

He pushed forward out of instinct with his left hand and thrust the short saber into the side of the beasts' massive collar of fur with a satisfying thump.

The wolf fell to the side, dead. He rolled to his feet to face the final beast. The creature looked towards the direction in which the arrow had come.

It was going to attack him, but thought better of it and backed away. The wolf turned, running towards the forest and was met in full stride by a shaft identical to the one that killed its pack mate.

The beast lay writhing in the snow flailing in its death dance before it stilled. A long arrow protruded from its breast where the heart laid, a pool of blood spread about the

FOREST OF SHADOWS

snow beneath it.

Jaziri looked to the tree line and spotted a dark cloaked figure in a hood out in the distance. As he picked up his weapons, the figure approached. When it was within fifty paces, he recognized the figure as Laila, the king's daughter.

The full light of the moon accentuated her striking, bountiful figure. Fire-red colored locks spilled around her face from inside the hood. She still held a shaft armed in her bow, prepared to let it fly at a moment's notice.

"Are you hurt, warrior?"

"No, I'm well. What are you doing out here in the dead of night no less," Jaziri said.

"I was seeking you out. I heard father's guards as they spoke in the courtyard. They told tales of running you out of the village with a bounty on your head and into the Forest of Shadows. Apparently, a bar-wench, the daughter of an innkeeper betrayed your intentions. Given the season, I figured that you'd wait it out and attempt to leave shortly after spring arrived. I escaped the castle and ventured here."

Jaziri barely contained a self-deprecating chuckle.

It would appear that one cannot trust an ample backside and a smiling face in a bar-wench these days, he thought.

Laila looked at him with an expression of consternation.

"Why does this amuse you warrior?"

"Never mind that, why are you seeking me out girl? Are you looking to claim your father's bounty?"

"Nay, I wish to join you on your journey if you'd allow it. How could I possibly want to remain with a man who would've no sooner seen me dead, than look upon me?"

Her porcelain skin glistened and her emerald eyes sparkled in the soft moonlight. He had always found her appealing, but even more so in the light of the moon. Her skills would prove most useful, considering she'd survived the treacheries of this forest. Her company would also serve to appease his desires until he reached his destination.

The piercing shriek of the witch snapped him back to the present. He'd almost forgotten about her after he'd vanquished her minions.

He and Laila stood back to back and moved in unison to make a tight circle. An odd drone rolled over the distance. Turning his head, five black, winged figures threatened to block out the moon itself.

Jaziri braced against Laila and waited. As the winged creatures dove at them and filled the air with a putrid odor of brimstone and rotting flesh, the dark demons produced a blood-curling scream. Their eyes glowed red. Taloned hands swiped at Jaziri and Laila, threatening to slice them into ribbons.

FOREST OF SHADOWS

Jaziri swung his saber in a wide arc at the lightning fast creatures, but to no avail. Laila let fly an arrow which struck one of the demon's wings. It howled and crashed into the snow in a large plume.

Another creature knocked Jaziri to the ground and circled back to swoop down upon him. Unhurt, Jaziri braced for the attack.

The demon flew into range, and Jaziri turned to his left side and rolled back with his long saber. His blade bit into the thick skinned torso of the creature and it sputtered in the air and flew in a reckless manner. The shrill whine of another arrow cut the air as it found its mark and penetrated the demon's skull.

Jaziri regained his bearings and turned towards Laila in time to see a demon grab her and take to the sky. Snatching his bow and notching an arrow he aimed, but he was too slow—one of the demons flew into him, knocking him to the ground.

As he struggled to his feet, he noticed the creature was the one Laila injured in its wing. It stood and faced Jaziri with glowing eyes and an eerie hiss. Razor sharp fangs dripped with saliva and snapped at the air as it circled him.

"What manner of devil are you?" Jaziri said. He looked about to see Laila struggling in the other creature's grasp.

They flew about forty feet in the air, circling the clearing.

The demon he faced shrieked, head to the sky. The other creatures stopped and turned. Jaziri presumed its cry had communicated with the others.

Another demon flew close in on the one holding Laila and attempted to grab her legs while the other held her shoulders. Jaziri knew they intended to rip her apart in mid-air, a grizzly fate. There were only seconds to act!

He lunged at the bow and arrow lying nearby in the snow. Grabbing them, he rolled away from the wounded demon on the ground.

Coming up into a crouch, he notched the arrow and raised the bow to the sky.

The arrow hit the demon holding the girl squarely in the heart. It fluttered toward the ground. It released Laila in mid-air, while the other flew off. She was tossed some distance, from where he stood and landed in a snow drift.

Even as he crouched while catching his breath, he knew that had she not been cushioned by the snow and avoided having struck a tree, she'd have likely died.

He attempted to get to his feet, but the demon was already upon him. It grabbed him around his neck and held him just above the ground. Its rancid breath would have caused Jaziri to retch had his throat not been closed in the

FOREST OF SHADOWS

creature's talon grip.

"Son of Atumba," the demon hissed. "You are the last of your clan and my only threat. I fled to the north to escape your clan, that threat ends this night!"

"You speak the truth demon, this does end now."

Grasping the amulet, he pressed it into the demon's claw.

The creature howled with pain and dropped Jaziri to the ground.

Feeling around, he searched for his saber.

The demon swung a taloned claw and avoided contact by an arm's length, felling a small tree. He struck at Jaziri in a reckless manner. Given its great size and the proximity of the trees, Jaziri could easily avoid his strikes.

Jaziri pushed off and dove through the demon's legs. The beast slammed clawed hands into the bark of the tree that had been behind him, snapping it in two.

Like a gift from Atumba himself, Jaziri's hand found his long saber. The demon moved to strike at him again, he turned on his back. As the demon lurched forward, its sharp talons aimed at his throat, Jaziri struck with his blade. His sword bit into the leathery, scaled flesh of the creature's neck and severed its head in one powerful arc.

Dark demon's blood spurted from its shoulders and its

head bounced off a nearby tree and rolled into the woods. Its body fell, first to its knees, then back on its haunches, then slumping lifeless to the ground.

The warrior sprang to his feet to find Laila. There remained one more demon and he feared it had likely killed the girl by now.

He looked out among the snowdrifts. Reaching the area, he spotted her body, partially covered in snow and lying deathly still.

He surveyed the area, but he saw no sign of the last demon.

Jaziri knelt, and brushed the snow from the girl. As he pulled her towards him, he searched for signs of life. When she began to stir, he held her tight in his arms to keep her warm. When she finally came to, he helped her to her feet and guided her to the stable, all the while he scanned for any sign of the demon.

He bolted the doors and tended to the girl. He sat her down on a bundle of hay and covered her with her own cloak. He looked to the back of the stable, grabbed some logs from a pile and arranged them in a steeple formation as his father had taught him when he was a boy. He gathered some fist sized rocks and arranged them into a circle. He then pulled a shard of iron and a flint from the pouch on his sword belt and used them to start a fire with the logs. After a few moments, bright orange flames licked the air, providing reassurance, warmth, and comfort.

Once they were settled he looked to Laila. She sat on a bundle of hay, her eyes following him. She rubbed her left hand and kept it hidden within her cloak.

"Are you well?" he said.

She smiled, "Aye, warrior, I am well. Are you?"

"Yes."

"Do you know where those creatures came from?"

"The witch Heolstor, they belong to her. She has enchanted the entire forest, and this is her stable. It would seem that she preys on all who travel through these woods, and I was to be her next victim."

"How did you manage to evade her?"

"She fears me because I'm the last son of Atumba."

She looked at Jaziri and pulled the fur cloak closer around her body. He rose and busied himself with fastening saddles on the two mares housed in the stable.

When he finished, he came to sit back near the fire, the girl eyed him warily, her gaze frequently drifting to his chest. He pulled the amulet from his tunic and pulled his fur cloak loosely across his shoulders.

"How did you come to be the last of your village?" the

girl said.

Jaziri stared into the fire. It was as though he were far removed from the situation at hand. His mind returned to the time he stood and watched his entire village burn to the ground. His parents, siblings and clansmen lay slaughtered in the streets. Women and children brutally mutilated in a massacre the likes of which he had never experienced.

Jaziri was no stranger to war. His father had been chief of his village and there had been plenty of skirmishes with rival villages in the region for centuries before his birth, but it was nothing like the total devastation of an entire community.

He drew a deep breath and answered in a calm voice, "It is believed that a witch came to our village to obtain the knowledge of our elders in an effort to bolster her power in the dark arts."

"So that is why you ventured into this haunted forest; you seek revenge?"

He regarded her with narrowed eyes and studied her expression with earnest. She smiled, and the catch lights from the fire danced in her eyes.

"Tell me, your father is sure to worry that you have followed me into these cursed woods. He will have no use of you if you were to be deflowered while in my company."

FOREST OF SHADOWS

Laila smiled. "Then we will have to keep our distance from one another I suppose."

With one fluid motion, Jaziri drew his saber and slashed viciously at her. Unlike the last time, he caught her unaware and connected with her torso. Her powerful magicks gave her inhuman strength and reflexes, saving her from complete evisceration.

He grabbed a flaming faggot from the fire and flung it towards her. The cloak caught fire. She spun in a circle and ripped it off. She held her belly with her left hand and a pitchfork with the other.

Her entrails were partially exposed.

"How did you know warrior? My disguise was flawless."

"Yes, but your knowledge of my intimate conversations with Laila was limited. You responded as though we had not already bedded and you asked questions which you already knew the answers to and despite your outward appearance matching hers without err; you cannot change your eyes. Not to mention you favored your right hand, Laila is a southpaw and your left hand bears the impression of my amulet, where it burned the flesh of your pet demon."

"Clever warrior, but it is no matter; even in my weakened state I still have the power to destroy you. This is my forest, my land and when you die nothing can stand against me."

"Yes, all of this is yours. I, however, I am not. I am the weapon of your destruction."

He moved with the speed of a black jungle cat and attacked with the strength of a river horse. Jaziri tore the amulet from his neck and tossed it at the witch. The amulet grazed her shoulder, and she leapt to avoid its touch. This brought her closer to the warrior, and with one swift thrust of his saber, he ran her through. Jaziri quickly pulled his blade from her body and cleaved the witch from crown to jawbone.

Her head bounced on the ground and landed in the fire. A whoosh of flame rose to the ceiling and caught. Jaziri grabbed the two horses housed in the stable, opened the door and led them out.

Once he was several paces from the stable, he turned and watched it collapse on itself. The burgeoning flames spread to the hut and took it as well.

A rustling near the edge of the woods caught his attention. He turned with his long saber in hand.

A lone cloaked figure leaned against a tree. Jaziri recognized Laila immediately. He jogged the horses over to her, tied their reins to a sapling and approached her.

He pulled her upright and steadied her in his arms. "I

thought I had lost you."

"Nay, not so easily, I'm afraid. I landed in a tree top, which broke my fall, and I remember coming to only to find an old woman bent over me. She began mumbling in some strange language, and the next thing I remember is waking to the sight of flames in the distance."

"The witch is dead, and so are her demons, I would wager. Come; let us take our leave of this place. It will only be a short time before your father's men pursue us through here. Perhaps they will figure that I perished along with you at the hands of the witch."

"Aye, we can only hope, warrior." She wrapped her arms around him and kissed him deeply. He broke their embrace and helped her mount one of the mares before he straddled the other.

As they rode past the smoldering rubble, he dismounted and walked towards the area cautiously. He bent to pick up the amulet given to him by his grandmother. He closed his eyes and held it to his heart in silent prayer to his ancestors.

His head snapped to attention as he heard the rustle of the thicket and spotted a cloaked figure fleeing into the woods. He could tell from her raven tresses it was Rasheeda, the bar-wench. She no doubt was on her way to lead the King's men to them.

JOHN F. ALLEN

"Come, let us hasten our leave of this place," Jaziri said.

The warrior hurriedly remounted his steed, kicked his mount into a brisk run and headed east into the Metrophian Mountain range. Laila followed suit and together they went in search of whatever adventures found them.

John F. Allen is an American writer born in Indianapolis, IN. He is an active member of INDIANA HORROR WRITERS and serves as it's Vice President and is also a member of Indiana Writers Center. He began writing stories as early as the second grade and pursued all forms of writing at some point, throughout his career. John studied Liberal Arts at IUPUI with a focus in Creative Writing, received an honorable discharge from the United States Air Force and is a current member of the American Legion. John's debut novel, The God Killers is planned for publication in Summer 2013 with Seventh Star Press.

John currently resides in Indianapolis, Indiana with his wife, son and daughter.

WEBSITE/BLOG: www.johnfallenwriter.com

EMISSARY

MARCELLA BURNARD

"I have not wrought evil... I have not done what the gods abominate. I have not plundered the offerings in the temples."
The Book of the Dead

When I walked out of the Red Desert into the thin strip of fertile land I'd left as a girl a decade ago, I barely recognized it. Farms still dominated the banks of the broad, dark river, defying the desert sands just beyond. Crops grew in the rich soil. But the people watched me pass with hollow, fear-stricken eyes. No one called out in greeting, nor hailed me for the news from the southern lands from whence I came, trailing the uneasy specters of those I'd killed in battle.

It didn't seem to be the sight of the sword and bow slung across my back, or the pair of lionesses striding beside me that excited dread in the populace. No one commented, nor even awarded us second glances. That remained as I remembered, at least. While the sorcerer, Prince Aukenhet, might have denied his obligation to the temples, his people, at least, seemed to recall the old ways.

The lionesses, Eburi, and her daughter, Sorqet, could accompany me safely into the city. As was Eburi's due, I'd dyed Sekhmet's marks into her fur. She wore white on her nose and on the backs of her ears. Red tear stains striped her cheeks, and red pigment marked her spine and ribs. The adolescent cub, Sorqet, bore the sign of the Goddess's protection, a collar of red-dyed leather studded with bronze. No one would mistake Sekhmet's Chosen or her daughter for feral lions.

Eburi's mother's mother had given up her life in the wild to serve Sekhmet. Whether the Goddess Herself had blessed Her Chosen with intelligence, or whether the cats were naturally smarter than anyone had believed, Eburi's intellect rivaled my own, though her thoughts walked a path unfamiliar to me. Much of our training since the day she'd chosen me so many years ago had focused on teaching us to value and trust our different perceptions.

We'd learned well. Just as the cats had given up life in the wild, I'd forfeited home and identity in order to commit my life, body, and soul to Sekhmet's Army. Never had I intended to return to the land of my birth. Yet, shortly after the height of the sun, I stood at the war-scarred sandstone block gates of my birth city. Menethes.

The statues of Horus that had stood vigil at the gates since the inception of the city had been shattered. Blackened fragments of stone littered the road. Deep scars marred the stone columns of the city gate. The rock appeared melted.

My heart stumbled and fell.

Why destroy the likeness of the God who'd protected the city from marauders, bandits and invaders throughout history?

Sorqet snuffled a blackened chunk of stone and sneezed.

Her mother hissed, not at her cub, whose fur bristled along her spine, but at the empty spaces where the statues of Horus had been.

I looked closer and shuddered.

The fetid stench of magic clawed at the back of my throat. I felt it, then, the cloying touch of sorcery enshrouding Menethes as tightly as the priests of Anubis wrapped a mummy. Misgiving weighed heavy upon me. I was a simple warrior, not one of Sekhmet's priestesses familiar with the kind of power that melted stone.

Still. Sekhmet, through the voice of Her high priestess, had charged me with curing what ailed Menethes.

Eburi, Sorqet, and I shuffled to the gates, doing our best to avoid stepping on the magic-tainted fragments of

Horus's statues.

The battle-hardened veterans who'd guarded the city in my youth had been replaced by baby-faced young men rattling around in leather and bronze armor that had clearly been made for full grown warriors. The pair snapped to attention, crossing their spears to bar my path.

Eburi growled at the blatant discourtesy.

Both young men twitched and eyed the three of us, uncertainty etched into the crinkles that appeared between their brows.

"Surrender your weapons," one of them demanded. His voice shook.

I was wrapped still in white traveling robes in the fashion of the desert nomads. They'd taught me to wear the robes thus when I'd nearly died attempting to cross the Red Desert for the first time as a girl. And for that reason alone, he could be forgiven for mistaking me for a common traveler. Fabric covered every inch of skin and hair, leaving only a narrow slit open so that I might see as I walked. I took the wrap shielding my nose and mouth from sun and dust away from my face and said, "Has Menethes fallen so far that it no longer recognizes the courtesy due warriors of Sekhmet?"

The young men traded a glance, wide eyes suggested

that they didn't know what to do. The bigger of the two tightened his grip on his spear, puffed up his chest and took refuge in bluster.

Beyond the gate, townspeople gathered, watching, worry and fear in the stoop of their shoulders and in the way men and women alike lifted garments to hide their faces. Whether from me or from the guards, I didn't know.

I frowned.

"It is Prince Aukenhet's command, Lady," the soldier snapped.

I drew my sword in a slow sweep so as not to threaten or alarm.

Sorquet sidled away, retreating out of the reach of possible battle.

"It is Sekhmet's command that I enter the city of my birth with my weapons in my possession," I said. "Let Aukenhet gainsay Her."

The guard drew breath to argue.

Eburi snarled.

In a flash, I swept my blade up to where their spears crossed. My sword shattered the ebony-wood hafts. I had no doubt they'd felt the blow resonate to their shoulders. Their fingers would sting for a while.

The bigger of the two cried out and stumbled backward, grasping for his sword.

A shout went up from within the city as I strode after the retreating guard and swung again.

He yelped as the flat of my blade rang against his knuckles. He snatched it away from his sword hilt to suck on his reddening hand.

Eburi and I stalked to his side. I yanked the still sheathed sword free of his belt.

Behind me, the younger man drew.

Both lions coughed a warning.

I spun on him as his blade rang clear of the sheath.

He knew how to hold the weapon, but from the sweat beading on his upper lip and the nervous shifting of his eyes as he tried to keep me, Eburi, and Sorqet in his sight, it was plain he'd never used it in anything but learning to use it.

Eburi grumbled. She turned her back on him and sauntered through the gates. Sorqet followed her mother's lead, expressing disdain in that turning of their backs. They'd plainly opined that the young guard wasn't worth their effort.

I fought back a smile.

The big cats paused to one side of the gathered watchers,

keeping an eye on me and on the crowd all at the same time.

"Hoktep!" a gravelly male voice called from the crowd. "Put away the sword, boy! Are you mad? The Emissary. . ."

"You were relieved of duty, old man," the guard facing me gritted, determination in the set of his shoulders and fear in his white-knuckled grip on his sword hilt. "I have my orders."

"And I mine," I said, pressing my tone flat. I'd wasted too much time protecting young men from themselves. I did not want to give Aukenhet time to send more experienced reinforcements to the gate.

The young guard attacked, driving straight for my chest.

A quick thrust across my body, hilt up, point aimed at the ground, knocked his sword well off target.

Momentum drove him past my left side. I turned, following his stumble, and struck a forceful blow to the small of his back with the flat of my blade.

He cried out, dropped his sword, and arms flailing, fell face down into the pale dirt of the road.

The gravelly voice sounded in anguished protest.

I tucked the first guard's sword under one arm, then picked up the second before turning to face the watchers.

A lean man, his craggy, sun-burned face ashen, stood

apart from the others. While he'd dressed in a farmer's tunic and sandals, his bearing and the lines of muscle showing through the fabric said 'soldier'. His wide eyes focused on the guard I'd felled.

I took the weapons to him. "He's bruised. No more. There is no honor in killing children."

He looked me in the eye, then. Relief broke across his visage in a grim smile as he took the guards' swords from me. He saluted. "Welcome home, Emissary of Sekhmet. It is not the Menethes you knew."

I nodded. "I am not the child who left Menethes over a decade ago. Change is life."

"And death," he murmured in response. "Gods go with you, Emissary."

I awarded the old soldier a brief smile before I sheathed my sword and strode into the streets of Menethes.

The spectators scattered before me, vanishing into houses and storefronts.

The aged soldier had guessed my mission.

Undoubtedly, the sorcerer, Aukenhet already knew I'd been sent to Menethes to destroy him.

Low lying, sandstone buildings squatted on either side of the road. No women lingered in the shadows tending to spinning or grinding grain for bread. Unnatural silence, broken only by the hot breath of the wind stirring laundry hanging over the window sills, blanketed Menethes.

The stink of too many people living close together assured me that the city was still populated. But I saw no one.

Where were the children?

Even the market, usually a crowd of carts and animals, bright goods, and shoppers gathered around the well at the city's center, stood all but deserted. Three merchants had set up shop in the achingly empty space. They'd picked spots equidistant one from the other, but not a single soul wandered through browsing the metal cooking pots, or fruits, or clay wares.

Eburi and Sorqet followed me to the well. I divested myself of pack, bow, and sword before I turned the dusty, slimy water out of the clay bowls arrayed at the foot of the well and drew fresh water for each of the lionesses. When they'd drunk their fill, I drew water to quench my thirst, and then to wash the dust of travel from my hands and face.

The white robes I unwound from around my body glittered pale red with sand. Even my companions' coats had taken on a reddish, rather than tawny hue. But the protection offered by the robes meant that my leather armor remained supple. The bronze studs still gleamed in the sun.

I stuffed the bundle of dusty fabric into my pack, then buckled my sword belt around my waist, slung my quiver and arrows across my back, and picked up my short bow.

The cats stepped into their places beside me, Eburi on my left where she could join a fight without being in the way of my sword arm, and Sorqet on my right where the adolescent could dodge away to avoid battle before it was joined.

I slung my pack over one shoulder and turned toward the tallest edifice in the city. The palace towered several stories above the surrounding structures. Sand-blasted, sun-bleached pennants, little more than dingy rags waved listlessly from the corners of the building.

Feeling eyes upon me, I glanced at each of the merchants.

The tall, dark-skinned man selling bronze goods folded his hands before his lips and bowed low.

"Emissary," he said as he straightened. His glance followed my line of sight to the palace before he returned his attention to me and came forward. "I live in the south lands. It is because of the Army of Sekhmet that I still have a home and family to return to when my business here is complete."

"I am glad of it," I replied, feeling as if his acknowledgement put a few of the dead men haunting me to rest. "It is a long journey north you have made to sell your wares."

He shrugged and lowered his voice. "In times of trouble, when few will venture into perilous regions to provide necessities…"

"A man can make a considerable profit," I noted.

"Business should benefit all," he said. "The buyer, the seller, and the Gods."

He drew breath as if he meant to go on, then frowned, and instead, reached into the folds of the saffron fabric of his flowing robe.

"When I first came to Menethes," he said in an undertone, "I went to the temple of Sekhmet to give an offering in thanks for my safe passage through the Red Desert."

I nodded.

"The priestess of the temple gave this to me and bade me to wait and watch, for, she said, another devotee of Sekhmet's would come. This was hours before the prince destroyed the temples and cut the priests and priestesses down in the streets."

Desolation swept me, replacing the beating of my heart with a deep ache.

This was why I'd been discharged from the army and sent to right the wrongs Aukenhet had committed. He'd offended not just my goddess, but all the gods by his actions. Sekhmet held dominion over bringing down the sorcerer who'd brought misery and death into Menethes. I just didn't know why she'd chosen me to Her weapon in this matter.

"Take it, Emissary," the merchant said. "I beg you."

I glanced at what he held. My eyes widened at the sight of the polished black dagger blade. The blood quickened in my veins. "A Dagger of Heaven?"

"The priestess said I would know when the dagger's rightful owner appeared," he said, reversing it to offer the hilt to me. "I have no doubt it was you that the priestess awaited."

Hesitating to take something that suggested yet more magic, I closed my stinging eyes.

"Emissary, please," he said. "It is not safe for me to carry this burden."

He was right. The Daggers of Heaven were rumored to be proof against magic both as shield and as weapon. If Aukenhet knew that the dagger existed, he would stop at nothing to destroy it along with whoever carried it.

"Do you believe I give this too lightly?"

"No." I opened my eyes and accepted the weapon from him. The hilt was warm, whether from exposure to the sun or from his skin, I couldn't say. "The priestess of Sekhmet in

EMISSARY

Menethes was my mother."

His black eyes widened. "I am sorry you learned of her passing from my lips, Emissary."

Twelve years ago, I'd left the city in anger, full of the arrogance of youth, certain my mother's unreasonable demands and restraints upon me were unjustified. Months of travel, years of training and then a decade of service to Sekhmet's Army had given me perspective. And maybe understanding. It tore my heart that I'd missed my single opportunity to reconcile with the woman who had only tried to protect me from my own childish foolishness.

I had to straighten my shoulders and found I couldn't look the man in the eye. I tugged my bronze dagger from the sheath at my left hip. "Take my dagger in its stead. Sell it, or use it for your protection, as you will. Your duty here is done. It would be safest if you returned to your home. I suggest departing within the hour."

He took my dagger, bowed again, and without another word, scurried back to his cart where he began packing away his goods.

I tucked the priceless dagger into the sheath at my hip so that only the leather-wrapped hilt showed. It might be any other bronze-bladed dagger.

Eburi rumbled, eager for battle.

Squaring my shoulders once more, I left the market behind and marched to the doors of the palace.

"Halt." Guards, proper, seasoned men who fit their polished armor, stepped into my path. "What business have you with House Menethes?"

Eburi's lips lifted in a snarl. The fur along her back rose. Sorqet fell back to stand behind me.

"The Emissary of Sekhmet requires a word with Prince Aukenhet," I said.

The elder of the two guards snapped to attention and bowed his head. "Emissary."

"You're armed," his younger companion said, frowning between us as if confused.

"It is good to know the guards of Menethes are so diligent and observant," I said.

The man flushed, and then bristled. "You can't enter the city bearing arms. Prince Aukenhet. . ."

His companion put out a hand to restrain what would have been an aggressive step into range of Eburi's claws and my sword.

"Omlin," the elder guard warned. "Your bruised ego will get you killed."

"No weapons in the city, Tamorek," Omlin snapped. "To keep the peace, to protect the citizens. . ."

EMISSARY

"It isn't to protect the citizens," I countered, letting my pack, then my quiver and bow, slide to the stones beneath my feet.

The elder guard, Tamorek, cut a sharp look my way. "Sekhmet demands an accounting?"

I didn't answer.

He dropped the hand holding his companion and stepped back. "I honor the old ways, Emissary. The destruction of the temples and of anyone who dared stand against Aukenhet, many of whom were my former comrades in arms, grieves me. I won't stand in your way."

"And so I pray you will not fail, because this one," he jerked a thumb at Omlin, "is Aukenhet's creature."

I met Omlin's calculating gaze and detected the glaze of insanity. I knew what he saw. A tall woman dressed in oiled leather armor, studded with bronze, a long braid of thick black hair, and a slender body marred by battle scars.

For a split second, he weighed his chances against me.

And made the wrong decision.

He charged, drawing his sword in the two steps it took to reach me.

Using an acrobatic trick Sekhmet's temple taught, I cartwheeled to one side, rounding off at the end to land beside him as he skidded to a halt.

Too late.

Eburi flanked him on the right, I, on the left. I drew my sword.

Roaring a battle cry, Eburi sprang, claws extended, and ears flattened.

Omlin went down screaming beneath the big cat's teeth and claws.

Eburi liked tormenting her prey, and normally, I wouldn't deny her the pleasure. But Omlin had committed no sin other than playing for the wrong side. I gave him a more merciful death than the lioness's teeth.

"Gods guard your path to the Halls of Judgment," I said, closing in and cutting his throat in one quick blow.

Blood staining her muzzle, Eburi lifted her head to glare at me. She snarled.

I dipped my chin to her. "Be angry if you wish. Or rise and follow me to better sport."

She blew out a sharp, disgusted breath, but she was already on her feet, whiskers and ears perked forward, tail twitching in anticipation of the hunt.

Bloody sword still in hand, I saluted Tamorek, and then scooped up my possessions before Eburi, Sorqet, and I strode into the palace grounds.

He returned the gesture. "Sekhmet guide your blade."

EMISSARY

Murmuring prayers for strength and guidance, I led the way into the courtyard. No guards blocked my path. I frowned, misgiving rattling down the inside of my ribs.

A trickling fountain stood in the center of the yard. Date palms, vines heavy with brilliant yellow flowers, and glossy shrubs grew along the walls. The sweet scent of flowers rested easily in the cooler air of the shaded courtyard.

I paused long enough to wipe the blood from my sword with a corner of the robes tucked into my pack.

Whispers and hushed footsteps suggested the cats and I had attracted onlookers. I cast a glance to either side, wondering if I faced spies or merely the curious.

An enormous, furred head nudged my hip, as if in reassurance. I rubbed Eburi's scarred ears. She wouldn't seek affection if she believed we were threatened.

She grumbled her pleasure.

Behind me, someone giggled.

A glance over my shoulder showed me a sea of children's faces. They clung to one another while craning their necks for a look at the big cats. The curious, then.

When I turned, smiling upon them, the littlest – I judged it was she who'd giggled at Eburi's expression of bliss – shrugged off the hands holding her back. She darted forward, heedless of the blood matting the fur of Eburi's muzzle. The child stopped well out of my arm's reach.

"Blessings, Little Sister. Where are your parents?" I asked.

"Can I pet them?" the child asked, staring at the cats and totally ignoring my question. Her eyes widened as she looked up to meet Eburi's golden eyes.

I hated to lose time, but above everyone in Menethes, the children were my charge to protect. I needed to understand why they were inside the palace. Perhaps I could coax an answer from her as she admired Eburi and Sorqet.

"You may," I said, "but you must first learn to be polite in lion language. This is Eburi. She is a veteran of many battles. See her scars and the red stripes painted on her sides? She has one for every campaign she's fought in. This is her daughter, Sorqet. She has no scars and no paint because she is too young, yet, to fight."

At my hand signal, both cats sank to the ground, forepaws before them.

"Come where they can see you," I directed, rounding to the child's side so I could demonstrate. "Approach from the front, like this. One must never sneak up on a warrior. Now. Let them get your scent. Hold out one hand. Yes. That's it."

Eburi obligingly stretched her neck to snuffle the tiny

fingers.

The child laughed.

The lioness crept forward to head-butt the girl's hand.

"You see? She has given you permission to pet her," I said.

The child stoked the lioness's short, dusty fur and began telling Eburi what a good girl she was in a cooing, singsong voice, as if the scarred warrior were the family dog.

"Where are your parents?" I asked again, glancing around at the rest of the children who'd edged forward to emulate their youngest friend.

One of the older boys shrugged. "At home."

"Yet you are here in the palace," I noted. "Why?"

"Prince Aukenhet says we are his guests," the boy answered as if parroting someone. Confusion showed in the furrows marring his forehead.

"I see no guards," I said. "How does he keep you?"

The boy paled. "He has demons, Lady. If we leave the palace, they come for us. They hurt us."

Solemn faces nodded in agreement and something icy twisted in my gut.

"They killed Lapheses," the boy went on. "Prince Aukenhet said the demons squeezed him too hard when they caught him. Then he laughed."

Heart hammering in horror, I stared at him. The boy might not comprehend, but I did. The city's children were hostages. Aukenhet controlled the populace by threating their children. If it was demons Aukenhet commanded, they hadn't merely killed the child. They'd consumed his soul, erased him from existence. His parents wouldn't be reunited with him, not even in the afterlife.

My grip tightened on my sword to quell the shaking in my limbs. "By your leave, Eburi, Sorqet, and I must attend to an errand. I ask that you remain here or in your rooms no matter what you may hear."

Try though I might to keep my tone friendly and reasonable, I managed to frighten almost all of them with my thinly disguised fury.

Eyes widened. Faces paled. Older children took hold of the younger ones, pulling them away from me.

I turned away feeling small for frightening children already separated from their families and homes. I caught up my belongings, then skirted the fountain and stalked into the palace.

Aukenhet clearly knew I had entered the city. Not a single guard stood at the entrance to the procession hall. When I walked up to the great mahogany doors adorned with patterns inlaid in gold, the court attendants opened it smoothly, without any trace of emotion on their brown faces.

I let my pack and my quiver slide from my shoulders into a pile against the back wall. "Sorqet. Stay with our things."

Grumbling, the lanky cub settled to the floor resting her chin on my pack.

"Eburi."

The lioness met my gaze, her golden eyes alive with cunning and anticipation.

"If the Dagger of Heaven confers any protection at all against the usurper's magic, it will shield only me," I said. I hoped. "It cannot also protect you."

Clearly not wanting to hear what I had to say, she flattened her ears and looked toward the distant throne.

"I must be the one to destroy the sorcerer," I said. "But I need the aid of your superior senses."

That brought her gaze back to me. Her ears swiveled forward in interest.

"Keep watch. Warn me of sorcery, treachery, or traps."

Holding my gaze, she came close and rubbed her cheek against my hip. Her agreement brought a smile to my face while a bittersweet pang pierced my heart.

I loved Eburi and Sorqet. Yet I walked into each battle

with Eburi knowing that it could be our last. I didn't think I could bear the loss of my remaining family.

Taking a deep breath, I nodded.

Sword in hand, Eburi at my side, I set a sedate pace into the wide-open throne room. Sun slanted in through narrow windows high in the sandstone walls on my left. It gleamed off the burnished gold adorning the carvings cut into the right hand wall, scattering yellow-orange light through the room like a handful of lotus petals.

Braziers burned on either side of the throne, casting sickly-sweet smoke into the overheated atmosphere. Behind the braziers, two statues stood. I didn't recognize the black stone from which they'd been carved. They had reptilian rather than human features. I caught the glitter of fangs and the opalescent gleam of scales cut in the polished rock. Their eyes glowed red as if lit from within. Each held a blade curved in the style favored by the people living far to the east.

Prince Aukenhet, thick of body and round-faced, lounged at his ease upon the ornately sculpted ebony wood throne. He wore a glittering gold waist cloth that fell to his feet and an elaborate lapis and gold bead collar.

What few courtiers remained, he dismissed with a flick of his fingers.

EMISSARY

A girl in white robes and jet black wig fled down the steps of the dais. Another young woman, clutching the rent fabric of her blue robe to her bare chest stumbled past. Her eyes looked red-rimmed and out of the corner of my eye, I caught sight of burns and whip stripes on her back.

A man, little more than a skeleton covered in an ooze of skin, followed the pair, grinning. His gaze, when it crossed mine, glittered with malevolent glee.

I twitched with the desire to cut him down as he passed, but I locked my muscles, forcing myself to stillness. The evil in Menethes began with Aukenhet. It clung to him and to the room. If I wished to end it, I had to start with the sorcerer who'd stolen the throne from his elder brother.

I shivered, chilled by the oily touch of Aukenhet's foul magic. When I looked again at the corpulent self-styled prince, one other man remained, standing at frozen attention on the step below Aukenhet's throne, an open white robe draped over his shoulders.

Soldier.

Aukenhet's body guard?

The man wore the striped waist cloth of an officer. Muscle stood out in his chest and crossed arms, showing through the fabric of his robes. Worse, intelligence rather than cunning shone from his black eyes as he assessed me in turn.

"Emissary of Sekhmet," Aukenhet said, satisfaction ringing in his voice. "I've been expecting you. I'd offer welcome, but already, you abuse my hospitality by bringing a pair of flea-ridden pets dripping dust, blood, and filth into my presence."

Swallowing the suicidal urge to charge him and stick my sword through his throat, I forced a chilly smile to my face. "Aukenhet, you have destroyed temples, murdered the priests, and defiled the sacred precincts. Your actions offend the Gods."

His beady black eyes glittered at me.

I fingered my mother's gift to me, the dagger she'd given into a merchant's keeping before she'd died. Whether the Dagger of Heaven knew by some means that I stood before the man I'd been sent to destroy, I could not know, but strength and resolve surged into me when my left hand closed on the hilt.

"You've been sent to rectify the situation?" he sneered.

"By any means necessary," I confirmed.

"Sekhmet has turned you from a warrior into nothing more than a common assassin?" He clicked his tongue. "Pity. You see, Kol defends my life with his own. Kol. Kill her."

As I'd feared, Aukenhet gestured to the soldier. The

man lips pressed tight in what looked like distaste at the prince's command, but he drew. Tightening his grip on his weapon until his knuckles showed white, Kol advanced on me.

"Sekhmet has no argument with you. Nor have I," I said, backing away and crouching in a battle-ready position.

Eburi stalked to the edge of the room. She put her back to the wall where she could keep her eye on Aukenhet and on me.

Kol said nothing. Instead, he circled outside of my shorter reach, watching me counter him.

Most fighters telegraphed their intent – attack or retreat – well before executing the move. Well trained warriors had learned to read their opponent's body language like a scribe reading a papyrus scroll.

I knew he watched me move, hoping to learn to read me. I knew this because I sought the same information from him and shivered when a thread of misgiving wrapped a noose around my heart.

I couldn't read him.

Eburi's growl echoed through the throne room, bouncing back upon itself until I felt as if my skull rattled with it.

"He is not our prey," I told her.

Aukenhet's champion imagined I'd left him an opening while I spoke to Eburi.

He darted in, aiming a swift cut at my sword arm.

I didn't bother parrying, since I suspected he'd use any contact of our blades to run up on me and lock us body to body. With his greater weight and strength, if I let him gain that advantage, I'd be dead in an instant. So I sprang out of the way, a simple leap, conserving energy.

Poised on the edge of the dais, Aukenhet muttered. His fingers twitched.

Eburi hissed.

Something cold and slimy slithered up my right leg, rooting me to the floor. When I glanced down, I saw nothing. Panic tightened barbed bands around my chest. In its sheath against my side, the Dagger of Heaven warmed.

The scent of bodies rotting in the sun wafted past, making my eyes water. The chill wrapped around my leg vanished. I could move unhindered.

Kol's eyes narrowed.

Did he know Aukenhet had tried and failed to bespell me? Did he care?

He opened his guard slightly.

Not quite taunting. A goad, maybe.

No matter. I'd take his dare. I dove into a shoulder roll

that brought me within striking distance. For a moment, as I let the momentum of the roll bring me to my feet, I caught the startled look in his face. His lips parted and I heard the rush of air sucked into his lungs as I aimed my blade at his ribs.

Kol backpedaled hard and barely brought his sword across his body in time to deflect me.

That he managed to parry at all spoke of agility and strength that could all too easily best me. Why then did my heart sing at the prospect of having found so worthy an opponent?

He followed the parry around as I danced past his left shoulder. He tried for a slice at my back, scratching only my tricep.

Flinging my heels over my head, I threw myself to the right, using my free left hand to push off the stone floor and land on my feet many sword lengths away from Aukenhet's champion.

No permanent damage.

Yet.

He didn't waste time or effort in reversing the direction of his intended strike. Turning full circle, he came back on guard.

The hint of a smile on his lips drove a splinter of

warmth into me. Kol brought his blade up in a salute. Respect glimmered in his dark eyes.

With a nod, I returned the salute.

"You aren't courting, are you, Kol?" Aukenhet taunted, still sketching symbols in the air, his face contorted in concentration. "Don't think I'm not tallying the price of your delay."

Rage flashed into my opponent's face, and then vanished, scoured as expressionless as the desert sands after a windstorm.

Another rumbled warning from Eburi.

Blue fire erupted from the floor behind me. More magic. Heat seared my back, driving me forward, into reach of Kol's blade.

Cold so intense it made my breath catch radiated out from my hip. The Dagger of Heaven.

The flames didn't wink out, but I no longer felt them. I backed through the wall of fire, putting it between me and Kol.

On the dais, Aukenhet cursed. His magical flames sputtered and died.

Kol rushed me. His first step alone closed nearly half the distance between us.

Slashing at my abdomen, he kept coming.

EMISSARY

Thinking he'd meant to body-slam me to the ground, I leapt aside. The sting of his blade parting the skin below my ribs registered in my brain. Too late, I saw him pull up short as if he'd anticipated my dodge.

He swung, bringing his sword down toward my head.

Too close. I had to block him. His blow drove me to one knee.

Eburi snarled, rose and paced the edge of our battlefield.

"No!" I cried at her, my heart stumbling in my chest at the thought that Aukenhet might focus his sorcery upon the great cat.

My fear gave Kol the perfect opening. He could kill me.

But the champion, his gaze locked on the blood I felt trickling down my stomach, flinched.

At the sight of my blood drawn by his hand? Why?

His sword fell away from mine, making both blades ring.

I staggered upright and saluted in acknowledgement of first blood.

He inclined his head and attacked.

I met him halfway, my sword poised to deflect the slice to my throat. At the last moment, I ducked beneath his blade and spun to slash at his sword arm.

The tip of my blade opened a gash where his arm met his shoulder before he caught my blade with his.

He grunted.

Gasping for breath, I looked him in the eye and said, "What is his hold over you, Champion? Why do you protect a despot?"

Aukenhet clapped, a slow derisive sound punctuating the noise of our labored breathing. "I'd heard that Sekhmet's Army trains the minds as well as the bodies of its soldiers. Clearly they failed with you."

I spun away from Aukenhet's reluctant champion, toward the dais, and the corpulent form clothed in gold-sewn robes. Not because of the insult to my intelligence. But because of the lines of worry and recrimination I saw creasing Kol's forehead.

I raised my weapon to drive it through the sorcerer's morbid body. Save that his champion moved too quickly. His footfall sounded right behind me. I whirled in time to deflect a vicious blow that would have severed my spine.

My arms took the shock all the way to my shoulders.

The blow notched my blade, possibly his, too. We stood locked together for a moment, the worst possible thing for me in any battle. But I had more than one weapon - the intellect Sekhmet's priestesses had trained and Aukenhet had maligned.

"Your family," I said. "It is the safety of your family he holds over you."

"A sweet-faced little sister," the repulsive tyrant said on a sound like he'd smacked his lips in enjoyment.

I shuddered in horror. One look at the torment in my opponent's eyes and I disengaged. I flung myself past his left hip, off the steps. I did not want to kill him. Not when he fought to protect his family.

That put me at a distinct disadvantage.

His sword and another pulse of magic whistled just above my heels as I tumbled away from the pair of men.

The sorcerer growled in frustration.

Rolling to my feet, I muttered thanks to my mother's spirit for the protection she'd afforded me from beyond the grave.

I spun on Kol and demanded, "Why have you not killed him yourself?"

Misery etched lines into the flesh around his eyes.

"Stupid girl," Aukenhet hissed. "If I die, she dies. Such is the power of my magic."

The air went out of my lungs. I hadn't counted on murdering innocents along with the sorcerer prince destroying the people of Menethes. Weariness clouded my limbs and dulled my reflexes.

The Dagger of Heaven did nothing.

Sucking in a trembling breath, I demanded, "Have you gotten your heir upon her, then?"

Kol stumbled. White outlined his lips as if I'd stuck him a mortal blow.

Aukenhet smirked but did not answer. Of course. Defy the Gods though he might, he knew enough of Divine Law to know I could not and would not kill a woman with child.

Kol met my gaze, regret and dread written in the furrows of his brow. "I can't let you kill her."

He leaped from the steps, his sword, already stained with my blood, aimed for my heart. And left his torso unprotected.

I stood my ground, bracing for impact, my own blade held at the ready. I'd taught him that I could and would dodge his blows until exhaustion took me. So I couldn't move. Not this time.

In the final second before his blade took my life, and I saw the dawning horror in his wide eyes indicating that he believed he'd kill me, I dropped to the ground.

His rush carried him past me.

I rolled to my feet and rounded, already swinging as we both turned.

My blade opened a stripe across his abdomen. Blood ran freely. I feared I hadn't pulled my cut sufficiently.

But he didn't fall. He took a step, winced, then drove for me again.

I recognized his strategy as I whirled away.

He couldn't force me to engage in a contest of strength, one I knew I wouldn't win. My fighting technique was unfamiliar to him, but he'd obviously worked out that I survived based on speed, agility and endurance. If he could wear me down, he'd have my life in his hands.

It was a blade that cut both ways, however. Sweat rolled down his forehead and moistened his chest. His ribs heaved.

No matter how I looked at this, I could see no triumph for me. I wouldn't shrink from killing any man who violated Sekhmet's tenets.

But Kol hadn't. He was a man driven to desperation by a tyrant.

I didn't want to kill him.

It appeared that he didn't want to kill me.

Yet he wouldn't let me near the man I needed to destroy, the man I wanted to kill for every depravity he'd visited upon Menethes.

A light went on in my brain. I gasped and stumbled away from Kol's jab at my thigh.

I wasn't fast enough.

The point bit my flesh. It hit muscle. Deep. I croaked a pained protest.

Kol jerked away, the move graceless.

Hot blood rushed down my leg.

Eburi yowled and disobeyed my request to stay out of the battle.

The great cat sprang. Her howl rattled my chest.

"Don't kill!" I yelled. "Hold! Hold him, Eburi!"

She screamed her displeasure, but she twisted to avoid landing atop Kol. She slapped him with one massive paw.

He made no move to deflect the blow.

Eburi swept him from his feet and sat on him.

Through the ringing in my ears, I thought I heard Kol wheeze in despair, except the sound resolved as a chuckle.

Aukenhet shouted something that sounded like a curse in a guttural, ugly language I didn't recognize.

Whirling to face the tainted throne of Menethes, I saw the sorcerer cloaked in a sickly yellow-green glow. Otherworldly power surged through the throne room.

I felt as if the stones heaved beneath my feet. Shock congealed the blood in my veins.

The statues on either side of Aukenhet's throne *moved*.

"Emissary of a useless god," Aukenhet snarled, "you

disappoint me. If your precious deity were of any use, she'd have whispered every one of my secrets to you. You'd have known that so brazen an attack upon my person could never succeed."

My throat went dry because I heard the ring of truth in his words. I couldn't see any possibility that I would get close enough to the sorcerer on the throne to destroy him.

Yet, Sekhmet taught that Divine Truth rarely matched human truth. What the prince believed to be true and what was actual fact might be very different things.

I was Sekhmet's instrument. The Goddess could and would make the rivers run red with the blood of those who'd offended the gods. As Aukenhet had done and continued to do.

Chanting again in a voice that hurt my ears, Aukenhet continued his spell. The sickly glow surrounding him spread, until it blanketed the entire dais. The scent of the incense in the braziers grew overpowering. Sweet with a layer of long dead corpse lingering underneath.

My gorge rose. I swallowed hard against it.

Yellow-green light washed the feet of the statues.

Eburi roared.

The demons flexed, the glow of their baleful read eyes intensifying. Black stone cracked, then shattered.

Shards whizzed past.

I choked on sulfur fumes. Cold terror washed my innards.

If the demons killed me, they'd erase me from existence as surely as if my heart weighed heavier than Ma'at's feather of Truth at judgment. It hadn't occurred to me until that moment how much I valued the promise of a blissful afterlife and the chance to embrace my mother, if only in our spirit forms and apologize for parting on angry words.

I heard the sorcerer's manic giggle as the demons jumped to attention with a clang of metal. Shaking, my hands slick and damp, I crouched to face them.

They'd killed a child.

Justice required that I put aside my fear and give Sekhmet their blood. If they could bleed.

As if they hadn't learned anything from my battle with Kol, they rushed me, curved swords brandished high.

Whispering, "Sekhmet, Powerful One, Eye of Ra, Goddess of Divine Retribution. You are the Terror before which the Demons tremble!" I pitched forward over my weapon and tumbled a complete summersault well under the swipe of their weapons.

Still tucked, I rolled to my feet, blade held to take one of the creatures across the gut. The metal bit. His momentum drove it deeper. Blood and darker gore sprayed out behind me. Hot drops spattered my back. The thing collapsed. It sounded remarkably like the sacks of sodden laundry temple servants tossed from the walls down to the river.

Behind me, the second demon clawed for purchase on the stone floor. It grunted.

I'd never turn in time. I shoved my sword up to guard my head.

The demon struck.

Metal screamed and my arm went numb to the shoulder.

The demon grumbled and I realized our blades were locked together, the bronze stressed enough to hold his weapon.

He heaved, ripping my sword from my grip.

Both blades crashed to the floor and slid to the far wall.

Leaping to my feet, I twisted, both feet planted, then at the last moment, lashed out with my left foot, catching the creature lower than I'd anticipated.

If demons had groins, I'd nailed him. It was enough to stagger him, momentarily.

I dove for his companion's blade, scooping it up in my left hand. Then, spinning, I took his head in one blow. The curved blade barely even paused in hacking through the spine, even wielded in my weaker hand while my right arm dangled at my side.

Pausing to suck in a breath and flex my tingling fingers, I turned back to the dais.

Eburi and Sorqet both shrieked in warning.

The sorcerer, face crimson with rage, had begun casting, fingers sketching symbols, lips moving as he muttered incantations. His malevolent gaze locked onto mine.

Cold sweat erupted on my forehead. Icy, unseen fingers clutched at my throat. My footsteps faltered and I swayed.

Gritting my teeth until my jaw ached, I forced myself up the first step of the dais. It grew harder to draw air into my chest. I closed reluctant fingers around the hilt of the dagger the merchant had given me as the pitch of the sorcerer's spell rose.

Perhaps I'd used up whatever beneficial magic had graced the Dagger of Heaven. The weapon offered no solace.

In a flash of insight, I saw that Aukenhet would kill me.

I had planned for that, but I'd intended to take him with me into death. Now, I knew. I wouldn't. I drew the Dagger of Heaven, anyway.

I'd face my end armed as was my duty and my right.

A blur of gold confused my sight. I braced, expecting the pain and burn of foul magic to blast me.

A shrill wail filled with terror and agony sank into the

stones like blood.

The tendrils of magic choking me vanished. I drew a full breath.

And I saw.

Blood. And Sorqet, backing away from Aukenhet.

My heart faltered.

"Sorqet!" I croaked above the sorcerer's snuffling groans.

She turned, her whiskers twitching in satisfaction, and her nose wrinkled in disgust. She spat a mangled hand to the floor.

The prince's left hand, rings still intact. My gaze shot to him, cradling his bleeding stump.

Cool breath slid into my lungs.

The blood wasn't hers.

I had asked her mother to sit out the conflict. It hadn't occurred to me to ask her to stay out of the fight, too.

Pride soared in my chest.

Sorqet had taken first blood in her first battle and thereby had become an adult. And a warrior.

I smoothed gore from her broad head as I tightened my grip on my dagger and made it a single step toward ending Aukenhet's miserable life.

He murmured over his wound, his chant broken by gasps.

The bleeding stopped. His wound closed, healing before my eyes.

He lifted his gaze to me once more. Rage and triumph mingled in his face. His attention flicked to Sorqet. The mumble shifted.

Sorqet screamed.

I screamed.

Where his blood touched us, we burned. I smelled scorched fur and skin.

Fury burst through me. I pounced.

With a warbling battle cry, so did Eburi.

We slammed into the man at the same instant, bearing him to the stone floor. I'd expected the impact to interrupt his vile spell.

But Sorqet still hissed and caterwauled in protest.

My left hand, where I'd smoothed blood from her fur, burned hotter than any fire.

Eburi's growl covered Aukenhet's mumble, but his lips still moved.

The pain in my hand doubled. With a rumbled command to Eburi, and shuddering in disgust, I straddled Aukenhet's chest. I cut his tongue from his head as his shriek of agony and terror ended in a gurgle of blood.

I flung his limp, dead flesh into one of the braziers.

EMISSARY

The reek of charring meat cleared the sickly sweet incense from the air.

His wordless screams and sobs sounded sweet to my ears, for Sorqet's cries had eased to grumbles at the first touch of the heavenly blade.

My left hand still throbbed, but the active sense of burning had ceased.

"Emissary, he deserves death, but by your mercy. My sister," Kol said.

Starting, realizing that Kol could have killed me at any time from the moment Eburi had left him, I heaved away from Aukenhet, writhing on the floor. Eburi glared at Aukenhet, her muzzle wrinkled in threat and her ears flat.

"Go," I told Kol as I straightened. "Find your sister. Aukenhet won't be casting again."

Save, when I glanced at him, he'd struggled to his knees. Madness shone from his contorted face. Yet, the fingers of his right hand twitched, sketching symbols.

The flow of blood from his mouth slowed. Healing. Again.

I snarled and lifted my knife.

The motion caught his eye. He opened his red, ruined mouth and uttered a cry that curdled my blood.

Before I could move, Eburi lunged.

SNAP.

She took his right hand and a good part of his forearm as well.

She spat it to the stone in front of him.

Aukenhet's shriek rose in pitch.

I stalked to the man, shredded his robes and cinched the fabric tight around his bleeding stump so he wouldn't bleed to death.

"Kol! Can he cast based on sight?" I demanded. "Must I blind him, too?"

Aukenhet whimpered and collapsed, groveling at my feet. I forced myself to look at my handiwork and to accept the flush of shame that followed. I preferred to deal in clean death. What I'd done bordered on what Set had done to Osiris. It was unholy. Even if I'd preserved an innocent woman's life.

"No, Emissary," Kol replied. "To my knowledge you have disabled his ability to harness magic."

With a sigh, I sank to the floor. Or would have, save for Eburi thrusting her shoulders beneath my right arm, lending me her strength.

"Sorqet, Eburi, go to the river. Bathe the monster's blood from you," I said.

Sorqet shook as if she could dislodge the touch of magic

like a cloud of flies. She mewed at me.

I held out my burned hand and touched her nose in salute. "You saved my life, warrior. You have earned the right to choose your own path."

She met my eye and closed hers slowly in a feline expression of affection.

I returned the gesture.

Eburi 'woofed' a question at her daughter.

Sorqet replied with a rumbly puff of breath, then she turned and padded out of the room.

Something sharp cut through my heart at the thought that she might not return.

I'd feared this, the further loss of family.

But the lioness cub had made an adult decision. She deserved the right to make her life her own.

"Kol," I said, my voice rougher than usual, "find your sister. Free her."

"After we tie up your wounds," he countered. "If you will permit me to assist, Emissary."

As he said the words, I recognized the source of my weariness. Blood loss. If I didn't bind my cuts soon, the weariness would be mortal.

"My name is Ahmeksut," I replied, nodding. "You had opportunity to kill me. You did not. Thank you."

"I say the same of you," he countered. He took my right arm and hooked it over his shoulder. "You had opportunity to kill me. It was clear you did not wish to."

He and Eburi helped me down from the bloody dais.

"Sekhmet's argument wasn't with you," I said as I sank to a relatively clean spot on the stones.

Eburi rubbed her cheek gently against mine, scent marking me, then she, too, padded away to wash Aukenhet's blood from her fur. She, at least, would return. A decade ago, she'd chosen me as her companion. We'd fight together until the day one or both of us died.

Kol called for servants.

Two men and two women dressed in white robes came, their eyes down cast, and their shoulders stooped. None would look up.

"Fear no more. Sekhmet has delivered us," Kol said.

The eldest male flicked a glance our way, then at the dais. Drawing an audible breath, he stumbled forward two steps. His posture plainly said he didn't trust the evidence of his eyes.

"Lieutenant Commander?" the servant queried, turning to face us. Hope and relief burned bright in his wide eyes and in the way he drew himself upright.

"Aukenhet is defeated," Kol confirmed.

EMISSARY

Cries of joy erupted.

"By your kindness and by your oath to serve the throne of Menethes," Kol went on, overpowering the celebration in a voice that had been trained to carry across battlefields, "I ask you to free my sister. And to bring water that we may cleanse and bind our wounds."

"It would be our pleasure, Lord Kol," the servant said, bowing low.

"Carry Aukenhet to the healers when you go," Kol directed, "his life is still magically bound to my sister's life. She dies if he perishes."

Beckoning the other three, the older man issued rapid instructions. He and his younger male counterpart carried Aukenhet from the room.

Kol picked up and tore his discarded robe into strips.

I wrapped my thigh with the fabric he offered, gritting my teeth as I pulled the bandage tight to staunch the bleeding.

He looped a strip around my right bicep.

A serving girl, her face pale, and her eyes round with wonder, brought water and rich, cool beer. She paused to whisper to Kol.

I accepted the water to drink and stuck my burned palm into the beer, both to wash away the blood and any lingering malevolence. It stung and breath hissed in between my clenched teeth.

The cuts on my torso weren't deep and had mostly scabbed over. I shook my head when Kol offered to cleanse them as the serving girl departed.

"Only the actively bleeding," I said. I'd wash my wounds from the sanctified spring within the ruins of Sekhmet's temple. "Your wounds must also be dealt with."

"I doubt I can find a bandage long enough to wrap this." He nodded at the still oozing wound I'd cut across his abdomen.

"Use this." I offered him the dagger. "I recommend washing his blood from it first, lest it poison you."

His chuckle sounded forced as he accepted the black blade. "What is this? I've never seen its like."

"The metal fell from the heavens in a flash of fire," I said. "The making of the blades is guarded as a sacred secret. They are stronger than any metal known to humankind. The blades fashioned thus are rumored to be proof against sorcery."

"And so it was, but only when wielded by your hand, I warrant." He stared at the weapon. "Will it take harm from water?"

"Only if it is not dried well after," I said.

EMISSARY

Reverently, he submerged the blade, washing Aukenhet's blood away. Once satisfied, he wrapped the blade in a fold of his ruined robes.

He hefted the dried blade a moment, then sliced through the fabric as I watched.

"A formidable weapon," he said, reversing it to return to me hilt first. "Keep it close, Emissary. A divine blade in your possession will reinforce your right to rule."

I frowned. "Rule? Kol, I was sent to redress a grievous wrong. Tell me you will restore the temples and honor the gods and as the highest ranking officer in Menethes, the city is yours."

"Me? I protected that. . ."

"You protected the innocent," I interrupted. "You're an honorable warrior. You saw and experienced one man's abuse of his power. You are unlikely to make the same mistake. This is the judgment of Sekhmet. My oath is to Her. I cannot and will not be foresworn by accepting responsibility for a kingdom I am not qualified to rule."

He bowed his head.

I took the opportunity to wind fabric around Kol's deltoid and bicep. It was a clumsy bandage, given my burned hand, but when I tightened down the knot to apply pressure to his wound, he grunted.

"I'm getting too old for this," he muttered. "Perhaps Sekhmet should choose a younger champion for Menethes."

"A younger champion who would become drunk on the prospect of riches bought on the backs of the city's farmers and merchants?"

He frowned and would not meet my eye. "Where will you go?"

I hesitated.

He looked at me then, a sliver of hope gleaming in his faint smile. "You planned to die here."

"Yes," I admitted.

"And Sekhmet's priestesses gave you no command for after Aukenhet's defeat?" he surmised.

"With Aukenhet's defeat and the promise you have yet to make to establish the temples once more, my obligation to Sekhmet's Army is done."

He looked at me, a light in his eyes I couldn't identify.

"Stay, then," he said. "See the temple rise again with your own eyes. We will send for a priestess, but Menethes would be the richer for having a teacher of your skill."

"Teach?" I echoed, unsettled. I had thought to return to the army — to the life I'd chosen with the family I'd chosen. Never had I contemplated a future in the land of my birth. I'd run too hard and too far to escape from it when I'd turned fifteen.

"The daughters of Menethes should learn to defend their homes. My daughter will be your first pupil."

The image of a serious eyed, dark-haired girl in Kol's likeness made me smile. "You have a daughter?"

"I do. My only child. We lost her mother three years ago."

"I am sorry."

He dipped his chin in acknowledgement. "Thank you. I'm told Nufehri approached your lioness companions in the courtyard."

"The brave one," I murmured. "Good."

His smile split into a grin, pressing crinkles into the corners of his eyes. "You'll stay, then?"

A shriek sounded in the courtyard, followed by childish laughter.

Eburi burst into the room at a lope, her tail arched in play. Dripping water, Sorqet followed on her heels.

My heart soared.

Both cats, mischief in the set of their ears, bounded for us.

Before I could warn Kol, Eburi and Sorqet shook.

Water sprayed us.

"Demon cats!" I bellowed.

Kol laughed.

Sorqet smeared her cheek against me to see whether I was really angry.

I rubbed her ears with my good hand, cautious of the bare patches of red, raw skin I could see dotting her head.

"We will stay," I said. "At least until Sekhmet's priestess arrives to naysay me."

"Good," I thought I heard Kol murmur. "I fancy another daughter."

Marcella Burnard writes science fiction romance for Berkley Sensation. Her first book, Enemy Within won the Romantic Times Reviewer's Choice award for Best Futuristic of 2010. The second book in the series, Enemy Games, released on May 3, 2011. An erotica novella, Enemy Mine, set in the same world as the novels was released as an e-special edition by Berkley in April 2012. Nobody's Present, a short alien abduction novella was released as part of The Mammoth Book of Futuristic Romance in January 2013.

THE DOGS OF WAR

DAVID WEST

Dawn rose blood-red over the Hellespont, turning the bay of the Golden Horn into an open wound. Upon Byzantine towers, defenders watched in horror as invading ships choked the gateway to Constantinople like maggots in carrion. A great taut chain between the city walls and the Tower of Galata repelled the invaders, but for how long?

Aboard over two hundred hundred Venetian transports, the wickedest dogs to ever wear the Cross donned their armor, chain-mail and thick woolen padding. They beat their shields and raised their broad-swords. Banners flapped in the morning breeze. Prayers and curses flowed equally. A tidal wave of men and steel, they were the greatest amphibious invasion ever assembled in Europe. From swaying ships they gazed upon massive sea walls, lofty towers, ornate palaces, and church spires reaching to an azure sky.

And they lusted for what they knew lay within.

Soon enough, they muttered, it would be theirs,

treasure and women, golden and wanton. Soon enough the decadent Queen of Cities would burn.

Among the largely Frankish and Venetian crusaders, a pair of unlikely allies, foreigners, readied their mounts aboard the horse-transport. Tyr Thorgrimson, a towering Swedish mercenary, passed a skin of wine to the poet and Templar knight, Wolfram Von Eschenbach. Whereas clean-shaven Tyr was broad-shouldered with flowing blond hair—Wolfram, a Bavarian, was bearded and lean with close cropped dark hair. They appeared to be complete opposites, one in the white tunic and red cross of a noble knight, the other with a collage of mismatched chain-mail, a barbaric fur cloak and studded leathers. Each had also joined this fourth crusade for divergent reasons. Wealth for one, absolution for the other. After their recent siege of the Christian city of Zara on the way to Constantinople, Tyr's goal was much the likelier.

"Mein herz brennt. Have you ever dreamt of its like?" asked Wolfram.

Tyr shook his head. "I would not have believed Valhalla looked so grand."

Wolfram shrugged at the mention of the heathen paradise. Tyr was the only pagan he knew and it surprised him that the Swede had joined the crusade at all. But with the double-dealing of the Venetians and the unscrupulous behavior of the Franks; it made Wolfram smile that the most honest man in the entire crusade was a pagan mercenary.

"The chain keeps us from violating the bay," shouted the divisional commander, Jacques of Avesnes, as he made a crude gesture, bawdy laughter followed. "We land at the Tower of Galata. And we will triumph! We'll enthrone Alexious and then you bastards, *then* you will feast!"

The men at arms cheered, but Tyr and Wolfram knew the truth. Restoring a dispossessed princeling was the Franks and Venetians smokescreen, the true goal would benefit the Roman papacy and make Venice master of the Mediterranean.

But a job is a job mused Tyr.

The rising Tower of Galata grew closer and the yeoman shouted at the knights to ready their chargers.

"For Alexious the fourth and the true church of Rome! We shall conquer!" called Jacques raising his sword and war-standard. "Death to heretics!"

The transports bridge splashed down as a hail-storm of arrows struck. The screams of men and horse shattered the arrogant cheer of seconds before. Bolts and ballista smashed into the crusader ranks as Byzantine pike-men lined the Bosporus shore.

The foremost crusaders either died or hesitated. Blood spilled over the deck and the thick scent of oozing copper punched into nostrils.

"If we sit—We die! Charge!" roared Tyr, kicking his war-horses flanks and forcing the beast to leap over the top of fallen comrades.

"Dann sind wir helden," grated Wolfram through his teeth as he and a dozen others followed. Crusading archers and footmen leapt into the fray loosing their own at the Greek enemy.

Tyr deflected a thrusting pike and slammed his great sword through the skull cap of the nearest Greek on the right as the war-horse bit the soldier to the left. The stunned bitten man lost his pike and then his life to Tyr's blade.

Wolfram's charger trampled a flanking Greek as the Templar took the beach.

Cutting a bloody swath through the enemy ranks, Tyr and his charger were splashed with gore.

The still clean Wolfram caught up to Tyr shouting, "Niemand gibt uns eine chance!"

"You'll get your chance. There are more!"

Six score Greek infantry rushed toward the crusaders, shouting righteous indignation. They were answered with unholy steel. The crusading knights hacked their way

THE DOGS OF WAR

through the bravest of defenders and made formation on the shore with lances poised.

Facing the terrible array of yet more mounted crusaders landing every moment and the coming wall of lancing steel, the Greeks did the sanest thing they could.

They turned and ran.

The charging knights ran down the more stalwart of the Greeks, though most dashed back toward the Tower in blind panic. A short wall of stone with an arch precluded the mounted knights from following, but sighting the lowered drawbridge and panicking Greeks, Tyr dismounted and ran after the fleeing Byzantines. His armor was heavier than that of the pike-men he raced after, but Tyr was not yet winded running along the beach front.

Catching up the last couple stragglers, he slammed them headlong into the cobblestones, knocking them senseless.

Spotting the hulking knight with more of his allies at his heels, the Greeks began raising the drawbridge. Cranking under the strain of a dozen men, the iron-buckled door jerked upward, abandoning six Greeks to the closing enemy.

The Tower did not have a moat, but a six foot ditch ran its perimeter. As the tip of the drawbridge was at eye level, Tyr leapt, grasping the lip with claw-like fingers. He and two other crusaders pulled themselves over the edge and slid down just as the gate slammed shut.

The three enemy knights stood within the tower.

"Surrender," Tyr snarled.

The astonished Greeks captain gasped, "You surrender! There are twenty of us to three of you!"

Grinning like a madman, Tyr drew his sword and went to his bloody work. The other two crusaders following suit.

Pike-men went for their weapons, but these were too long and ungainly to use within the shallow courtyard. A crossbowman shot a bolt at Tyr from scant few feet away, but this glanced off the fold of plate armor protecting his heart.

The angered North-man sent his blade through the crossbow and the breastbone behind it. That simple red fate was repeated a dozen times.

Shouting for help, Greeks ran for the stairs as the Swedish juggernaut mowed them down.

Tyr glanced for the release mechanism on the gate, but was too hard pressed with his work to release the chained lock. The other two knights slew the archers and Greek captain, then set to work opening the gate.

As Tyr struck down the last man, his senses prickled. Something moved just out of clear sight in the shadows. Too thick and low to the ground for a man, Tyr's mind reeled at the imagined threat of demons and trolls. The unseen nightmares his grandfather spoke of lurking in his Nordic homeland.

A growling revealed the new threat. A pair of great dark hounds bolted from the shadows, massive beasts with spiked collars and fearsome temperaments. Both eyed Tyr and his companions readying to flank them. These would prove much more difficult than the Greeks.

Tyr backed toward the gates release lever, though he daren't let his guard drop against the big black hounds. Seconds counted, any moment more Greeks might arrive with crossbows and feather him.

The hounds worked in concert, leaping at a crusader from two sides. As one knocked and pinned him down, the other tore out his throat and face. The knight, helpless as an overturned turtle, screamed and then gurgled his frothing terror. Tyr and the other knight moved in with swords, but the wily hounds leapt back, the damage done.

"I'll hold them off. You open the gate."

The knight balked. "No. I'll hold them off. You open the gates."

Tyr snorted but went to the gates wheel-lock. He pulled at the chain, locking the lever with his left hand—keeping his sword at the ready for the hounds. The lever would not budge for a single hand, it might not for both hands. Tyr supposed it took a half-dozen Greeks to shut the thing.

The baying hounds remained just out of sword-swinging reach.

"Hurry, I can hear the Greeks coming!" cried the knight, as he waved his sword at the hounds inching closer.

"Then slay those dogs and help me," retorted Tyr, throwing his shoulder against the lever.

The knight glanced over his shoulder at Tyr for a fraction of a second and the hounds leapt. Again they knocked the knight over and this time each had at his decorated neck. Fangs crushed flesh beneath chain-mail and the knight had no breath to scream.

Wheeling, Tyr slashed the ear from one and barely cut the other across the foreleg. It was not a mortal wound but would slow the beast down. Keeping his back against the wall, Tyr left no room to be flanked or knocked over.

Barking as if possessed, the ear-less hound on the left came snapping to within a foot of Tyr.

Swinging cold steel at the brute, Tyr sent his blade too far.

The hound dodged and leapt, clamping down on Tyr's mailed right forearm.

The iron links held, but the canine pressure was intense.

THE DOGS OF WAR

Kicking at the hound charging on the left, Tyr slammed the biting dog against the lever. It yelped and let go, but the other bit down on Tyr's cloak yanking and pulling him off balance.

Recovering, the ear-less dog lunged with jaws wide.

This time Tyr met it with armored elbow and knocked teeth loose. Slashing his broadsword, backhanded, he caught the second along the ribs, and dispatched it.

The toothless and one-eared hound wasn't ready to give up. Howling like Cerebus it came on again.

Tyr swept it aside but not without the hellish hound scratching his face as it strove for his throat. The clawing and snapping knocked the sword from his grasp. Drawing his dagger, Tyr cut the hound in one fell motion. It dropped near its mate, not to rise.

Greeks scampered down the stairs with short swords, spears and crossbows, shouting in chaotic astonishment at the courtyard littered with torn bodies.

Dropping his sword, Tyr wrenched the wheel-lock like a titan, releasing the drawbridge. Waiting behind the gate, dozens of crusaders rushed inside and took the Tower in an orgy of bloodthirsty ruin.

Wolfram appeared beside Tyr. "Gott im Himmel. I hate big dogs."

"You mean you're scared of them?"

"Ja."

Mere moments and it was over, the crusaders held the beach and Tower of Galata. They called Tyr "the Gatekeeper" afterward, because Murello the minstrel, sang that Tyr was the golden hero whom opened the Tower. Regardless of that bravado and verse, the rank and file soldier acknowledged he saved them a prolonged siege on what should have been a formidable obstacle.

An impatient Venetian war-ship, the *Eagle*, tore through the great chain of the Golden Horn just moments before the crusaders could have lowered it. The harbor and poor Byzantine fleet fell with but a whimper.

Tyr could only laugh at their nearly rending the ship for naught. He had only scorn for the Greeks that surrendered without a fight.

The noble lords, Baldwin, Boniface, and Jacques entered the captured tower as conquering heroes, yet with clean swords.

Baldwin clapped bloody Tyr on the shoulder, recognizing him from an earlier encounter in Zara. "Good work North-man. I told the Doge you were an asset."

"Ha-ha! The Greeks haven't been worthy fighters since the days of Alexander," said Jacques surveying the carnage in the courtyard. "Their decadence makes them weak."

"They did not expect such an attack," added Marquis Boniface.

"They thought to frighten us with their superior numbers. They should have known better, but I suspect this warm climate makes them soft," said Baldwin. "After all, a cold Swede took the Tower by himself."

Shaking his head, Tyr answered, "Not by myself your lordship. I but opened a closed door."

"I know a worthy man when I see him. Your wounds show those beasts did more damage than the Greeks. Lets us pray they don't have anymore of those damned hell hounds."

Tyr grimaced and rubbed his bruised forearm. The hounds teeth almost made it through the old links. He would scrounge and find new mail if he could.

It was not long before Murello the minstrel was ordered to sing no more of Tyr "the Gatekeeper" and instead praise be to God and his chosen nobles, namely, Baldwin, Boniface, Jaques and the Doge. It was ironic to Tyr that so quickly they praised and then swept aside his contribution for themselves.

Was this the way of the greedy civilized west? Perhaps it would be better to return to the frozen North where a mans deeds were his own.

Other nobles landed, congratulated each other and marveled at the hasty retreat of the Byzantine usurper and the Greek horde. Count Boniface led a troop into the Imperial camp that was located just beyond the Tower, Tyr and Wolfram followed to gain what spoils they could. Fabulous pavilions were scattered across the grounds where the usurper had recently held court to watch what he must have believed would be a victorious battle. In their hasty retreat, they left succulent wines and meats, soft silken divans, and other delicacies from rich Cathay.

"Sterne! Das ist gut. Opium," said Wolfram, extending a jar to Tyr.

The North-man shook his head.

Rummaging through tents behind what was likely the Emperor's own, Tyr found a vestment beneath a black fur cloak that made him pause.

"Was ist es?"

Tyr held it up for Wolfram. A large iron-scaled tunic with Nordic runes emblazoned across it. A fearsome helm with short bull horns lay beside it as did a shield splashed with an image of Thor's hammer. It matched the one that hung about Tyr's own neck. The magnificent sword which surely must have accompanied such a collection was missing.

"Was bedeutet das?"

THE DOGS OF WAR

"It means there are Varangians here. North men who serve as the emperors elite guard."

"You're sure?"

Tyr grinned, "Aye. My father was one long ago. I wager we'll see them tonight."

* * *

Twilight fell with no moon, only cold stars to pinprick at the curtain of night. After the Imperial pavilions had been stripped of their decadent wealth the surrounding meager suburbs were next. On this side of the Golden Horn the undesirables were represented, odoriferous tanners and pig farmers even a colony of lepers. Some valuables were yet found amongst the reviled Jewish silk merchants but all paled in comparison to what the crusaders knew waited across the bay in the city proper.

Tyr and Wolfram sat beside a dying fire with Count Boniface and a dozen of his sleeping henchmen.

"We'll march to the Lion Gates on the morrow while the Venetians assault the sea walls," said Boniface over his cup of wine. "I want you beside me Gatekeeper. Together, we'll take this city."

Tyr nodded. He enjoyed the wine but not the company,

guessing the Count only wanted to seize the glory for any victories he might accomplish the next time. Such was the way of nobles.

"I'll tell you this," slurred Boniface. "We're damned lucky to be fighting Greeks instead of Saracens—those bastards can fight."

Tyr sipped his wine, listening to the night more than the noble.

"This here," Boniface gestured absently about the decorative encampment, "*this* will be an easy war," he said, before slumping upon his silken divan in a snore.

Wolfram eyed the wine bottles greedily. "Nehmen sie seinen wein."

"*You* take his wine then," said Tyr, striding out into the night. He listened and watched for things unheard and unseen.

Wolfram followed after snatching two of Boniface's wine bottles. "Nordmann. Ist gut idea to wear the Varangian armor?"

"Spoils of war, Templar. It's better made than what I had. You have yours," he took a bottle from Wolfram and guzzled a deep pull, adding afterward, "and I have mine."

Wolfram said, "I wouldn't want anyone mistaking you for one of them."

Shrugging, Tyr gazed into the abyss of darkness. "Maybe I was wrong. Maybe they won't attack tonight."

"Vertrauen sie ihrem instinkt."

"I'll go walk the perimeter then."

"Ich bleibe."

"Stay then." Tyr drew his sword, musing that Wolfram only reverted to speaking his native tongue when he was truly afraid. "If I haven't returned by morning...you'll know I found a Jewish princess."

Wolfram laughed and took another sip of wine.

Beyond the looted Imperial camp Tyr walked toward the makeshift perimeter. Constantinople had been alight with torches and fires all along its great wall at dusk, but the lights were now extinguished. The Franks had continually shot arrows at any targets but something was amiss. There should be watch lights at least at the Lion Gatehouse.

Bordered by palpable darkness, Frankish spear-men dozed at their posts. Weak torches guttered every hundred paces along a wide open avenue that marked the border. A trampled field was the widest spot yet, here only a few scattered trees could be seen in the gloom, shadows stretched beyond like a dark lovers kisses.

Tyr noticed a spear-man leaning against the broken wall of a tanners shop. His torch was extinguished and his warning trump hung well out of reach. The guardsman farther past him had his light snuffed as well.

"Wait, fool!" called someone far out in the palpable darkness.

Tyr wheeled, expecting an attack, but none came. He waited a moment, watching the shadows before smacking the spear-man awake, half expecting him to be dead.

The spear-man started at Tyr's perceived sudden appearance. "Gatekeeper?"

"Aye. Why did fall asleep at your post? Who else is further on?" he gestured into the shadowy fields.

"None. I am to let no one pass."

"I hear men."

"Impossible. We chased the dogs beyond the bridge and to the Lion Gates."

"Dogs?" asked Tyr, glancing about.

"The Greeks."

Tyr nodded, "Wake the man down the way. Be vigilant. Something isn't right."

The spear-man trotted to the next dozing man down the line and woke him. As one of the men struck flint to relight his torch the other gasped, "Demon dogs!"

The torch blazed to life casting just enough light to catch the baleful eyes of dozens of horrible shaggy forms in

THE DOGS OF WAR

the gloom.

"Werewolf!" screamed the spear-man as his own blood showered the guard beside him.

A black mass materialized out of shadow, vaguely illuminated by torchlight revealing a dog-like snouts and pointed ears.

Tyr's mind reeled at the hideous reality of a horde of hounds and what they might do.

But these raised up on two legs and ran, roaring blood and thunder.

The second guard was slain with a swift hideous leap as the furry legion washed over the Frankish perimeter howling bloody retribution.

Like frenzied two-legged wolves they came. Wolves with axes and spears and swords in their taloned paws. They howled and roared in chaotic abandon as the remaining Frankish spear-men only cried in fear. Then Tyr heard them speaking—shouting! in the tongues of his fathers. This was worse than the hounds. The Varangian guard, Northmen like himself, the savage mercenary army of the Byzantine emperors.

The wolf-skinned bezerkers slashed the few Frankish spear-men to pieces.

Tyr blew the warning trump left hanging by the now

shredded spear-man. He then turned to face a sure road to Valhalla as the bezerkers closed on him. He raised his sword and shield, bracing for their horrific onslaught.

The Varangian's, hundreds of them, glanced at Tyr and ran on heedless.

One recognized the armor. "Ulfhamer, I am with you!" shouted a bear-skinned bezerker, before he too disappeared into the night chasing toward the Frankish camp.

They thought he was one of them! Such was the only reason he was not cut down immediately.

Screams of terror erupted from the foremost Frankish tents and Tyr's allies of earlier that day died in bloody-handed ruin.

The war-drums throbbed in his heart and the pipes blew the song of death. Blood ran hot through his veins and called for him to join the cold madness of the North, his homeland. To be one with his wolf-skinned brothers, to delight in the slaughter and tear down the civilized dogs, the Franks and Venetians. Always the battle raged within, what would he choose?

He stood motionless as the pack swarmed by. It would be so easy to join in. To right the wrongs and take back the dishonor heaped upon his name. He had but to reach out and take it.

THE DOGS OF WAR

No.

Tyr shook off the bloodthirsty temptation. He was no traitor to men he had fought and bled beside. He could not allow harm to come to the Templar poet, his new blood brother, Wolfram.

Tyr raced toward Boniface's tent. He struck down a dozen bezerkers on the way, lamenting that at least they died with swords in hand. They could yet venture to Valhalla. They could expect no better from the outcast son of Thorgrim.

Nearing the center of the Frankish camp, Tyr tore off his wolf-skin cloak and threw away his shield of Thor. Even his valued horned helm was tossed aside to better distinguish himself from the bezerker horde. Spying Wolfram fighting for his life near a drunken Boniface, Tyr crashed into the bezerkers.

"Begrüßen sie bruder."

"Welcome yourself brother and slay!"

Men fell in droves before Tyr's sword and the howl of the dying was a siren song to his ears.

"You!" shouted a man in Swedish. "You're the dog who stole my armor!" came a guttural voice, deep as the pit.

Tyr faced a black-bearded giant with a dripping ax. "Ulfhamer?"

"You know my name? And took my armor? This insult

will be met with Death!" Ulfhamer dropped the ax and drew the great sword that Tyr had suspected was companion to the fine armor.

"I take what I want, dog!" shouted Tyr. "And now, I want your head!"

The two northern warriors stared across the gulfs of time at each other. Iron wills smashed headlong and the pair hammered at one another souls with bloody steel and streaming sweat.

Oaths came rampant and free as the world around them blurred and went still. Everything Tyr hated was encompassed in this one enemy, all the anger at the nobles, his clan, his father and his people melded into Ulfhamer.

Blow and parry exchanged and then reversed. The Viking titans were too evenly matched in fighting prowess and cunning for victory.

Something would have to give.

Tyr's eye caught a single dangling link in Ulfhamer's mail. A lone link loose from its shield brothers opening a tiny fissure in a stalwart foe. Tyr pulled a dagger from his belt and reached. Ulfhamer redoubled his efforts, pressing down with his blade at Tyr's neck.

Locked in an embrace of death, Tyr felt sweat and blood drip from his opponent; the salty tang foul and fierce.

THE DOGS OF WAR

The sword edge hungered for his flesh. Ulfhamer's eyes, like a ravenous dogs shone with an insane light.

"I shall drink mead from your skull, whelp."

Tyr pushed, striving, feeling the dagger tip scrape across Ulfhamer's mail until it found the open link, the break in the shield wall.

He shoved.

Hard.

Biting steel tore through the exposed weakness in Ulfhamer's mail and opened his belly. The Varangian chieftain cursed the Norn's, pressed his blade harder for a moment and then rolled away as all his strength seeped out in crimson rivulets. Nothing in his death was dignified or glorious, but he held onto his sword which was the most he could ever hope for in this life.

Those bezerkers nearby joined Ulfhamer in the crossing of Bifrost, the rainbow bridge to Valhalla, as shafts from Venetian archers rained like welcoming Valkyries. The bloody tide turned as more bolts found their wolf-like targets.

Gore-covered and exhausted Tyr, helped Wolfram get Boniface to his feet. "Werewolves, I tell you. Who knew the Byzantines had such sorcery?" asked the Marquis.

"Sie sind weg."

"What?"

"He said they are gone," answered Tyr, as he cleaned off his sword.

A troop of striped Venetian's entered what was left of the encampment. The blind old Doge was guided between corpses to his allies. "Seems we saved you yet again."

"Hardly," countered Boniface. "We had these dogs on the run. Where is my wine?"

"We came only when we heard the trump. If not for that warming blast, we may not have arrived in time and you would be overrun."

"Bah!" answered Boniface, shaking an empty bottle in his quest for drink.

"Whoever blew the warning trump then," muttered the Doge.

"Only the men at the front lines had them," said Boniface. "They are surely all dead now."

"Dead heroes are best," grinned the Doge.

"What we need is more dogs of war like these two," slurred Boniface, pointing at Tyr and Wolfram. "These bastards sat here the whole time and did naught but steal my wine. Now that's a true soldier."

"Dog's," chuckled the Doge. "Away with you. Let noble men discuss the morrow."

Wolfram frowned but Tyr shook his head whispering, "I won more than they can ever guess. But I know, and that's enough for now."

"Thank you brother," said Wolfram producing another bottle of wine from beneath his cloak as they made their way toward the Jewish sector. "What would I do without you?"

Tyr laughed, "You'd be dead!" He pointed toward the red lights hanging in the distance, "Let us go and find those wanton princess's and truly make this a night worth remembering!"

David J. West can't remember a time he wasn't writing. His first writing award was in the second grade for a tale about a wolf pack that killed and ate the hunters and their dogs that were stalking them . . . his stories are slightly worse now. From the primordial splash of a drowning Atlantis to a pair of vigilantes' six-guns blasting raw justice in the old west. From obsidian tipped arrows raining down on Cumorah's slopes, to crusaders' broadswords sweeping over shadowy terrors, and on to the cold vacuum of space and the birth of a new star, David is there, recording all that he sees for your edification and amusement.

You can visit him at http://david-j-west.blogspot.com/

THE RED HAND

ALEXIS A. HUNTER

Darkness – it surrounded me.

Even worse, it filled me.

Where was the rest the dead should find as a reward? Where was the serenity my priests promised me as the last of my blood spilled out into the earth's greedy jaws? There were no bright lights after death. No sweeping clouds, or beautiful women clothed in purest white.

When I succumbed to death – when I pressed my mortal eyes shut – there was only darkness.

And when I opened them again?

Only darkness remained.

How long I lived in that torment I cannot say. But I did not there remain.

For a bright hand, saturated by a scarlet hue, reached out to me. It grasped me firmly, though I had no form, and pulled me through the inky veils of death.

And when I blinked, my eyes found light again.

Bright, searing light that made me cower and moan.

The echo of my cries resounded off the cliffs as I fought away the red hand. My moan climbed to a roar as the light burned into my brain. And as I bellowed my wrath and confusion, a softer voice whispered in my ear.

A woman – the red hand – her full lips pressed against my temple.

"Raamiah," her voice called to me, somehow managing to filter into my ears, despite the violence of my roaring.

"Come to me."

The shattering yell died in my throat, frozen by her words. I did not know why she had this power over me. I struggled to open my eyes, but the light seared them shut and tears streamed down my cheeks.

I rolled my face into the earth and inhaled its scent. Rich, warm and fresh.

"My eyes will not open," I rasped, suddenly finding my throat dry and blistered.

I felt her shift, and a moment later her shadow fell over me.

Soft fingers reached out to touch my face. I felt her hand slide down my shoulders, tracing my spine until she reached the rest of me.

I wondered if she had ever seen a centaur before.

THE RED HAND

"Open your eyes, Raamiah," she ordered, her hand returning to my face.

After several faulty attempts, I managed to tear my eyelids apart. She was the first thing that I gazed upon – a fragmented vision obscured by my bloodshot eyes.

"Who are you?" I asked, cocking my head to take in the sight of her almond shaped eyes and shock of bright red hair.

She smiled, but her gaze darted toward my neck.

Caution fluttered behind that smile. "I am your savior."

Curious as to what kept drawing her gaze, I glanced down.

I blew a decidedly equine snort through my nostrils as my hazy gaze rolled over my own body. The skin on my human torso hung in great, heavy shreds – like a bolt of cloth half unwound, but with thick, inky blood and putrid mucous underneath. And my equine body? Covered in decayed, gaping holes, where my enemy's blade had sliced through flesh, and muscle and sinew, exposing the glistening white bones beneath.

And at the very last I saw her blade – the woman's dagger – pressed against my throat, resting lightly between the notches of my collar bone.

My dark gaze finally returned to her, my heart quickly filling with rage and numerous other vile fluids. "What is this? What have you done to me? You tear me from death only to send me back to those foul depths?"

I did not give her time to answer.

My body felt on fire, as if seeing my death-wounds reactivated the pain they had initially created. Rage rippled through me stronger than an ocean current.

Rage at the lies of the priests.

Rage at my untimely death.

Rage at the woman who had torn me from my grave

I bolted to my feet, sending the slight woman flying under the power of my massive body. She fell to the earth with a muffled grunt as I reared up and scraped the sky with a bellow of unadulterated rage.

With another scream, this one more of anguish than anger, I slammed my hooves back into the earth.

Only narrowly did I miss crushing the woman's skull.

Although initially stunned, she recovered with a grace and speed I had not expected. Rolling, she leapt to a crouched position. Low on her feet. Dagger extended toward me in a defensive stance.

I froze again.

Not because I feared that blade.

THE RED HAND

The thought made me snort.

What has the undead to fear? Having tasted death, there was nothing, I thought, that could harm me. Though there was something about that glistening piece of steel that sent a chill down my spine.

No, I stopped because her eyes captivated me. And because, looking at her standing like a crouched lioness, I suddenly knew I felt no rage toward her.

The muscles in my back – what few were not shredded by my death - relaxed as I unclenched my mighty fists

"Truly," I growled. "You are my savior."

I turned away in disgust, my gaze rolling over the canyon in which we stood. Patches of rusty brown dotted the empty soil, and a foul stench filled the air. Coupled together, the two signs indicated that yet another battle had been fought here.

"Does that anger you? The emptiness you found in death?"

Her voice was soft, and I tilted my head to view her out of my peripheral vision

"Only because it meant my mortal life had been filled with lies."

She stepped up beside me, and I caught a whiff of her scent. She smelled of spices and sunshine. Her skin shimmered a healthy copper tone under the sun's gaze.

I skittered a little to the side, not with nerves, but with the knowledge of my horrible appearance.

Even the undead can be self-conscious.

"The priests, you mean?" she asked.

I nodded.

"I lived thirty and two years in their service. I gave my blood and my sweat, and every ounce of my strength for a cause they said was worthy. For gods who would bring me peace after death. For honor and valor. And what did I find at the end of my journey?"

She shuddered a little. "Darkness."

I scanned her face, wondering at the unease that filled her voice

"You have been to that place?" I asked.

"I have been to that place." She swallowed hard.

My heart swelled with compassion. And I did not think it strange that an undead creature could feel such things. For my heart, shredded though it was, still pumped with righteous anger, and affection, and pain.

"Thank you," I said. "For pulling me out of that hell."

She looked up at me and I looked down at her, admiring the emerald green hue of her eyes. "Do not thank me yet. You do not yet know who I am or why I brought you back.

THE RED HAND

Or even the conditions of such a monstrous evil."

"Evil?" said I. "Yes, the priests did call this evil. You they would name an usurper. One who plays with the power of the gods. Many of your kind have I slain. And yet standing here, I find I do not think your deeds so evil."

A smile tugged at the corners of her lips. She extended her hand and I took it in mine, a gentle handshake.

"I did not think you would be so understanding. So many come back and attempt to slay me for what I do. I am glad you are not angry with me, Raamiah."

"You know my name, and I assume my history, but who are you then?"

She pulled her hand back out of my grasp with a certain reluctance that I found pleasing. "Tashia."

I froze.

Tashia.

I knew the name well, though never had I seen a face for the character. She was the daughter of the great Necromancer. The lord of the undead who had surrounded our noble cities and sought to destroy them for the past decade. A blood feud existed between the centaurs and the necromancers, although I had never cared much how it had begun.

"It was your people then that killed me," I muttered,

more to myself than to her.

She moved closer and tilted my chin toward her, looking up into my eyes with a desperate kind of longing. "But it was not I, Raamiah, not I who killed you. I have long sought to stop this senseless bloodshed. No one even recalls for what it began. It is an altogether useless war."

"And your father," I said. "Is he not evil?"

She wrinkled her little elfin nose.

"Evil is not always clear. My father is not good. But nor are your priests. They war because they have been taught to war. And because they fear to lose their power. And who suffers the most at their hands? You and your fellow warriors. For the legions of my father's undead will always rise again. But your kind will lay forever wasted by my kin."

A deep shuddering sigh escaped my lips as blood sprinkled out from my underbelly.

"What then can we do? What will stop this madness?"

She did not answer right away.

Her sweet brow furrowed with thought.

Mentally, I tried to curb my thoughts. It wouldn't do to fall in love with my savior.

"I cannot let my men continue to die for a shallow and empty cause. Tell me what I must do."

"You must stop the lies of the priests, Raamiah. This

violence must end."

This idea caught me off guard. I shifted back a half step, switching my tail to shoo away the flies buzzing around my rotting corpse.

"Kill them?"

She hesitated.

"Or make them speak the truth."

I considered the options for a moment as I stared at her face. She seemed so open and honest. Gentle and sweet like a pure spring bubbling down the mountainside.

But the hand that had pulled my through the veils of time and death - the red hand - it had been a powerful one. A cold one.

"Did you have help pulling me out?" I asked, almost without meaning to.

Her right eyebrow arched toward her flaming red hair.

"What?"

"Pulling me out of death's clutches. Did someone help you? The hand that pulled me out did not feel like you. It was colder. Stronger. More…"

I shuddered, remembering the sensation.

"Evil."

She blinked once and then nodded.

"Yes. I did not want to tell you, but…"

She hesitated again before spitting her next words out like a dirty confession.

"My father helped me. He often pours his strength into me that I might do these acts."

"Then he knows you wish to stop this war?"

"Yes, but he does not think it possible," she responded. "It is a bit of a bet between us."

Betting over the lives of centaurs?

I frowned at the thought, but did not address it.

"Very well. I will go to the temple and see what I can do. May the gods grant-"

I did not finish my sentence; the words died in my throat.

There were no gods to grant me strength.

I stood utterly alone now.

***

Night had fallen by the time I reached the temple.

A hundred miles of rough terrain I crossed that day, finding my body as powerful - if not more so - than the day my life ended. The only negative side effects I felt was the pain, and that lingering sense of emptiness.

The pain came in flashes. More intense now, and then

receding like waves on the seashore. This I could bear, and the smell of my own flesh as well.

But the emptiness, it hounded me. It clung to me, and gnawed away at my exposed innards. As I galloped across the blood-soaked wastelands, I struggled to understand the feeling that left me hollow.

Why should I feel this way?

I was alive, albeit in a rather mutilated and disgusting way. I knew the truth now about life. I had found in my savior a very wonderful and strange kind of affection. She was a creature I hoped to know and understand better.

So why, with all of these things to comfort me, did I feel as if something still was missing?

When I neared the temple, trotting through my own capital city, it suddenly hit me. As I stared at the glistening white walls, and heard the soft chanting of the priests within, I knew.

I missed the peace. The purpose. The reason.

Without a god, there was no purpose.

And here in this temple I had so many nights found a sweet relief. In the knowledge that my life was not lived in vain.

"But it was," I whispered to myself, as I strode through the double arched doors, "It was in vain, Raamiah. And these men, these are to blame."

As I made my way through the temple, I left a wake of gasps and ashen faces. The chanting stopped as soon as I entered a room, and the whispered cries went up as I moved down the hall.

I felt their gazes sharply.

Felt their horror and disgust like a sharp knife in my breast.

And I felt shame.

Shame for being undead. For defiling the temple of the gods I now knew did not exist. For believing the lies for thirty and two years.

A bell rang far away, not the steady soothing kind, but the sharp, alarming one.

When I approached the doors to the inner sanctum, I found them barred shut. And one lonely centaur priest stood in front, arms folded across his chest. His face twisted into an attempt at bravery.

But I noted how his knees trembled and his tail flicked incessantly from side to side.

"Barten," I growled. "Let me pass."

"Raamiah?" he gasped. "I…I did not know it was you. Great Troll's Breath, can this be true? Oh, Raamiah, what have they done to you?"

THE RED HAND

My face flushed red under his gaze and anguished words. The torchlight sent shadows dancing across the walls as I mustered the strength to push forward.

"Move, Barten, I do not wish to harm you. I have been to the other side and I have seen that there is nothing. There is no truth in the words of the priests, and I will not let others live, and die, in vain as I have."

Barten danced uneasily, but kept himself in front of the doors.

"I don't believe that, Raam, I cannot believe that. You speak lies of the Necromancer. You are under his sway."

Anger flamed to life within me. And even as I gave a throaty roar, I realized my reaction did not make sense. Why should I be angry at Barten? He who took my confessions so many late evenings before battle. He who took it upon himself to nurse me to health upon more than one occasion.

But the rage that sprang up within me controlled me. It put an unholy power in my limbs so that when I swung my massive forearm at Barten, his body - human torso, and equine form as well - flew across the hall. He hit the marble wall with a sickening crack and sank down.

A streak of blood marked the end of his existence on the cold, uncaring wall.

Half a sob tore through my throat as I bolted through

the door. Not caring to open it, the wood splintered around me and into me as I burst into the inner sanctum.

I spoke no words, under the complete sway of my rage, but flailed about, striking down the seven altars.

Hatred and anger.

Agony and turmoil.

They tore at me. They ate my undead flesh and spewed it back out in my face.

The priests cowered in terror as I tore about the room. In my eyes a red, savage light burned.

In that moment, there was no Raamiah.

There was only the flame.

The red hand and the flame.

I did not hear their cries for mercy. I did not discuss their lies in a calm and reasonable way. I gave them no room for retreat, no room for surrender.

My hands wrapped around their throats and squeezed the air and life out of them. My massive, quivering arms filled with power and smashed their heads into the walls.

When all was done, I stood alone in the inner sanctum.

Blinking rapidly, I fought to see the carnage that lay around me. But all I could see was red. I swiped a hand across my brow, and felt the warm stickiness of the priests' blood.

THE RED HAND

Revolted, I heaved up the contents of a empty stomach onto the floor of the sanctuary.

The walls were smeared with screaming inky scarlet. The priests' bodies lay crumpled and trampled about me. The altars I had torn down. The tapestries I had shredded.

The inner sanctum I had defiled.

"W-what? What is this? How…?" I gasped out between the sobs that shook my entire frame.

"This is true power, my precious one," said a familiar voice behind me.

I did not have the strength to turn. My quivering limbs gave out and I collapsed into a puddle of blood on the marble floor.

"Tashia," I gasped, knowing it was she that stood behind me. "What have you done to me?"

She stalked around my side, dragging her fingers across my body. On her face a proud smile danced. Her beautiful eyes lit up with excitement.

"You were beautiful, my love," she whispered, sliding to her knees in front of me. "Such power I have never seen. Such rage."

She uttered a strange, delighted little groan and pressed her lips against mine.

But I recoiled from her touch.

My vision cleared and I saw her for what she was.

"It's you," I said, voice laced with horror. "You are the great Necromancer."

She flashed a grin at me, a wolfish expression that exposed glittering white teeth.

"So powerful and so intelligent. You figured out the game faster than the others. But you will outlast them, my love. You I have chosen especially. You I watched in life. I saw your prowess and your nobility, and I desired you. We will live together forever, for your body, undead though it be, delights me as much as it did when you lived."

"But…your father?"

My mind felt hazy now, lost in confusion and the growing horror of what I had done.

She did not noticed my blanched face, her own excitement held her so captive.

"My father is an old and fragile fool. I have used his name for decades in order to reign over the legions of undead. Isn't it a wonderful thing, my precious one? Now no one stands between us and the world that shall be ours."

She reached her eager fingers out toward me, but now instead of looking soft, they seemed like greedy talons to me. I used the last of my strength to stumble to my feet, swaying with dizziness and guilt.

THE RED HAND

"You used me."

The brightness of her smile dimmed as she stared up at me.

"You used me," I repeated. "And you lied to me, just as did the priests."

At this she laughed, a cold edge lacing the raucous noise.

"Ah, but there you are wrong, my love. For the priests never lied to you."

My eyes widened as I retreated further back. She stood and pursued me as I stumbled out of the sanctum.

Barten's glazed, lifeless eyes taunted me. The streak of blood on the wall tormented me. And looking at Tashia's eager, dark face, I realized why I had felt the emptiness.

Because lies are empty, and truth is full.

Thus in life I was satisfied, and in undeath restless.

Tears streamed down my face in torrents as I snatched the blade from her hip. She paused, awaiting my next move. Subtly she shifted her position.

Defensive again. Ready for attack.

But she misread me. She did not see the despair that permeated every inch of my shredded body and soul.

"You have betrayed me, Tashia, and I, fool that I am, allowed myself to be your pawn. You have won. And stolen me from the grips of my faith. But know this as I now know - my gods live. They live and they avenge. And if they will wreak their vengeance upon me, tenfold will they wreak it upon you."

Only for a moment did fear shimmer in her eyes, but a loud and dry laugh replaced it.

"Tell your gods I do not fear them, Raamiah, for I have taken and used their greatest warrior. And their priests lay slain by his hand."

The grief was too much for me to bear. A soldier of war, I knew the guilt of bringing death to many. But always my foes had been of the undead kind. And now I had slain the living - worse, the priests of the living. The servants of my gods.

What would become of my people? Would they fall into the clutches of the fiery necromancer? These thoughts I could not bear to consider, for they caused my heart to quake within my chest.

"Forgive me," I whispered, eyes turned toward the sky. "For I did not know."

And with those words, I plunged the Red Hand's blade deep into my chest. Only it could slay me. As the last of my undead blood spilled onto the floor of the temple, I closed my eyes.

THE RED HAND

Unwilling to see last of all the Necromancer's laughing face.

Unwilling to see the carnage I had created.

And praying with a broken urgency that the gods whom I had served in life, would forgive the horrible deeds done in my undeath.

A lifelong fan of speculative fiction, Alexis A. Hunter specializes in all things mythical, ethereal and out of this world. Her work has appeared most recently in At Year's End: Holiday SFF Stories, Goldfish Grimm's Spicy Fiction Sushi and more. To learn more about Alexis visit www.idreamagain.wordpress.com.

WHERE THE RED BLOSSOMS WEEP

JAMES R. TUCK

Ravens.

Tens of thousands of ravens.

They sat and feasted on thousands of corpses, their cries filling the air, raising a din that would wake a dead man.

As if that were possible.

None of their meals rose up, none lifted an arm or shifted a mangled body to brush away their tearing beaks or shake loose their gripping claws. Instead they lay, loose-limbed and sprawling, uncaring and growing cold as they gave their flesh to scavengers one gobbet at a time.

The ravens were not alone. They shared their banquet table with a multitude of kin. Thousands of crows, owls, and vultures crowded the carnage, taking their portion of the bloody harvest and adding their voices to the orchestra of gluttony.

Mostly though, it was the ravens.

They screamed and cawed and cried at the bloodstained barbarian who strode slowly through the corpse littered field, bristling blue-black feathers and blinking ebon, insolent eyes as he stepped over their feasting board.

And he didn't give a damn.

Pain throbbed his knee from pushing forward, pressing shield to shield with countless enemies. Sharp burning raced along his side with each step from a vicious cut taken early in the day. Bruises and scrapes painted his skin over the tattoos lodged underneath, blanketing him in a dull sheen of ache. He would live, but as he stepped over fallen sword brother and enemy alike, he appeared to be the only one.

He'd fought the day long, hewing and hacking, swinging his axe for the promise of cold, hard coin. He did not count the number of men fallen at his hand. He wasn't paid by the kill, just by the slaughter.

At the end he faced a tallow-skinned Assyrian just as battle-weary as he. They clashed and Theok's axe split the man's shield and then the skull behind it to the teeth.

When he turned to face the next man he found himself alone on a field of corpses.

He'd won victory for the man who hired him.

Huzzah.

King Taranth was a fool.

WHERE THE RED BLOSSOMS WEEP

A fool with money to spend on swords and men to swing them but a fool nonetheless to think he could invade and conquer Assyria with his mealy-mouthed army of highborn sons with soft asses in new leather saddles and a motley assortment of hired dog-soldiers like himself. Near eight thousand men met on this plain at dawn. When they arrived that morning short-cropped grass and tiny red blossoms covered the field.

Now the grass had been churned to bare earth and the few flowers not crushed under booted foot wept the shed blood of those eight thousand men. It fell from their petals and mixed with the rich, black earth.

Theok's boots were covered in mud.

Movement made him pause and turn, lifting the axe in his right hand. With his left he knocked the dented helmet off his head. The visor cut his vision in half and he would have no further use for it now. It rolled off his shoulder and clunked to the ground. A raven, busy worrying an eye free from its socket, moved too slow and lost a handful of tail feathers on impact.

It choked out an insulted caw around a beak full of eyeball.

The cloyed stink of spittle-wet leather and old bronze that crowded his nose throughout the battle left him, replaced by the piss and shit and torn gut stench of the battlefield.

The breeze was cool against the skin of his scalp.

The world opened outside the helmet. Eyes narrowed, he looked over the rolling plains and rising dunes of dead soldiers. He'd been wrong. The birds and him weren't the only things alive on the field. Low-slung shapes darted among the dead, four-legs creeping and leaping. Wolves trying to snatch the ravens and their kith for a live meal, jackals and hyenas content to hunker down among them and share in slowly cooling man-flesh.

None of them turned a lambent eye toward him, choosing easier prey and plentiful scavenging. As long as he cleared this place by nightfall, he wouldn't have to deal with them.

On the other end of the field two-legged shapes also crawled over the dead.

He watched them dragging baskets laden with weapons, armor, and jewelry looted from the fallen. They stooped and pulled free their bounty, picking steel and bronze and iron from bodies. He felt nothing. He'd wielded swords once used by dead men. They came cheaper for the buyer. Not so much for the original owner. Other sellswords refused them, thinking they were bad luck.

He had no use for superstition.

Yahweh blessed.

Yahweh punished.

Beyond that a man made his own way in the world.

As he watched, some of the shapes knelt around a stack of corpses. Together, they pulled limbs, severed and attached, from the pile and lifted them to their mouths.

Ghouls.

Revulsion churned his stomach. He let the axe fall to the end of his arm, in no danger of dropping it. His fingers were locked around the haft from hundreds of swings and blows that day and glued in place by a thick layer of dried gore. He would pry it free once there was untrampled grass beneath his boots again.

Once he was gone from this abattoir.

The corpse-eaters were an abomination, but the dead were dead and not his business to defend.

Then came the screams.

He froze, scalp tingling with a jolt of adrenaline. He scanned the field, looking for the source of the human noise. The ravens, the wolves, the ghouls, and the mounds dead were all he could see.

But the screams were close.

Growling a curse, he climbed to the top of a dune of dead soldiers, muddy boots slipping on slick dented armor and disjointed limbs. Blackbirds flew away as he clambered, flapping in a cloud of feathers and shreds of meat. He didn't think about what he stepped on, what he grabbed to hoist himself to the top, even when white-rolled eyes glared at him and swollen-tongued mouths licked at him. Settling his feet on the shifting mound, he looked again for the screams.

There.

Several dozen yards away was a veritable mountain of dead. It rose into the darkening sky like a monument, rather than as a side effect of the debris of war being pushed aside by the engine of war. Around its base, a group of shambling ghouls circled, closing on a figure that lay on the ground, trying to crawl away from them.

Trying to stay alive.

Theok leapt.

Pain shot from knee to hip as he landed. He shoved it aside, moving, calling on reserves of barbaric strength from his North-born breeding. He pushed forward, fingers tight on the haft of the notched axe in his hand.

He rounded a pile of broken chariots taller than himself, not breaking stride as he swiped the axe's edge across the throat of a horse that was trapped, still strapped to the stays of her chariot. Spine broken, back legs twisted into the air, she feebly pawed the mud in front of her. Lather painted her from jaw to stomach, foam dripping from her mouth as she rolled wild eyes at him.

The mercy stroke did not slow him.

She settled, slumping, legs slowing as her life flowed onto the ground.

The ravens closed in.

He kept moving.

On the other side of the chariots he came upon the circle of ghouls.

They shuffled forward, arms outstretched, moans of hunger rolling from chapped lips, reaching toward a meal of living flesh. All of them shared an unhealthy pallor, all of them possessing the same matted, dark hair that lay lank against skin gone greenish and waxy from inbreeding and a diet of only human meat. They squinted in the twilight under heavy brows, both men and women, young and old. One of them could have been his own mother in age, two of them could have been his own sons, the rest were between the two extremes. Filthy rags hung off them, scavenged from the dead and never washed, simply worn until they wore out.

Theok's eye picked out scraps from dozens of uniforms. Some were armies he'd fought, some were armies he'd fought in.

He slowed his run, breath bellowing from his lungs, knee throbbing in time to his thundering heartbeat.

The ghouls turned as one. They fell silent, watching him draw near. Holding his axe at the ready, he kept walking, slowing his breathing even more, bringing his body under control. The ghouls shuffled, parting around him. He didn't turn, didn't look back but tension drew the muscles along his spine taut as cables on a bridgework as he heard them shuffle to close the gap, felt their rheumy eyes on him.

Back pressed to the mountain of corpses leaned a young Assyrian soldier. He'd torn the sleeves off his uniform and tied them tight to his leg with a wheel spoke from a chariot. Bone jutted from skin below his knee.

Theok assessed the man, years of battlefield experience in his judgement.

He'll have a limp, but if I can find him a surgeon he'll keep that leg.

The Assyrian swung his short bronze sword in a slow arc, to and fro, a razored serpent looking to strike anyone who got too near. His eyes were wide, white showing all around the near black irises. They skittered about in their sockets, trying to see everything at once. Blood coated one side of his face, steadily seeping from a gash that ran ear to eyebrow. More blood soaked his tunic across his stomach.

WHERE THE RED BLOSSOMS WEEP

Gut wound.

Theok stepped close, out of reach of the short sword, but close enough for the soldier to hear him. He spoke in the middling, mishmash language used by merchants and mercenaries to communicate in this area. "Will you live?"

The Assyrian stared up at him. He opened his mouth to speak but no sound came out. He swallowed hard then tried again, his voice a croak of pain and thirst. "You are the enemy."

"We're beyond that now. Will you live?"

The Assyrian looked past Theok. "Not if they have anything to do with it."

Theok stared down at him.

The Assyrian turned his eyes away. "With Ishtar's blessing, I'll live."

"To hell with your pagan whore-goddess. Yahweh has sent your salvation this day." Theok turned to the gathering of flesh-eaters. Their numbers had grown, nearly twenty crowded close. He stepped forward, making distance from the wounded man, giving himself room to move.

A large ghoul stood at the front. Tall and thin, bunched muscles strung over bones in sharp definition. Weird symbols covered his skin, painted in filth and shit and dried blood. They made Theok's skin crawl.

Corpse-chewer.
Defiler of the dead.
Necromancer.

The corpse-eater's eyes danced with intelligence, a hard edge of malevolence glittering inside. He opened a mouth full of teeth filed sharp, better to cut flesh for eating, and spoke, voice ringing hollow through his drum-tight ribcage. "Why do you stand between us and our rightful prey, outlander?"

"This man is still alive, abomination. Go fight the crows for your meal."

"Flesh pulled still living has more power." A tongue swiped the necromancer's rubber lips. He smacked them together. "And is much tastier."

"Piss off."

"He's your enemy. Why should you care?"

"I am a servant of Yahweh."

The necromancer blinked at him. "You're not an Israelite."

Theok shrugged. "He is the One True God no matter where I was born."

"Their god only cares for them. He's nowhere to be found on this field, here with these dead." The necromancer spat. "You are alone."

Theok said nothing.

The necromancer gestured toward the soldier. "He is Assyrian! Sworn enemy of the Israelites! You should leave him to us because of that."

Theok growled. "*You* are an abomination. *He* is under my protection. Walk away," he dropped the tip of his axe to the dirt, cutting a shallow line between him and the ghouls. "or feel the wrath of my God at the end of my axe."

A harsh laugh barked from the necromancer. "You *are* a man of conviction! You can barely stand and yet you defy me."

"Go eat the dead or join them. The decision is yours."

"We desire the flesh of the living and now you have given us two morsels." the necromancer snarled, "You've already been tenderized by the battle. You will provide us a meal for hours." Splinter-nailed hands swung through the air. Three ghouls shambled forward, drawing even with the wizard. "Take him."

They shuffled, reaching toward Theok. He settled back over his good leg, axe held low and to his side. He didn't retreat, he just stood. His mind slid sideways, disengaging from logic, dropping into the raw, barbaric spirit that dwelled inside him. It rose and he became a creature of instinct, of reaction. The trappings of civilization always rode outside his skin, never reaching his core, never diluting the untamed, primal force of the barbarian he was raised to be.

Lips pulled back, his teeth showed in a silent snarl.

The ghouls drew close. Bony fingers, the skin chapped back from the tips and split around pointed bone phalanges clawed the air toward him. Teeth filed sharp and set in black lined gums chomped, snapping at the air, waiting for the hands to drag meat, his flesh, to them. They weren't people any longer, they were ghouls. Dead-eaters. Corpse-grinders. Abominations.

Side by side and shoulders rubbing, their dirty feet crossed the line he'd cut into the mud.

Theok swung the axe.

Pulling from the shoulder, muscles contracting in a chain of power from hip to hand, he struck the three ghouls in one long swipe. The notched edge of the axe-blade bit deep, taking the first ghoul just under its ribcage. The heavy blade, wider than the chest it carved through, burst him like an overfull wine sack. Entrails spilled from the gash in a gout of dark fluid. A stench of old death washed over Theok, tightening his throat.

The weight of the axe and the power of his arm carried it through, not slowing, shearing the bone and flesh of the next ghoul. The corpse-eater hinged backwards, chest yawning open to reveal blackened, shriveled lungs and an unbeating heart nestled between them.

The axehead smashed into the third ghoul just below the jaw, ripping flesh and tendons. The jawbone flew away, spinning through the air. It bounced off the skull of a ghoul in the front of the gathered crowd.

All three of them stopped moving forward.

But they did not fall.

"Devil's balls." Theok snarled. Behind him the Assyrian began to pray loudly, calling to Ishtar, Enlil, Moloch, and their kin to save him.

"You cannot kill that which is already dead, barbarian." The necromancer laughed. "You can only join them or feed them." He raised filth covered arms, spindly fingers twisted in a sorcerous gesture. Behind him the horde of undead began to moan, a deep, undulating, call for human flesh.

Theok's scalp crawled.

Dark magick sparked along the necromancer's skin, tracing the symbols painted there. It flashed and popped, a grease fire of eldritch energy. The death-head carved into Theok's back burned, the lines of scar tissue responding to the call of sorcery.

The necromancer capered, feet hopping in the mud, arms swinging wildly. A mad grin split his face, pulling the skin tight under his eyes as if drawn by wire. "I feel the mark on you, outlander. You have been touched by Namtar. The god of death has marked you." A cackle burst from his lips in a shower of spittle. "I will claim you for him. I will finish the job started by someone else."

Movement to his left made Theok glance. The Assyrian was on his feet, using a broken spear shaft for a crutch and hobbling on his uninjured leg. Sweat sheeted his face, running in streams across skin gone waxy with pain. His knuckles were white on the handle of his bronze sword but he stood.

Theok nodded in approval.

"You will serve me like the others, barbarian," The necromancer pointed at the Assyrian. "and you will partake in that man's flesh with the rest of us." His hands waved, slinging magick out over the horde of zombies to each side. "Go my children! Go and claim your brother!"

The undead began to shamble. Dragging one foot in front of the other, they lurched, each thudding step causing their open mouth moans to pulse in the air.

"It's the end but we'll fight together." The Assyrian spoke from the side of his mouth, voice bitter, jaw set in a hard line, and his eyes locked on the approaching dead. "It will be a good death."

The battle-axe flew through the air, spinning head over haft.

It struck the necromancer in his jutting breastbone.

The mighty blade hewed deep, splitting the wizard like a chicken in the hands of a butcher. Blood showered out around the axe-head in a hot rain of red. The impact lifted the necromancer off his feet, flinging him back to land in the muck made runny with his life's blood. His mouth worked silently once, then twice before falling open and slack as the god he served swept him up. Life ran out of his eyes like water from a broken cup and they glassed over, useless as sticky marbles.

"Fucking wizards never learn." Theok spat. "Yahweh is the God Above All Gods."

The horde of ghouls jerked to a stop, the magick sustaining them dying with their master. One by one they fell to the earth, puppets with cut strings.

"Well," the Assyrian said "I didn't see that coming."

"Neither did he." Theok walked to the fallen wizard. Reaching down, he pulled his axe free from it's resting place in necromancer ribcage. He turned to find the Assyrian watching him warily.

"What happens now?"

"Now we get the hell out of this cursed place."

"I won't be a prisoner of King Taranth. They don't live long enough to be pardoned."

"I won't be taking you in. I'm done with Taranth, his bitch-queen, and his pack of mewling bastards." Theok dropped the axe-head to the ground and leaned on the handle. "There is a wide world outside of Assyria, son. You should see some of it."

The Assyrian nodded. "You know it was you who knocked me off my horse and broke my leg."

Theok shrugged. "I think we're even now." He straightened, lifting the axe. "I'm done talking. The sooner we leave this place, the sooner we can find some ale and you a surgeon."

Theok hooked the arm of the Assyrian over his broad shoulders, lifting the man's weight off his injured leg. They began the long walk off the field.

Behind them came a growl.

Theok looked around. The wolves had gathered, yellow-eyed in the falling twilight.

He raised his axe.

"Piss off."

One by one the wolves turned tail and slunk away.

The ravens continued to feast.

James R. Tuck is the author of the Deacon Chalk series of

Dark Urban Fantasy novels and the editor of this anthology. A professional tattoo artist for nearly two decades, he lives in Metro Atlanta where he owns Family Tradition Tattoo. His time not slinging ink on skin or page are spent with his lovely wife and children or taking pictures of cool and interesting things.

Find out more at:
www.jamesrtuck.com

THIEF OF SOULS

LORIANE PARKER

A painful tingling filled Alexian's bones, warning him of dawn's approach. He needed to find shelter before sunrise. The old fort at the top of the hill had fallen to ruin, but one of its towers remained intact. Dark vines crept across its weathered stones. Only the crossbow slits near the top of the tower would let in the sunlight; the bottom sections of the tower would be filled with shadow all day. Alexian trudged up the hill. His black plate armor hovered magically over his bare bones as though his flesh and muscle still bulged beneath the metal. He shoved open the tower's heavy wooden door and stepped inside.

He closed the door behind him. In the darkness, he could see clearly. Ladders led to the tower's upper levels, but the wooden floors had mostly rotted away with time. Alexian's spectral vision cast his surroundings in an eerie green glow. Like everything else, the silk scarf tied around his arm appeared to be green, but he knew it was blue. He tried to picture the day Lyssa had tied it there, her blond hair shining in the sun. The images and colors had faded from his memory over the years. A specter never sleeps, and the long hours of the days and nights stretched on unbearably without her. What troubled him the most was that Lyssa suffered too.

Outside, the sun slipped above the horizon. The cool blanket of night slid from Alexian as the sun stabbed through the crossbow slits at the top of the tower, casting slanted pools of light upon the wall high above. Even this distance from the sun, Alexian's bones ached. He crouched in the safety of the dark.

The door creaked open.

Alexian drew his sword. Who else could be interested in a dark, empty tower? Perhaps some roadside bandit or other outlaw seeking a hiding place for the day. It didn't matter. The tower sheltered him, and no one would drive him from it.

A torch flared as it was lit, then tossed into the center of the room. The blazing flame blotted out an area of Alexian's vision, creating a bright blind spot.

A slender figure dressed in dark clothing stepped into the tower. Alexian leapt from the shadows, blade flashing in the torchlight. At the last moment he stopped himself.

It was a young woman. She was slender but strong with her hair in a long braid. She held a longsword before her, prepared to defend herself. Alexian took a step back.

The woman stood her ground. "Are you Sir Alexian Graystone?"

"I am." His deep voice echoed in the tower like a wind moaning through a tomb. "Who are you?"

"Kyra Kadir."

"The thief hunter. What do you want?"

"Revenge against Lord Darius Trent."

Alexian lowered his sword.

"Last night," Kyra said, "a man at the inn said he'd seen the Dark Knight in the area. This tower looked like a good place for a specter to hide during the day. I was hoping to find you here."

"Why?"

"I can kill Trent if I can sneak into his castle undetected. You escaped from there; you must know a secret way in."

"I do," Alexian said. "But I won't take a lady to her death."

"Your confidence in my abilities is overwhelming. I'll make you a deal. You seek Trent's prized sword. If you get me into the castle, I'll bring you Shadesplinter. After I kill Trent."

"With Shadesplinter, Trent is undefeatable."

"When he's at home in his castle, he leaves the sword in his gallery. He likes to spend some time away from the sword. Apparently, it 'pains him.'"

If Trent and Shadesplinter were separated, if Alexian could get the sword . . . this could be his best chance to free Lyssa. "You are a woman of honor," Alexian said, "so I will help you. But I'll have to meet you in Valeria. I can only travel at night, and the paths I must take are ones you cannot follow."

"Meet me? Can't you just draw me a map?"

"No. The secret passageway into Trent's castle leads through Valeria's vast network of catacombs. It's a labyrinth under the city. I'll have to guide you through myself."

Kyra was silent for a few moments, and Alexian wondered if she was changing her mind. At last, she spoke. "How soon?"

"Three weeks." He sheathed his sword. "Meet me outside the city on the morning of the Summer Solstice, in one of the Dhareg Caves. You'll find its entrance hidden behind a fire bush."

"Three weeks," Kyra said. She retrieved her torch and strode out into the sunlight, leaving Alexian alone in the dark.

THIEF OF SOULS

* * *

The old mine where Alexian had sought shelter from the sun during his escape from Valeria was now sealed with heavy stone blocks and mortar. He drew back his fist, then punched as hard as he could. An unseen force threw him backward and he slammed into the ground. The stones blocking the entrance remained intact. Though a specter was much stronger than an ordinary man, Alexian was no match for such a powerful spell. He'd already tried two other possible hiding places in the area: a haunted mausoleum and the ruins of an old royal manor. The mausoleum's entrance was sealed with stone and spell just as the mine's was. All that remained of the old manor were piles of broken stones. Trent had done everything he could to prevent him from reaching Valeria.

Alexian now stood in the open countryside, far from the cave in the forest that had sheltered him yesterday. Between him and Valeria stretched the vast plains of the Ronel Prairie, half a day's journey to the city.

Alexian's bones tingled. To the east, the stars had faded from the sky.

He sensed only one more place nearby that could shelter him from the sun--a small underground cave. He hoped Trent hadn't sealed it as well. With sunrise only minutes away, he sprinted in the direction of the cave.

A soft glow filled the horizon.

He saw it: an old oak on the edge of the prairie. He could sense the cave below ground, its entrance hidden under the tree's roots. He reached the tree and knelt on the grass. He dug furiously, his fingers raking the earth. The sky brightened. Searing pain swept through him. If he was caught out in the open, then the sun would destroy him, and Lyssa would stay imprisoned forever. Dig, dig, dig . . .

The ground shifted, then sank, opening into the cave below. As the sun slipped above the horizon, Alexian dove head first into the hole. For a split second the sunlight touched his lower legs and feet as he fell down into the cave.

He cried out, slamming into the cave floor several feet below with a loud clanging of armor. The cool darkness snuffed out the burning in his bones with a loud hiss. Smoke rose from his legs and feet. Trembling, Alexian unfastened one of his front greaves and lifted it back, then pulled off his boot. His tibia and fibula and all the bones in his foot were blackened. He checked his other leg to discover the same damage. His singed bones throbbed. Carefully, he flexed his feet. The bones creaked, but did not crack. When he touched them, they did not feel brittle. Slowly, he stood.

THIEF OF SOULS

His legs supported his weight, but strength no longer surged through them the way it usually did in darkness. If he blocked an opponent's sword, the impact sent through his body might shatter his normally unbreakable bones.

Alexian slammed his fist into the cave wall, creating an indentation in the rock. Though Kyra had agreed to get Shadesplinter for him, he wanted to face Trent. Alexian had often thought about the things he'd like to do to the man. But Lyssa was more important than revenge. Alexian could not risk his own destruction, or he would lose her forever. He leaned back against the wall of the cave. Soon, the sun would bleed its light through the opening above. He stayed in the shadows, beyond the sun's reach.

* * *

He remembered the last time he'd comfortably spent time in sunlight. He had followed Darius Trent down a hallway in a fort where Trent was stationed. The sun streamed through the tall, arched windows and reflected in their armor. Alexian and Trent wore the surcoat of King Ivtar. Alexian knew the surcoats were red, embroidered with a golden phoenix, but he couldn't remember what the colors looked like. Even his memories were tinged green.

The heavyset Trent led him down a winding staircase into the lower level of the fort. Trent glanced back over his shoulder, curly dark hair straying in front of his eyes. He swept his hair back. "I fear King Ivtar's reign will be short-lived. He can't keep the five cities united."

"He is far wiser than we are," Alexian said. "What he lacks in manpower he makes up for in resourcefulness. He is a good man, and a good king."

"You have too much faith in people. Ivtar doesn't have the army or monies to keep order and bring true stability to the kingdom. But I've found a way to make his dream a reality." They stopped at a door at the bottom of the stairs. Trent rested his hand on Alexian's shoulder. "Remember when we vowed we would sacrifice everything to bring peace to the land?"

"Our knightly oath," Alexian said. "I meant every word of it."

"So did I," Trent said. His face hardened. "So did I."

Trent pushed the door open and stepped back so Alexian could enter first. The door opened up into a room. On the wall, a young woman hung by chains, wrists and ankles shackled. A shrunken figure shrouded in dark robes pointed a longsword at her. The woman struggled, rattling the chains, but the gag tied around her face smothered her cries. As Alexian stepped into the room, she met his gaze. The shrouded figure shoved the longsword into her chest.

"Lyssa!" Alexian cried.

A misty white shape rushed from Lyssa's body and into the longsword.

A forceful blow struck Alexian's back and he heard the scraping of a blade piercing armor. The point of a sword emerged through the front of his breastplate. For a split second, he felt nothing. Then pain exploded through his chest, stabbing down his arms.

Trent leaned close to Alexian's ear. "It's nothing personal, friend," he said. "In order for my new sword to work, you had to be the last thing Lyssa saw before she died. Of course, I had to kill you too, so you wouldn't seek revenge against me." He pulled his blade free.

Alexian collapsed. His blood pooled around him, soaking his beard. The cold of the stone floor seeped into his face. The unbearable pain dashed his thoughts to pieces. He could *feel* his body falling apart inside, could feel himself sliding from consciousness.

Then, his pain ceased. He started to pass through his body.

With all his might he strained against the irresistible force that tried to pull his soul free. He pushed himself back into his body. Lyssa's soul was trapped in the longsword, and Alexian couldn't, *wouldn't*, leave her there.

The shrouded figure chanted, waving its gnarled hand over the longsword. The blade glowed briefly, then turned dark red.

"It is finished, Sire," the figure hissed. Its breath stirred the hood draped over its bowed head.

Trent took the sword. He tilted it, examining the blade. "It should have a name," he said. "Every powerful sword has a name." He pursed his lips for a moment. "I shall call her . . . Shadesplinter."

A fierce chill smothered Alexian. His flesh crumbled to ash; his armor dropped and clanked against his bones. His eyes dissolved. Darkness swallowed him.

A pinpoint of green light burned in his vision, then spread, until he could once again see the room. His chest no longer rose and fell with his breath, the warmth of his flesh replaced with the cold, dry hardness of bare bones. Glowing sinews appeared and wound around his joints, binding them together. His armor lifted and hovered in its normal place.

"Curse you, witch!" Trent shouted at the hooded figure. "You didn't tell me he would become a specter!"

The witch shrugged. "I didn't know his love for her would be as strong as her love for him. Her love powers the sword; his holds him bound to this world."

Trent raised Shadesplinter over Alexian, preparing to strike.

"No, my Lord!" The witch cried. "You mustn't slay him with this sword!"

Trent halted. "Why?"

"To slay him with it will destroy it, great Lord."

"You said the sword would be indestructible!"

"It is--unless you use it against the specter."

"But he'll never stop hunting me!"

"I will enchant another sword for you later. But for now we must leave, before he rises. The sun outside will hold him at bay and give us time to escape."

Trent sheathed Shadesplinter. He strode from the room, the witch scuttling behind him.

Energy surged through Alexian. He leapt to his feet and raced after Trent. Halfway up the stairs, Alexian stopped. Sunlight filled the hallway above, spilling into the top of the stairwell. An irrational terror filled his mind. Every fiber of his spectral being warned him against the deadly power of the sun. He would have to wait until nightfall to go after Trent.

Alexian retreated downstairs. He pulled the chains that held Lyssa and ripped them free from the wall. For the rest of the day, he cradled her body in his arms. His screams made the walls shudder. He swore an oath that he would find Shadesplinter and set Lyssa's soul free.

* * *

In the cave, Alexian stared at his singed bones. He had failed to save Lyssa that day in the fort; he could not fail her now. The scarf tied around his arm reminded him of Lyssa's suffering, and of the vow he had sworn to keep.

The sun slipped below the horizon.

Cold swept through Alexian, snuffing out the tingling in his bones. His legs stopped throbbing, though they still ached. He pulled on his boots and strapped on his front greaves. Reaching up, he grabbed hold of the opening above, then pulled himself out of the cave.

He stood at the edge of the Ronel prairie. In the distance, Valeria City perched atop a small mountain, the jagged dark shapes of its stone buildings blotting out the stars. Trent Castle overlooked the city, its tall slender spires stabbing the sky.

Alexian trudged through the prairie, the tall grasses striking his chest and swishing as he passed through them. After several hours, he reached the mountain. The main road was the easiest way up the slope, but Alexian wished to avoid travelers, so he chose a more difficult path. He grasped at rocks to grab hold. He heaved himself up the mountain. As he climbed, the moon rose high overhead, bathing the boulders and scrubby bushes in soft light. Near the top of the slope, just below the city, a series of caves pockmarked the cliff face. Narrow paths led to several of the caves, with steps hewn into the rock by ancient people who had lived there a millennium ago. The caves had all been sealed. Again, Trent had taken away any possible shelter from the sun. But there was one cave entrance Trent didn't know about. As dawn approached, Alexian spotted the fire bush, its thick clusters of leaves flashing in the wind. Fire bushes did not normally grow on mountainsides, and this was the only one near the Dhareg Caves. Alexian reached behind the bush and felt the surface of the rock. His fingers found the edge of a crevice. Pushing back the whip-like branches, he squeezed himself behind the bush. As cool air enveloped him, he knew he'd found the cave's entrance. It was little more than a large crack, just wide enough for a person to squeeze through. He turned sideways and stepped in, inching deeper and deeper into the dark.

The narrow crevice opened up and he stepped into a wide cavern. On the other side, a tunnel led into the mountain. Alexian headed down the tunnel far enough so that when the sun would later filter through the crevice, it wouldn't touch him. Now all he had to do was wait for Kyra.

It was mid-morning when footsteps sounded in the crevice. Kyra stepped into the cavern. She lit a torch, then reached into her pack and took out a vial of thick, sap-like liquid. She smeared some of the liquid over the soles of her leather boots, then took a few steps. Alexian saw nothing unusual where her boots had touched the ground. Kyra took a leaf from her belt pouch and placed it in her mouth. After a few moments, she studied the ground where she had stepped, and smiled.

Juntar sap.

Alexian had used it when hunting in the woods, back when he was alive. The resin on Kyra's boots would last for days, and would leave behind footprints she could see when she ate the leaves. Though Alexian admired her resourcefulness, he wasn't sure why she bothered. He would guide her to the castle and back; she wouldn't have to find her own way.

Unless she feared he might double-cross her. Alexian's heart sank. She didn't trust him. And why should she? She didn't know him. To her, he was just a specter.

Alexian's armor clanged as he stepped from the shadows.

Kyra turned to face him, her torch held high.

"Are you ready?" He asked.

"Yes."

"Good. Follow me, and keep the torch back. I see best in the dark."

Alexian led her into the tunnel. "This passageway leads under the city, to the southern courtyard of Trent Castle."

"How did you find it?"

"I came here years ago to take Shadesplinter from Trent, but a powerful spell protects his castle from the walking dead. It drained my strength and I was forced to flee. Trent and his witch thought they had me trapped, but specters can detect paths that lead underground, away from the sun. I sensed this passageway and found the secret door that led into it."

"Did you hear what happened to his witch?"

"I heard she died a few months ago."

"No," Kyra said. "She cast so many powerful spells, she used up all her magic. Trent threw her out into the street. When she heard I wanted revenge against him, she came looking for me. She's the one who told me you had escaped from his castle."

"I can't say I pity her, but I'm grateful she helped you."

Alexian and Kyra passed through a narrow section of

the tunnel. Rumbling echoed throughout the passage and the ground trembled.

"Look out!" Alexian shouted as the ceiling caved in.

Kyra ducked, covering her head with her arms. Alexian crouched over her, shielding her with his body. Warmth emanated from her, the comforting warmth that only life could give. He could steal that warmth for himself with a mere touch, could take her life and warm his own bones for a little while. But it was not the warmth of the living that he sought. He took great care not to touch her. Rocks thudded against his armor and rolled off his back.

The passageway grew still.

Alexian straightened up. "Are you all right?"

"Yes," Kyra said. "Thank you."

"You're welcome."

They picked their way around the rocks and continued down the tunnel.

Alexian glanced back at Kyra over his shoulder. "What did Trent do to earn your wrath?"

"Trent has grown wealthy by stealing from merchants. My father was the bodyguard of a merchant named Rishad." She stared at the ground. "When Trent's thieves attacked Rishad's caravan, my father gave his life defending him. The thieves killed Rishad too."

"I'm sorry," Alexian said. "Is that why you hunt thieves?"

"Yes. I stop as many as I can." She ran her fingers over her hair, brushing off the dust from the cave-in. "Why do you want Trent's sword so badly?"

"Shadesplinter steals the soul of every victim it kills. My wife Lyssa was its first victim."

* * *

They reached a dead end. Just inches above their heads, a wooden trap door was set in the rock. A thick layer of cobwebs coated its cracked boards and large, iron handle.

"I can't tell what time it is," Kyra said. "The witch said the best time to sneak in is just after sunset, at the changing of the guard."

"Then we must wait a while," Alexian said. "The sun still shines. I will sense when it has set."

Kyra leaned back against the wall of the tunnel, and Alexian gazed off into the distance. Their shadows danced on the wall in the flickering torchlight. If things went well tonight, Alexian would soon see Lyssa again. He touched the scarf tied around his arm.

"Was that your wife's?" Kyra asked.

"Yes."

"What was she like?"

"She was a Shira," he said, "a magical spirit of exceptional beauty. Shiras rarely take on human form. Even when they do, they almost never fall in love with mortal men. But when a Shira does fall in love, that love is pure and eternal. Lyssa only trusted two people with the secret of her true form; myself, and our closest friend."

Kyra scowled. "Trent."

"Yes. Trent needed Lyssa's soul to forge Shadesplinter. It's her love for me that gives the blade its power. Her soul desires so much to be with me that it unwittingly draws in the soul of each of the sword's victims in the hope that it will be mine. If I am slain by the sword, my soul will join Lyssa's. Our reunion will break the spell and set both of us free."

"How long has it been since you've seen her?"

"Twenty years."

"That's a long time."

A fierce cold smothered Alexian. His vision sharpened; energy surged through him.

"The sun has set," Alexian said. He grasped the handle of the trap door and pulled. It trembled, then gave way, opening with a tremendous groan. He pulled himself up through the opening, then reached down to help Kyra through. When Kyra touched his hand, she gasped.

THIEF OF SOULS

Alexian pulled back. "Are you hurt?"

"No." Kyra rubbed her hand.

Alexian cursed himself. How could he have forgotten? "Forgive me. I didn't mean to harm you. It's just that, you're a lady, and...it's an old habit."

Kyra smiled. She passed up her torch, then pulled herself up. Alexian realized that she had reached for his hand too. For a moment, she had forgotten that he was a specter.

They stood in a small room, barely large enough for the two of them to fit in comfortably, and Alexian's closeness made Kyra's breath frost over. The walls and low ceiling were made of stone and mortar. In the wall beside them was a door.

"We're inside the wall that surrounds the courtyard," Alexian explained. "The castle proper is to the left, and the gallery wing is directly across from here."

"Good," Kyra said. "The sword should be hidden behind a secret panel in the gallery."

"Be careful," Alexian said. "Shadesplinter is cursed. If you attempt to wield it, you won't be able to put it down, and your hand will catch fire and crumble to ash. Only handle the sword if it is sheathed. I'll wait for you here. I'll leave this door open; when closed, it blends in perfectly with the stones that surround it on the other side." He yanked open the door and fresh air rushed into the room. A thick network of tangled vines covered the doorway.

Alexian pushed aside the vines. Outside, the courtyard was just as he remembered: clusters of white blossoms lined a series of pathways, and the breeze scattered their soft petals across the dark stones like snow. The leaves of majestic oak trees shimmered in the moonlight. On the other side of the courtyard, a wide balcony overlooked the gardens. Its tall doors were opened to let in the breeze. To Alexian's left was the side of the castle, with a small, arched door.

The bell's deep knell rang outside, its sound hollow and distant, signaling the changing of the guard. Kyra stepped out from behind the vines and ran to the castle door. It creaked softly as she pushed it open and went inside.

Alexian arranged the vines slightly to make certain they covered the open doorway. He waited, listening to the leaves rustling in the breeze outside.

A man cried out from the gallery, his words carrying across the courtyard. "Thief! Guards!"

The tromping of armored boots thundered into the gallery, followed by the clashing of blades. Alexian shoved the vines aside. Shadows moved behind the gallery curtains, wavering in the flickering torchlight: the silhouettes of people engaged in combat. Kyra could handle herself in a fight, but against how many men? And what if Trent heard the commotion and came to dispatch of the thief himself? What if he was wielding Shadesplinter? If he killed Kyra, her soul would be trapped along with Lyssa, and Alexian might lose his best chance to save them both.

Alexian leapt into the courtyard. Pain stabbed through his feet and up his legs with such fierceness that he stumbled and fell to his knees. For a few moments, all he could do was double over, shaking, his armor suddenly heavier than normal. He forced himself to stand straight.

The commotion in the gallery stopped. A man spoke, but Alexian couldn't make out his words. Then one blade clashed against another, the sounds of one-on-one combat. A woman shouted, and the man laughed.

Alexian knew that laugh. Trent. The bones of Alexian's fingers creaked as his hands clenched into fists. Then two figures stepped onto the balcony.

Kyra backed against the railing. She raised her sword in time to block the blow from her opponent, a man in a light-colored tunic. Then the man swung his dark blade and shattered Kyra's sword in one mighty blow. Shards of splintered metal flashed in the moonlight as they clinked and scattered across the stone balcony.

Alexian recognized that dark blade all too well. Kyra

faced Trent and Shadesplinter with no means of escape. From the balcony, it was a two-story drop down to the courtyard, too far for her to jump down safely.

Alexian gritted his teeth against the pain that shot through his legs and sprinted toward the balcony. Kyra looked down over her shoulder. Alexian stopped below the balcony and motioned for her to jump. She threw the broken hilt of her sword in Trent's face, then swung herself over the railing and dropped down into Alexian's arms.

Her warmth surged through Alexian's hands and up his arms, driving the chill from him. Kyra gasped. Alexian quickly put her down on the ground. "Are you all right?" He knelt beside her.

Kyra's eyelids fluttered. Then, she nodded. Alexian looked up at the balcony.

Trent stared down at him. Gray streaked his dark hair and neatly-trimmed beard, and fine lines creased his gaunt face. The muscular knight from Alexian's memory had faded into a thin, wiry man. Trent paled, then ducked back into the gallery.

Kyra stirred. When she spoke, her voice was barely a whisper. "I thought you weren't coming."

"I heard sounds of a struggle."

"We have to get out before Trent and his guards get

here."

"He won't bring his guards," Alexian said. "He'll want to face me alone."

Kyra tried to sit up, but fell back to the ground.

Trent burst through the door and into the courtyard. In one hand, he held a torch; in the other, he wielded a silver sword, runes glowing on the blade's surface like liquid fire. Two empty scabbards hung from his belt. One was for the sword he wielded, but the other…where was Shadesplinter?

Alexian whispered to Kyra. "Trent doesn't have Shadesplinter. He cannot use it against me."

"Maybe he left it in the gallery." The color returned to her face. "When I can move again, I'll get the sword." Her fingers brushed her empty scabbard. "I should be able to slide this onto the blade."

Alexian nodded. "I'll deal with Trent." He turned to face Trent and drew his sword.

"Sir Alexian Graystone," Trent said. "You shouldn't have come back."

Alexian charged at Trent and their blades clashed. The force of the swords' impact sent a shock wave reverberating down Alexian's arm and through his ribcage. It was as though he had thrown all his might and steel against a stone wall. The bones of his legs creaked, but remained sound. Still, he wasn't sure how many strikes he could withstand.

Trent shoved his torch in Alexian's face. Blinded, Alexian staggered backward. He glimpsed movement on the edge of the blazing light and barely raised his sword in time to block Trent's blade.

Again, Trent shoved his torch at Alexian. This time, Alexian anticipated the move. With a sweep of his sword, he knocked the torch from Trent's hand. The torch sailed through the air and landed on the stone path.

Trent struck back. Alexian blocked the blow. He pressed close, staring at Trent through their crossed blades. The green orbs of light in Alexian's empty eyesockets reflected in the pupils of Trent's dark eyes.

"Thief," Alexian growled. "Give back my wife's soul."

Trent pushed back. He circled, poised to strike. "It's your fault she's trapped. If you hadn't won her heart, I could never have forged Shadesplinter."

Alexian glanced over Trent's shoulder. Behind Trent, Kyra took a rope and grappling hook out of her pack. She cast up the hook and it caught on the balcony's railing. She pulled herself up the rope, hand over hand. Above her, the gallery was quiet; the guards had likely returned to their post by the door.

Trent didn't notice her. He stayed focused on Alexian.

"I told you I'd bring order to the mainland," Trent said. "Four of the five cities are now mine. With Shadesplinter, I'll conquer the fifth and become king."

"But at what price?" Alexian said. "Shadesplinter may strike fear in the hearts of your enemies, but the more you use the sword, the more Lyssa's pain affects you. If you had Shadesplinter with you right now, she might compel you to use it against me. You may control most of the mainland, but you can't control yourself."

"That will change once you're gone."

Kyra pulled herself over the railing and disappeared into the gallery.

Trent attacked Alexian, who parried the blow. The clang of metal striking metal rang throughout the courtyard. The runes on Trent's sword burned bright in the night. Alexian slashed Trent across the face, severing the lower part of his ear. Trent snarled. He stabbed Alexian's shoulder. The wound stung and Alexian's arm fell limp. He quickly switched his sword to his other hand.

Alexian dodged Trent's swinging blade. It whispered through the air just above his chest. Alexian limped as he fought. Every step on the courtyard grass stabbed him as though knives sank deeper and deeper into his feet.

Kyra climbed down from the balcony. She carried her

swordbelt slung over her shoulder, Shadesplinter in the scabbard from her shattered blade. If Alexian could hold off Trent long enough for her to escape, then he could follow her into the secret passage. There, beyond the reach of the spell on the courtyard, he would regain his strength. He and Kyra could lose Trent in the catacombs.

Alexian forced his limbs to move. His legs dragged, as though he struggled against the swift current of a river. With each swing his sword grew heavier. He struck at Trent, who parried the blow. Trent raised his sword and slammed it down at Alexian.

Alexian blocked the blow, but the force of it sent a tremendous shock wave down his body. His right tibia and fibula snapped. He fell to one knee and his arm sailed out to the side.

Trent plunged his sword through the center of Alexian's chest.

Alexian cried out. Pain ripped through him and his entire frame shuddered. His armor fell and clanged upon his bare bones. His joints' magic sinews began to unwind, the glowing strands fading into darkness. "Lyssa!" Alexian's voice died to a whisper. "Lyssa, I'm so sorry."

Trent pulled his sword free. "Now you shall haunt me no more." He sheathed his sword, then turned and strode toward the castle door.

Alexian's mind raced with panic as his hands fell apart. The bones of his forearms separated, then slipped from his elbows. His vambraces clattered on the ground. He remembered Lyssa's face, creased in pain as the witch shoved Shadesplinter into her chest. Forever would she remain trapped in that blade, frozen in the final, agonizing moment of her life. He had failed her.

Kyra gaped at Alexian, her eyes wide as she ran toward him. She grasped Shadesplinter's hilt and drew the blade. Smoke rose from her hand with a hiss as she shoved the dark blade through his chest.

Again, Alexian's body shuddered as the blade struck home. An unseen force broke Kyra's grip on the hilt, setting her free and sparing her hand.

"Thank you," Alexian said.

Trent spun around. His jaw dropped.

Alexian let out a great sigh that rippled across the grass in a wave and stirred the leaves of the surrounding trees into a loud whisper, making it sound as though the entire courtyard exhaled with relief. He collapsed into a pile of armor and bones.

Abruptly, Alexian's pain ceased. He passed from his body as though plunging through the surface of a lake. For a moment, he held up his transparent hand, his ghostly form taking the shape of the body he'd had in life.

"Shadesplinter!" Trent cried. He rushed toward Alexian.

The dark blade sucked in Alexian's soul. He plunged into shadow. Then other souls rose around him, glowing bright, and pressed against him on all sides. Their white faces twisted as they screamed. Alexian couldn't squeeze between the souls, so he pushed through them. He tore through their gauzy shapes with ferocity. "Lyssa!" Alexian shouted.

One of the souls snarled, "Who be this 'Lyssa?'"

"She is the lady who gives this sword its power," Alexian said, "*my* lady."

The souls fell silent. They jostled one another as they struggled to part, forming a narrow path through the horde of misty, writhing shapes. A short distance ahead, a lone woman stood, her head bowed, her forehead creased in sorrow. Her long hair floated about her head as though caught in a breeze.

"Lyssa!" Alexian cried.

She raised her head. "Alexian?" Her voice was faint, hesitant.

Alexian flew to her and swept her up in his arms.

Memories burst into his thoughts in vivid colors: Lyssa's deep brown eyes; her flaxen hair; the flush of her cheeks in the cold. The red roses and purple irises in her bridal bouquet. The orange and yellow hues of a sunrise. The silver-green forest and steel-gray ocean with whitecaps rolling upon a brown sandy beach. The fall colors of the oak leaves. A bright blue summer sky. Alexian remembered the softness of Lyssa's skin, how her heart beat against his chest as he held her tight. The warmth of her sweaty body against his when they made love. The lavender scent of her perfume. Her presence enveloped him.

"You came for me," she said.

"Of course I did. I love you."

She clung to him. "I love you too."

A wave of force rippled through them. The souls burst away from them as the darkness shattered with a mighty crash.

Alexian's surroundings snapped into focus. He and Lyssa floated above the ground in the courtyard. The dark red shards of Shadesplinter lay scattered across the ground. Trent dropped the broken hilt, its black leather grip stitched with strands of Lyssa's blond hair.

The other souls from Shadesplinter swirled around Trent. With slender fingers they grasped his arms and clung to his blue tunic. He tried to pull free, but they wound around his limbs like the tightening coils of white serpents.

In the center of the courtyard, a large shadowy disc appeared, a doorway that opened up into darkness. As the shrieks of tormented souls sounded from its impenetrable depths, the ghosts in the courtyard dragged Trent toward the dark portal.

"Guards!" Trent called out.

The castle door flew open and several armored guards wearing yellow surcoats ran into the courtyard. When they saw the attacking souls and the dark portal, they hesitated.

Trent clawed at the ground, grasping at stones and twisted tree roots in an attempt to stop his plunge through the portal. "Save me!" He cried.

The guards drew their swords and slashed at the thick misty shapes without any effect, as though slicing through empty air. The souls flew at the guards, who turned and ran for the castle door. They barely managed to escape inside, abandoning their master in the courtyard.

Trent grabbed hold of a large tree root. He kicked hard, struggling to twist free from the souls' grasp.

Lyssa floated forward and hovered before Trent.

Trent tried to turn his face away, but his gaze remained fixed on Lyssa's feet. His lower lip trembled. As he clung to the tree root, his knuckles turned white. Slowly, he looked up, and met Lyssa's gaze.

Lyssa screamed a terrible, high-pitched shriek filled with the intensity of her long years of torment. Trent winced at the unbearable sound. He let go of the tree root and clapped his hands over his ears.

The ghosts dragged him through the portal. Too late they realized they had clung to him too long, and they fell into darkness with him. The doorway shrank smaller and smaller until it disappeared completely, shutting out the souls' tortured cries.

Alexian's armor and loose bones crumbled to dust, tatters of black ash fluttering like feathers as the wind dispersed them. Only his longsword remained--a fine blade, his parting gift to Kyra. She could escape through the underground passage, and his sword would defend her well in life. Alexian hoped it would be a joyous and prosperous one. She had risked her right hand to reunite him with his beloved, and he would forever be grateful. He raised his hand in farewell, and Kyra raised hers in return.

Alexian took hold of Lyssa's hand. She had substance, but felt differently than flesh. It was a strange but wonderful sensation. She smiled at him. For twenty years he had longed to see that smile. Her joy radiated from her and flowed through him, their souls now joined forever. A bright light enveloped them. Despite its intensity Alexian could still clearly see Lyssa beside him. The light's warmth and comfort beckoned to him. It spread, completely blotting out the courtyard from his vision. Together, he and Lyssa left behind the world of the living and passed into the Realm of Light.

Loriane Parker writes classic sword-and-sorcery and urban fantasy. She is a huge fan of stories where a sympathetic hero struggles to defeat a great evil to preserve the force of good. The clashing of blades and the weaving of spells in speculative fiction has always captivated her. A high school chemistry teacher, she has a passion for ancient languages, and is a graduate of the 2011 Odyssey Writers Workshop. To find out more about Loriane and her writing, visit her website at www.lorianeparker.com

THE GNAWED BONE

W.E. WERTENBERGER

"Tighten up that line you son's of whores! I will personally skin the next man who takes one step back. I swear by every god in heaven and all the demons of hell!"

The uneven column of armored men shifted as one. The once ragged line now forming, more or less, a solid front of shield and steel. Occupying a fortified hill made a parade ground formation impossible, even for elite troops like the Varangian Guard. The fortifications were sparsely filled, their numbers well below full strength.

They began the campaign with nearly eighty men. Now, just over half that. The fighting had been bitter and prolonged.

"Next time faster", bellowed the company's Centurion Ragnar as he stalked the line, ever present personal guard at his side. Personal guard was a term Ragnar bestowed upon them. The rest of the troop knew them as *Ragnar's Boys*, a motley collection of petty murderers and rapists.

Kol watched as they passed, removing his simple steel helmet to allow the little breeze there was to cool him. He kept his thick dark hair shorn short for just this reason and never understood why most of the Guard insisted on growing theirs long.

He leaned to his right, speaking from the side of his mouth. "I'd give this whole season's back-pay if he'd just shut up. I swear by *my* sweaty ass and itching balls."

A snort of agreement and a tired chuckle came back at him.

"Soulless bastard." Kol spat in the general direction of the hated Centurion. A figurative gesture, his mouth was dry as his empty water skin. The intense heat of the midday sun had dissipated, but choking clouds of fine dust kicked up by every charge and counter charge hung in the air like a soiled death shroud. "We've already beaten them back three times. No reason we can't retire, let a fresh company replace us."

Another snort came again from Kol's right, "What fresh company would you suggest replace us my friend?" This time, the chuckle was at Kol's expense.

"How do I know old man? I'm not some dung-headed officer", Kol turned to confront his ever shifty comrade

"No, you are not an officer, I'll give ya that. But if that

THE GNAWED BONE

thick Saxon skull of yours gets cracked open in the next rush, I'll not be givin' odds that shit instead of brains don't come spilling out."

Kol glared at the wide, unshaven face grinning crookedly back at him from under a dented steel galea. The helmet one size too large for the rangy veteran.

"Hakkon, you wicked fiend," Kol laughed, "if I wasn't preoccupied with killing these Delyanian fools, I'd find that jackal's den you call a home and regale them with tales of their father's mirth."

"If you do find that den, tell their mother she's a cheating harlot. And I miss her so" Hakkon said, right hand placed over his heart.

Kol shook his head and let out another laugh. If this be the day the fates decreed for his death, he could think of no better company to do so with. Raising his shield to block the sun, he surveyed the Bulgar line. What he could make out through the haze and buzzing flies didn't show him much. Just an indistinct mass of men, which could be as likely going as coming.

"Oh, they're heading over for another go. Don't ya worry about that Saxon." Hakkon said. "Hear that dull roar? They're building themselves up some courage to charge."

Kol had come to rely on Hakkon for such information,

and with good cause. What Kol knew about the doings of a battlefield could be fit into a sack and still have room for a half week's rations. And sure enough, that indistinct image he had only moments ago grew into a distinct, solid wall of warriors. The howls of the attackers cut across the uneven field.

"Get ready dogs! Show these turn-cloaks the Emperors justice. Let them hear you sing!" Centurion Ragnar bellowed, and the Centuria joined in.

Kol let out a war cry to match the others around him, hatred of his commander temporarily forgotten in the heady rush of impending battle.

Even through the surge of adrenaline, Kol kept enough of his wits to follow events around him, knowing his company was but a small part of a complete Cohort spread along a sloping ridgeline. On the Bulgars came, a solid block of infantry much deeper than the thin line opposite them. These rebels were professionals armed with pike and shield, more traditional arms for Byzantine auxiliary infantry. An imposing sight that Kol had begun to tire of.

Three times today these followers of the dead Peter Delyan rushed forward and were three times beaten back. If the enemy wanted Kol and his comrades gone, they'd have to scale these heights once more and face the blooded steel of the Varangian Guard.

"Seems our archers are taking their time finding the range" Kol said, noting the distinct lack of any missile fire.

"Aye, hear tell there's a shortage of fletching or some such cock and bull" Hakkon snarled. "Letting these bastards march up here, across that open field as brazen as you like. Shameful way to wage war I'd say. Give me a mess a slingers any day. Never see them run outa stones now do ya?"

It was no matter now, Kol could clearly make out faces in the advancing host. Angry faces, scared faces, young and old faces, and every one of them wanting his head. Kol shrugged and inhaled deeply, "This is the coin that fills my purse." With a final hoarse cry the faces faded and the host charged.

The blast of a tin whistle compelled Kol's shield up and level with that of his comrades. A second blast had him leaning forward, ready to accept the enemy, this action so ingrained in his psyche he barely took note. When the first pike slammed home, nothing remained but wild instinct.

The shriek of grinding metal accompanied a flash of sparks as the iron head of a pike skidded off the metal bands on Kol's shield, deflecting the attack down and into the hard packed earth. Kol brought his ax around in an overhead chop, hacking through shaft of the spear, making its wielder stumble and fall. Kol fought the urge to step forward and finish the man. A moment later, the soldier behind the prone man stepped up to take his place, trampling the unfortunate fellow in his haste.

Kol intercepted this one's pike as he did the first, feeling it bite deep, threatening to wrench the shield from his arm. Kol shifted his stance, pivoting to his right, allowing the point to slip free. This time the pike went high, and when Kol brought his ax around for a counter blow, it wasn't the wood of a spear shaft he connected with.it was the left shoulder of the eager Bulgar replacement. Kol felt the satisfying crunch of bone and heard the cry of the wounded man.

This one fell forward onto one knee as he tried to free his sword with his good arm. Kol did not restrain himself this time, bringing the edge of his battered shield down hard on the top of the man's head. It careened off the conical helmet and into the side of the man's neck. The wounded Bulgar solider fumbled his attempt to draw steel, his right hand dropped away to catch his fall. Kol's second blow with the shield landed directly behind the prone man's head, dropping him into a crumpled heap. The young Saxon warrior was certain he heard his opponent's neck snap under the weight of the blow.

And so it went, one charge after another beaten back,

THE GNAWED BONE

a grim replay from the day's earlier carnage. No matter how many men the Delayans threw at the Guard, the Northmen's line would not break.

"But for how long," Kol asked himself as he gulped in air during a rare moment of relative calm. He watched as the Bulgars pulled back a few yards to regroup for yet another push, dragging their dead and wounded with them. Even with this gallant act, they could not help but leave scores of their fellows in heaps at the base of the rise. As grievous a loss as they inflicted on the enemy, the Varangians did so at a cost. Kol surveyed the line and his assessment left him cold.

"We'll not hold another rush like that last" Hakkon said, reading Kol's thoughts. The veteran guardsman had his tall shield jammed into the ground, leaning on the uppermost rim like he would a saloon serving hitch, all the while casually cleaning blood from the short stabbing sword he favored. "Fiber's gone soft in the line, like this shield," he rapped the offending piece of equipment with his knuckles. "Few more good blows and it'll splinter for sure."

Kol nodded, taking a long draw on the full skin he'd plucked from a dead man. The lukewarm wine was bitter, but Kol could scarcely remember a sweeter vintage. "So this is it then." he said with a determined nod, taking another swig before replacing the stopper and tossing it to his friend.

"Not by a long league Saxon," Hakkon said, snatching the skin from out of the air. "No need that this sad piece of ground be our cairn. Time comes, you follow ol' Hakkon's lead and take to the heel."

"Run? From these cretins?" Kol asked bitterly. "I'll not take the coward's route."

Hakkon shook his head, swallowing a mouthful of wine. "Ain't cowardly when it's called a tactical redeployment, ask any old soldier," he said with a wink. "Besides, being dead takes all the fun out of life."

Kol grimaced, searching for a quick rejoinder when "To Arms! Prepare yourselves!" An alarm from somewhere on his left.

"Remember what I said Saxon," Hakkon reminded him, calmly strapping his shield on and bringing his deadly steel to the ready.

Kol needed no further encouragement, but it looked like today Hakkon's last piece of advice wouldn't be needed after all.

"They're pulling back…" Kol said in astonishment. "And in poor order at that…what could be-"

The sight of the Emperor's purple standard and the famed Byzantium Calvary thundering into view on either end of the far horizon answered all. The lack of reinforcements,

THE GNAWED BONE

inadequate support, all to keep the bulk of the rebel forces on the field and focused in the wrong direction.

"Rotten bastards. They used us as bait," Kol said in disbelief.

Hakkon laughed. "Such is the life of a Legionnaire. One moment you're bait", he said hauling up the defensive wooden stakes in front of him, "the next you're weighed down by a dead Bulgar's loot! Come on Saxon, we hit them now, we rout them all the way back to their camp!"

"Where the booty is plentiful," Kol said, a smile creeping onto his grimy face. "At em lads!" Fatigue forgotten, he charged, leaping the stakes, not bothering with them as Hakkon had done, and slammed into the now retreating Delayans. His blood-stained ax wove a pattern of blood and carnage with renewed gusto.

* * *

"Take a good look ladies," boomed the Centurion. "This is what happens to good Roman citizens when they place trust in these barbarians."

Kol eyed the two men laid out on the large wooden table, their unattached heads propped on one corner facing the legion. Dead eyes and lolling tongues mocked the living contingent gathered in their honor. He knew both of them, more by reputation than in any meaningful way. One a drunk, the other a cheat, and as far as Kol could tell, they were the only ones that could stand the other as company. Whatever events led to this gruesome fate, he had no doubt both richly deserved.

"Going against my better judgment, I allowed small groups their leave beyond the camp stockade. Seemed the decent thing to do, despite the piss poor performance of this troop of late. And this is my reward," Ragnar stabbed a finger at the guilty party. Kol noted the heads did not seem the least bit moved by the accusation. "As of now, no one is to leave this camp without official sanction. Do I make myself clear?"

"Aye Centurion," came the lackluster reply from the gathered soldiers. Kol could not bring himself to join the chorus.

It did not go unnoticed.

"You Saxon dog! Have you lost your tongue as well as what's left of your good sense?" Ragnar exploded, bulling his way through the gathered Varangians to confront this one man.

"Gods be good…you stepped in it now lad," Kol heard Hakkon mutter then step away as the unpredictable officer

THE GNAWED BONE

approached.

"I asked you a question, worm," Ragnar hissed. The Centurion stood nearly a full head taller than Kol and his sour breath and mane of unkempt yellow hair conjured images of some beast from legend.

"Lost my tongue? No Centurion, misplaced more like," Kol said, as casual as if he were discussing the weather.

Ragnar's blood red face took on a hue closer to purple. The air vacated the large tent, leaving a hollow void where the mere shift of a man's cloak might sound of crashing thunder.

No man dared even breathe.

"You see sir, your skills as an orator so moved me I lost the ability, momentarily, to speak myself. It is a great comfort to know just how you feel about the soldiers under your command," Kol finished.

With cold eyes and no inflection, but plenty of volume, Ragnar said "You lot, get out." With a flurry, the collected men at arms dispersed like eunuchs from a butcher's guild. The last man out, Hakkon, mimed placing a noose around his neck then swaying back and forth, all the while pointing at Kol.

"Hakkon, you reedy bag of dung, lose yourself," Ragnar growled, seeing nothing but knowing plenty. Eyes wide like a boy caught in some misadventure, Hakkon exited through the tent flap with speed. Despite his current situation, Kol couldn't help but grin.

"Oh ho, it's all one big farce with you isn't it?" Ragnar hissed, looming over Kol in an obvious attempt at intimidation.

The young Saxon merely shook his head and said, "No Centurion."

"Enough with the formalities, your comrades are gone, no one left to impress. Look me in the eye you dog and answer my question or so help me I will throttle you where you stand," the Centurion said through clenched teeth.

Taking that as license to speak his mind, Kol met his commander's gaze. "I take this work seriously enough. It's you I find farcical. Bellowing like a mindless ox when men need words of valor and inspiration. Striking them when they're down instead of helping them to their feet. You treat these free men little better than a drover treats his cattle, and every member of the guard hold you and your bully boys in contempt because of it."

"That so?" Ragnar growled.

"Aye. I hear the veterans speak highly of your abilities as a warrior before being elevated to that of centurion, and am inclined to believe them. But it is clear to me that skill in the killing arts is not necessarily transferable coin to that of leadership," Kol said, full of righteous courage.

Ragnar laughed in his face, "I suppose a half-breed like yourself thinks he can do better? These wolves," he jerked a thumb over his shoulder, "would chew you up and shit you out before you got three words into one of your pretty speeches."

Kol shrugged. "Maybe, but I'm not fool enough to think I'm ready for such responsibility."

Whatever bitter humor had shown on the Centurions face, vanished in an instant.

"And Ragnar, the next time you threaten my life, be prepared follow it with action," Kol warned. "I think you'll find throttling this half-breed more of a challenge than the mewling kittens you've become accustomed to of late."

"Oh, that time is fast approaching, you can be sure of it" Ragnar jabbed a finger in Kol's chest. "But to fill the void till then, let's have you report for work detail. New latrines are going in past the east wall, I expect them dug and ready for use before I return from council with the general."

"Yes Centurion, am I excused?"

Ragnar said nothing, just nodded and Kol left the tent. His mood surprisingly light, Kol whistled a tune on his way to requisition himself a shovel and bucket.

W.E. WERTENBERGER

* * *

Kol strode across camp just as the sun began to set. He was determined to put distance between himself and the newly excavated east wall latrines. Not that he minded the actual labor, he'd yet to meet a man that could outwork or outfight him. But three long days in the company of laggards, dullards and perpetual malingerers made one crave the sanity of everyday folk.

"Ahhhh, gather round fellows, our friend Kol has returned from exile. And with his head still intact. We were sure ol' Ragnar would have it removed for housing such a wicked tongue."

Kol smiled broadly as he approached a row of familiar tents and took in the scent of cook fires. "Well met, Hakkon. I have returned. And with tales of the mighty trench I did slay with naught but spade and pick ax." Kol struck as heroic a pose as he could recall from the many stone and bronze statues that populated the parks of Byzantium. "But all that must wait as I have survived on watery gruel and dull conversation for too many nights. Make way lads!"

And with that, Kol joined his friends at the fire and ladled himself a large bowl of boiled mutton and vegetables. His stomach groaned at the fine aroma, and he savored the

THE GNAWED BONE

first few mouthfuls. He ate heartily, downing the first bowl with gusto. Helping himself to another before slowing down to listen to his comrades banter.

"So she screams at me from the doorway, *My mother! You pig, I turn my back for a moment and you slip between my own mother's legs?*" Said the large Numidian, fire light dancing on his dark skin. "I turn to her with complete shock and genuine surprise and say, *Your mother? Sweet dove, I would have never done such a thing if I'd known she was your mother. She claimed she was your sister! Aw haw!*" Jumma roared with laughter, soon joined by the rest of Kol's usual band of compatriots. Though to call it his band belied the fact he was its junior member.

"That tale is as stale as this hunk of bread," said Harald. His bushy red beard twitching as he pulled a heal of dark bread from his cup and gnawed on an end. "Bout all this boiled water is good for."

The group acknowledged their agreement with a chorus of grunts. Kol swirled the cloudy liquid around in his own mug and made a face as the smell of rotten eggs assaulted his senses.

"Takes a truly petty man to ban all wine and spirits from a camp on account of one malcontent, eh Kol?" This came from fair haired Sigurd, his face perpetually red, be it from too much sun in the summer or biting wind in the winter. Kol guessed it didn't help the man's already bitter disposition.

"But Kol gave voice to all our dissatisfaction, now didn't he brother?" Asked Sigmund, the near identical match of his red faced brother. But where Sigurd was serious, Sigmund took life in a more relaxed manor. "And besides, this year's fighting has filled my purse to overflowing. Njorr has been kind to us all."

"To the hells with your back country superstitions and your Njorr. And throw in your overflowing purse while you're at it," said Sigurd. "A wealthy man is no different from a poor when you have nowhere to spend your coin."

Kol smiled broadly, and Hakkon took note.

"You have the look of a crooked horse trader with a dim witted pleb on the line," Hakkon said, squinting at the burly Saxon over the smoky fire. "Out with it lad, what scheme have you cooked up?"

Kol leaned back on one elbow and made a show of emptying his cup of boiled water onto the dusty ground. "Hardly a scheme my skeptical friend, more a guarantee of a good time had for all. I've secured passage from these confining walls and been given the name of the best, and by all measures only, drinking hole this side of the Iskar."

THE GNAWED BONE

Kol took great delight in seeing his companions lean in like children listening to a late night tale of specters and goblins. "It's nary a league distant and it's named The Gnawed Bone."

* * *

"I didn't appreciate how that farmer looked us over," said Sigurd. "He's probably gathering his neighbors as we speak, planning to ambush us unawares."

"Nonsense," Kol said, pushing a limb from a low hanging pine tree out of his way. As the sky blackened, it became harder to follow the narrow forest trail the self same farmer directed them onto. "He was an old man living alone. I'd say he acquitted himself well considering he faced six armed men from the army that just recently burned his village to the ground."

"Just the same, stumbling blindly through a dark forest, on hostile ground no less. I prefer to not test the patience of Amun so," Juma said, holding his flaming torch out in front of him. Like Kol, Juma was considered an outsider in the guard because of his heritage.

"It's not your gods that should worry you. It's Ragnar if he ever catches wind of us slipping his leash," Harald countered.

"All this bellyaching over a deed already done! Kol told you he'd be gone a fortnight, maybe longer," Hakkon assured them all, though Kol noticed Hakkon looking to him for some reiteration of the point.

Kol did not bother. The party emerged from forest path onto an open plane dominated by a single hillock. The lonely mound of towering earth and vegetation, silhouetted against a dark blue sky of the gloaming, stood as sentry to the open ground beyond.

"Here we are. Just as I was told," Kol said in triumph. "The cave entrance should be nearby."

When first told of this solitary tavern, Kol found it nothing unusual. Many an eatery and drinking establishment had been placed in such outlandish locales. He recalled one of his favorites located in a tree. The owner simply laid out a platform in the bough of an old oak and began selling drink. You even had to scale a rope ladder to gain access, and in turn, were lowered by basket once sufficiently soused. Deadbeats found an even quicker exit, right over the side and twelve cubits straight down.

Soon enough, the well-worn footpath lead up the side of the mound and produced a warmly lit entrance. The party stopped before entering, all taking in the sign hanging over

THE GNAWED BONE

the cave mouth. A crudely drawn, bestial face, clenching a white bone between fanged teeth.

"Just as promised," Kol said, slapping his hands together and rubbing them. "First drinks laid on my coin!" No soldier ever turned down a free drink, and the companions pushed and shoved their way inside.

"This is my kind o' place," Hakkon said, taking in the spacious cavern. "A place I could see myself operating one day."

"Just like you to choose the lowest rent space you could find," Kol slapped his friend on the back.

In all, it was a nice space. The ceiling was high and well braced with log beams to protect against falling debris. The smoke from the makeshift hearth and oil lamps easily filtered through the rock formation above, leaving the room dimly lit but well ventilated. At the center of the room sat a scattered collection of stools and mismatched, battered tables. A serving station consisting of a heavy, flat beam (probably scavenged from the skeleton of a burned out house, if the scorch marks were any indication) was placed along the wall. Four large barrels, one already tapped and laying in an elevated cradle, sat behind it.

"Welcome, friends," said a burly man in a clean white apron tending the barrels. He wore a long mustache, as was custom in these parts, and sported a red, puffy scar along the side of his face. "All sit. We bring" he said in broken Greek. Waving over an even burlier woman with tangled dark hair, and some impressive facial hair of her own.

Kol ran a finger along the side of his own face, "Looks painful, and fresh, myfriend."

The man shrugged, "War comes. Pain companion of war."

The Saxon nodded his agreement. He had no doubt this man was a rebel, or at least a Delyan sympathizer, but the war was over. If this man provided honest service to his troupe, Kol had no more quarrel with him than he did the King of Siam. He joined his fellow Varangians, already rearranging the tables more to their liking, then sat with the cave wall to his back.

The serving girl arrived soon after, with tall, sweating tankards topped off with nice foaming heads. After laying each drink out, Kol dropped a handful of silver onto her tray and said, "Keep them coming." Her tiny blue eyes bulged, and she nodded, fully understanding.

"To life! And a full purse to enjoy it!" Kol said, hoisting his mug on high.

"To life!" his companions repeated, as they all took tentative sips at first. The beer was dark, bitter and cooled the throat as it went down.

THE GNAWED BONE

Quite excellent, though I can't place the odd aftertaste. No matter, it is still delicious. The next round arrived Kol found himself caught up in the sudden festive atmosphere. The libations continued to flow, bawdy songs were sung off key, and even an impromptu wrestling match erupted between the brothers.

"Whos did you wager on again?" Asked Juma, his speech slurred.

"It matters not..." Kol said, squinting at the two combatants. "Can never tell 'em apart anyway," and he waved off the question.

Juma found this answer hilarious and smacked Kol a violent backhand blow to the chest that sent the inebriated Saxon off his stool and into a heap on the floor. This brought a fresh round of hilarity to all those not otherwise engaged in mock combat.

"Juma you thrice damned molester of sheep" Kol said through his own laughter, "You'll pay for that once I find where I left my feet." Kol made one or two honest attempts to do so, then surrendered to the absurdity of the situation and contented himself to the embrace of the cool floor. *Has it been so long since I had such strong spirits?* He shook his head and stared into the dark recesses of the cave ceiling above. He tried to count just how many rounds the companions had actually gone through, but found it too difficult to suss out. *Maybe after a quick . . . nap . . .*

He closed his eyes, still chuckling at something Juma, or was it Hakkon? said, or did.

* * *

Kol opened his eyes and sat up, regretting the action immediately. The dim light seemed like a blazing sun and his head felt like an overripe melon fit to burst.

"Gods be good…what did those Delyan bastards serve us?" Kol whispered, forcing himself to his unsteady feet. He scanned the room with bleary eyes. The lamps had all burned out, leaving only the central fire. It was down to a few flickering flames over glowing coals and ash.

Juma lay sprawled on one of the tables, his large body draped over the top like some obscene centerpiece. Kol gave the nearest table leg a couple hard thumps with the heel of his boot. Juma snorted, mumbled something in his native tongue then lifted one leg and broke wind. To Kol's drink abused senses, it sounded akin to the blare of a trumpet.

Kol left the Numidian alone and shuffled his way to where he remembered the entrance to be. His bladder full, his first priority was to make for the bushes outside. Along

THE GNAWED BONE

the way, he could make out another of his band, one of the brothers. Didn't know which one, the upper half of the man lay in shadow, but he recognized the boots as quartermaster issued like his own. Beyond the red glow of the near dead fire, figures moved, speaking in low tones.

"Barkeep, I'd have words with you about this rotgut you serve. I believe it has turned," he said, finding the cave mouth only to be confronted by a massive wooden door. "I'll not lie to you friend. It was fine going down, but the after affect is akin to being pummeled by a mule," Kol said, pushing on the door. It didn't budge. "*Or a roll with that serving maid of yours,*" he said in more muted tones. Having no success applying outward pressure, Kol felt around for a latch, "Blast it to hell man, do you mean to cage us in?"

His hands moved over the roughhewn door, the scent of old wood strong now that he was this close. Deep, darkly stained gouges were dug into the planks, more or less placed the width between a man's outstretched fingers as if someone had tried to claw their way out.

In that instant, Kol's abused mind fell into gear with a surge of adrenaline, washing away enough of the fog. He spun about and grabbed for his weapon. It was gone, along with scabbard, belt and all his money. The bastards had no doubt spiked the drink and stripped the group bare while unconscious. But why imprison them too?

Kol's heart raced as he peered into the gloom beyond the dying fire, trying to make out the mysterious figures his addled brain dismissed moments ago. Not knowing for certain what game was being played, the muscle bound Saxon reached down and grabbed a discarded stool, the closest item on hand that approximated a weapon.

"Juma. Juma you lout, rouse yourself. We are put upon by rogues," Kol said in an urgent but hushed tone.

The big Numidian murmured something similar to what was said before, but gave no indication that Kol had gotten through the spiked brew's effects. Crouching low, he made his way along the wall, trying to stay in the shadows himself until he could ascertain their situation further. He cursed himself a fool for getting his band involved in this affair. His vanity and need to act against Ragnar clouded his judgment on the matter. For sure the rest were just as culpable, for their own reasons, but none of this would be happening if it were not at his urging.

Having reached his intended target, the prone twin in the middle of the floor, he reached down to see if this companion could be urged out of his stupor.

"Wake up," Kol said. Reaching a hand out to shake the man to consciousness, he never took his eyes off the

THE GNAWED BONE

surrounding dark. "We are in danger friend and your brother needs you." Getting no response, Kol risked a glance to his companion, his heart sank immediately. Sigurd or Sigmund, he would never know, for the most identifiable aspect of each was gone. Bile filled Kol's throat when he took in the ragged remains of the man's upper torso. Both head and right quarter were gone, ripped asunder as the hanging hunks of meat would attest.

"You will be avenged," Kol said in a sober voice, anger swelling within his breast at the horror. "On my father's honor and my mother's grave, I'll make these people pay dearly for what they've done."

A guttural murmur, seemingly defiant of his oath, answered him from deeper in the cave. His blood now up, Kol rose to his feet, defiant. "You dogs! Not only do you drug us then pick our pockets, you now take pleasure in murder and mutilation?" The Saxon strode forward, makeshift cudgel clenched in his right fist.

"Your poison has worn off. Do you have the stones to face a man standing on two feet? Come out from the shadows cowards!"

Again the murmuring interspersed with wet snapping noises, as Kol approached, with revenge in his heart and blood on his mind. What he saw materialize from the darker end of the cave froze him to his core. A vision from some psychotic's nightmare, five hunched figures tore at the remains of Kol's comrades. Only their jostling for position and occasional looks toward Kol interrupted their feast.

At first Kol thought they were some sort of wolf, emaciated and malformed. But closer inspection showed muscle definition ripple under pale, wrinkly skin. That skin, covered with patchy grey fur had an oily sheen that shone in the dim light like tiny strands of pearls. His own hair stood on end as the largest of the group separated from them and turned his way. Bat-like ears twisted back and forth on its massive skull while a gore stained muzzle sniffed the air.

"Blast my soul," Kol said in hushed tones, regretting it immediately as the twitching ears stopped and locked forward onto him. The creature snarled, seeming to see Kol for the first time. Not surprising, considering the beady little black eyes the creature possessed. It approached at a cautious, lurching gait, sizing Kol up as a potential challenger to the pack's kill.

When it was no more than a few paces away, the strange beast did something even stranger.

It rose slowly onto its hind legs.

Standing nearly as tall as the awestruck Varangian, the beast stretched a clawed hand in his direction, issuing

THE GNAWED BONE

a wordless challenge. Never one to back down from any challenge, (for the Saxon warrior feared no man he'd met, and only a few women) the sudden urge to flee caught him by surprise. When he began to step back in retreat, he found he could not stop himself.

This stalking abomination before him touched a deep seated terror. A terror buried in the dark subconscious of pre-human civilization, before man huddled secure behind high walls with their steel and the glow of a night fire. This was the fear of a prey animal with a certainty of death at the hands of the hunter in the dark.

So Kol retreated, grabbing at the wall beside him as a guide, unable to tear his gaze away from the pale horror.

It was then he tangled his feet upon a crumpled heap on the cave floor. Stumbling, Kol caught himself before falling straight on his backside. Glancing down, he saw it was Hakkon! Not sure if he was even alive, but sure he was in one piece and not torn to shreds like his other companions, the sight of his oldest friend shifted the balance of his emotions, allowing him to regain some control.

"Damnable beast! You'll not get the satisfaction of seeing me run," Kol growled. "Come then, and let us see who is the true master of this dank realm." The pale nightmare paused, its ears twitching again, as if uncertain of its position of dominance held only spare moments ago. It cast a reassuring glance and excited yip to its pack members still around their kill. Kol paid no heed to any of this as his fear fled and his courage returned. He leapt at the monster, delivering a thunderous overhead chop, the heavy stool connecting on the side of his opponent's skull. A satisfying crack echoed off the cave walls, staggering the wolf creature. Kol felt a shock run through his arm as if he'd connected with the stone wall instead. He was sure it was the stool and not bone that cracked. Undaunted, he pressed his attack, bringing his crude cudgel around for a swipe across the muzzle then jabbing for its midsection. The beast grunted in an all too human fashion and rolled away. Separated now, the beast bloodied from a nasty gash on its head, Kol clutched the remnants of the stool, whose only use now would be that of kindling.

Casting his useless weapon aside, Kol faced the creature bare handed. Its snarling visage seemed more a mocking smile, belittling him for all his wasted effort. The two combatants circled each other. Kol tried to maneuver the fight to where he originally picked up the stool, hoping to arm himself again. The beast pressed closer, blocking the attempt.

Kol shook his head in disbelief, thinking until this

THE GNAWED BONE

moment he faced an animal aping human mannerisms. Now the realization of the opposite sent a fresh wave of revulsion through him. Then the creature attacked.

In a feat of astounding agility, the thing shot up into the air, coming down onto the surprised Saxon like a living avalanche of tooth and claw. Bowling him over onto his back, Kol barely got his right arm up in time to block the massive jaws from closing on his exposed neck. The two rolled across the cavern floor, the beast raking his chainmail covered chest with his fore-claws, trying to disembowel him with the rear. Kol, no novice in the martial skill of wrestling, was hard pressed to gain any advantage. The strength and ferocity, coupled with the creatures oily coat, made gaining any meaningful leverage near impossible. It was all he could do to keep the beasts jaws at bay.

Desperation driving him more than inspiration, Kol slid his right forearm, the one wedged against the creatures throat, under its chin and toward the slavering jaws. His gambit, that the beast could not pass up an opportunity to latch onto to something solid worked, and Kol grit his own teeth in anticipation of what came next.

"Arrrgggh!" The Saxon bellowed as the powerful jaws clamped down on his forearm. Even through the thick leather bracer, Kol felt canines pierce his flesh, the pressure threatening to snap his bones. Yet through the white hot pain, Kol felt some give in the anaconda-like grip the thing possessed.

"Bad move," Kol grunted, his face grimy with a mix of his sweat, blood, and the creature's saliva. He began pulling the massive head toward him. The beast resisted, calling upon its own reservoir of strength, twisting to and fro as a dog might with a caught hare. Kol's bicep and shoulder muscle burned with effort, and slowly he began to gain the edge. With one last desperate effort, Kol twisted the head about until he came even with one of the beast's ears. Then he snapped his own teeth onto the concave wedge of cartilage.

Blood exploded into Kol's mouth as his incisors latched on, then tore away a hunk of the flesh. The creature let loose a high pitched, surprised yelp, immediately letting go Kol's mangled forearm and wrenching its own torn flesh away. Taking advantage of the space offered him, Kol kicked his legs free and then spun, gaining a superior position, and more importantly leverage.

Burying his face and shoulder in the beast's side, Kol drove forward, slamming the thing into the rocky cave wall. He did this repeatedly until he felt the body go limp. He straddled the wolf-thing and used his uninjured left arm to hook around its neck. With one last mighty effort, the Saxon wrenched back. The stunned creature clawed desperately at him but to no avail. The contest was over. The repeated popping of vertebra and a final death rattle signaled the end.

Kol gained his feet and staggered back from the hard won contest. He stood, breathing heavily, not fully believing he'd won. Familiar growling caught his attention. Only then did he remember the extent of the peril. The rest of the pack left their meal and were spread out as if spectators at an arena. Kol got the impression they were none too pleased with the outcome and their dead Alpha.

With what wits he still possessed, Kol snatched up Hakkon and bolted. With his attention split between the pack of ghouls and the reckless retreat, it was little wonder he managed to crash into the table where Juma, now sitting upright with his head in hands, was perched. Hitting with the force of a panicked bull; Kol, Hakkon and Juma all tumbled over the ramshackle piece of furniture, ending on the other side in a heap.

"You bastard son of a lame milk cow! Have you lost your mind?!" Juma bellowed at the unexpected assault. "I feel near death and you-"

"No time for that now." Kol exclaimed, peaking over the turned table, thankful at least his panicked flight didn't incite the pack to run them down. "We are beset by unnatural forces friend, and half our number already fallen. We need to get out." Jumna looked confusedt. Instead of trying to explain again, he grabbed the Numidian by the collar and hoisted him to his vantage point.

"Amun protect us." Juma whispered as he took in the unnatural scene. The beasts milled about, yipping at one another in that guttural communication of theirs. They were uneasy, perhaps unable to determine how many foes they faced.

"Amun, Thor, nor all the gods in the east can do anything for us. If we survive this night, it will be by our wits alone," Kol said, taking a steadying breath.

"Damn it Northman, how do mortal men kill demons? We have no weapons even!" Juma exclaimed.

"They are not demons, and wringing their necks seems to kill them just fine. But you are right Juma, there are too many for a straight up fight" Kol said, eyes darting about, frantic to find a solution. Then his gaze fell on just the thing they needed.

"Juma, help me." Kol said, jumping to his feet and kicking away the planks that served as the surface of the table.

Juma grabbed at him, trying to pull him back into hiding. "Keep down, they'll see us Saxon!"

Kol swatted away his hand. "The base of this table!" he said, pointing to the heavy, charred beam holding the whole piece together. Standing on end, Kol judged it to be nearly twice his height and thick around as a small ham. "It's more than heavy enough to batter down that door."

Juma understood immediately, his eyes flashing with hope. He joined Kol in dismantling of the construct and, in short, frenzied order, they had what they needed.

Kol kept a wary eye on the pack. They were more agitated and their calls became more urgent. As his friend wrapped discarded rags around the solid beam to act as handholds, Kol grabbed a plank with his good arm from the dismantled table.

"Back!" he yelled at the pack. Making a big show by waving the plank overhead and mock charging. "Keep your distance you mongrels. This hell-pit is yours and we aim to be leaving it far behind!" Kol felt a little foolish in his declaration, especially considering these things had no idea what he was saying.

"Kol! It's Hakkon. He's coming around!" Juma called out. Kol, satisfied he'd bought them the spare moments they needed, rejoined his friends.

Kol watched as Juma slapped Hakkon into full consciousness. Hakkon fought weakly. Then with a bit of familiar vigor, ". . . easy now ladies . . .there's enough of ol' Hakkon to go around . . ."

"On your feet you old brigand!" Juma said, lifting the confused legionnaire upright and leaning him against the wall. "Or we'll leave you to the mercies of them fiends!"

"What's all this then? We under attack?" Hakkon asked, searching for his weapons just as Juma and Kol had before him.

"We are in mortal danger old friend," Kol said as he and Juma grabbed their makeshift battering ram. "Just stay awake and don't wander off."

Wrapping the loose end of the rag around his left wrist, Kol looked to Juma as he did the same. Then as one, they heaved the ram up and charged the door. The first impact sent them reeling back a few paces. The door was solid but old, must have been braced from the outside.

"Take it toward the corner. We'll shake it loose from the hinges," Kol said.

They hauled the beam back, then again hurdled themselves against the door. This time they felt some give. The next and the time after they heard an audible crack and cool air seeped in through a cloud of sawdust. This fired their purpose, and the duo repeated the task again and again.

"We almost have it," Kol said, puffing out air like a

bellows. "Few more and we got it."

Juma nodded his agreement, his breathing as labored as Kol's own. The Numidian's eyes went wide as he gaped at something behind the Saxon. Kol turned and saw that the pack was upright now and closing in and, worse still, more had joined their ranks from deeper in the tunnel system. At least a score now crowded the narrow entryway to the cave.

"Never mind that! The door, concentrate on the door damn it!" Kol said and motioned that they should give it another go.

They launched themselves a final time at the stubborn barrier and cheered as it gave way. They could see trees and a clear, near morning sky. Juma dropped his end of the ram and went for the opening.

"Too small, I can't fit! Hakkon!" He said in a choking cry, waving over his groggy companion and literally shoved him through the opening. "Get out there and unlatch this door!"

Kol paid little attention to any of that as he'd returned his interest to the pack. Seeing the possibility of their quarry slipping free, they focused on the nearest antagonist.

Kol cursed his Saxon luck.

Two of the pale killers leapt at him just as their Alpha had done. He lifted the beam over his head and pitched the heavy lumber in an arcing throw. Glancing off one beast, then spinning fully into the other, the weight of the object carried on into the white mob of death, disappearing, as a stone thrown into an open sea.

Kol grabbed the discarded plank he'd used earlier to intimidate the beasts. He held no illusions about his chances to pull off that trick again, and no intention of trying.

"Come on then!" The now fatalistic Saxon taunted. "Let's see how many of you it'll take to kill an honest Northman!"

The first challenger came at him from the left. Slung low and silent, only letting out a snarling yip as it lunged. Kol stepped back with his left, using the momentum of that movement to lend force to his back swing. Catching the beast-thing in the center of its thick skull, a familiar crack rang off the cave walls and floored the creature. Being much smaller than the Alpha, even an off-hand strike was effective. Kol followed up with a stomp to the now split skull.

Another came on from the right and Kol reversed his previous action. Dropping his right and bringing the bloodied wood in an overhand strike. The solid plank landed on an outstretched, white limb. The bone gave way and bent the appendage like a strung bow. The beast howled in its near human tone, only cut short by another blow from the

THE GNAWED BONE

trusty piece of timber.

"Ha! Two down, and uncounted multitudes yet to wade through!" The fever of battle now gripped Kol in its iron gauntlet. His good arm never tired as he landed one solid shot after the next. Expelling his anger and guilt over lost comrades, reveling in the knowledge of the two survivors. So, when the inevitable tide of tooth and claw overtook him, he couldn't help but laugh., Just as a pair of slavering jaws made for his jugular, an enormous black hand engulfed his face and the cave went black. He fell back, landing hard amongst green foliage and fresh soil. Sitting up, Kol was greeted to the sight of Juma and Hakkon leaning heavily on the outside of the door to the Gnawed Bone, with the sign swinging overhead as it had the night before. Juma kicked a large wedge into place. The door stop Kol guessed.

With barely a glance, Juma sprinted past him, pushing Hakkon before him. "That door won't hold!" was all he said and Kol knew he was right. Clawed hands and white snouts crowded the breach their ram had created, Kol wasn't far behind his friends after that.

The sprint to freedom down the twisting path ended up resembling more a comical acrobatics exhibition. Kol found himself falling and rolling as much as he did in a proper run. Being a step or four behind his friends, he nearly ran up their backsides when he rounded a thick hedge and found them stopped, hands in the air.

"Oh ho! And the ringleader appears."

Kol could scarcely believe his ears. After all this, everything they'd been through the night before, the fates did find humor in mortal suffering.

"Imagine my distress when I arrived back at camp. The conference being canceled and not finding my favorite ditch digger to punish further" Ragnar said, not surprisingly surrounded by his men. "Didn't take the wisdom of sages to figure where a group like you would have headed" he said, nodding in the direction of the footpath leading to the so called drinking establishment.

"Ragnar you fool, we have to flee. For the very hounds from Hades are nipping at our heals" Kol tried to explain.

"I will enjoy watching you suffer you boastful Saxon worm. When we get you back to camp-what is that damnable noise?" Ragnar asked as the bray from the pack of ghouls echoed from atop the hillock.

Despite the situation, the three surviving companions burst out in exhausted laughter. "Why it's our drinking companions from last night. Centurion, you'll get on well I think. Their smell is no worse than your own and they have a similar disposition," Kol said with a broad flourish and a

THE GNAWED BONE

bow, as if he were announcing the arrival of the emperor himself.

And right on cue, the pack tore out of the surrounding brush and descended on the Varangians. Ragnar and his guard watched in stunned disbelief.

"Run!" Juma shouted, and Kol did just that. He bowled over the gawking Ragnar, leaping his prone body. When he made the tree line he paused to gather the others. Only Juma and Hakkon had made it out. The rest had drawn swords and circled around Ragnar, their paymaster.

"Should we go for help?" asked Juma.

"No, we need to tactically redeploy ourselves as far from this army as we can" Kol answered. "A wise old soldier told me about that once."

"Damn shame. Had a nice haul o' loot back at the camp" Hakkon said, seeming to be back in full possession of his senses.

"We will find more gold. Nothing left for us here but death."

And with that, the strung out trio made for a southward path. Kol spared one last look over his shoulder. Ragnar and his boys had cut down many of the creatures but more were lapping at their perimeter. He gave them even odds at best. And he couldn't swear for sure, but he thought he glimpsed the tall form of the centurion come into view for only a moment, thinking maybe he even caught his eye.

With a shrug, the Saxon joined Juma and Hakkon on their long walk to the border.

W. E. Wertenberger grew up in northern Ohio and currently lives and works in Frankfort, KY. Having a lifelong interest in history and a deep admiration for the writing of pulp era giants such as Robert E. Howard, it's not surprising that these elements find their way into much of his writing. He is also co-host of The Abysmal Brutes podcast. This is his first published work.

willardwertenberger@gmail.com

www.theabysmalbrutes.com

ALL THE LANDS, NOWHERE A HOME

STEPHEN ZIMMER

Ice blue eyes lanced into the fear-filled gaze of the brigand. Towering over his battered form, lengthy blond locks flowing wild and free over her shoulders, the female warrior was the embodiment of an indomitable will. Strength and grace wove the aura surrounding Rayden, as time itself halted.

He gagged weakly as she pressed the cold iron of the spear tip harder against his throat. Only moments before it had been his weapon, when his intention had been to kill her. The murderous look had vanished from his eyes, and what was left resembled dead embers soaked through and extinguished of any hint of flame.

"What did he do?" Her voice was firm, her words not for the man whose life teetered precariously in the balance.

Sobbing, the young woman huddled a few paces away against the trunk of a tree replied, "I … I do not wish to speak of it."

Her bruised face and torn clothing testified to an atrocity, and the woman's shaken response was enough to tell Rayden the vile nature of it, but she needed to be sure about one thing. She could not proceed without the woman's absolute confirmation.

"This man?" Rayden asked, her piercing stare remaining locked upon the brigand. "I must know. Was it him?"

Choking back a new burst of tears, the woman finally muttered, "Yes. It was him."

The man's eyes widened in terror, and he tried to speak, but he could not get a single word out. Blood gushed where the spear plunged mercilessly into soft flesh, burrowing through his neck and lodging in the soil beneath. Rayden loosed her grip upon the weapon as life fled the brigand, leaving it skewering the body.

Her only regret was that she had not been traveling through the area a little while earlier. The faint cries of the young woman, from well off the woodland pathway, had been her only alert to the ongoing tragedy.

Rayden looked around the scene of the fighting as wind rattled the branches of the trees. A deep quiet had settled, broken only by the sounds of the young woman's sorrow.

The bodies of four other brigands lay strewn about the forest floor. Rayden walked over to the one with her hand axe buried in its skull. Setting her foot against the corpse, she yanked the weapon free. Wiping it on the brigand's clothes, she returned the well-familiar item to its loop at her belt.

A she-wolf among jackals, Rayden had unchained a primal fury and set it loose when she fell upon the brigands. Her stealthy approach brought her close enough to see the carnage they'd made of an ill-fated family, leaving only the one survivor for their own sport. The blood-soaked vision had swiftly elevated the simmering flame of Rayden's rage into an inferno of righteous wrath.

Hell feasted on a war-torn land, but those wicked men were held accountable that day. The instrument of their doom, Rayden exacted the heaviest of tolls for their transgressions. Condemned by their own cruelties, the men would beset no more victims.

Final judgement had been rendered.

Rayden grabbed the hilt of her blade and pulled it from the gut of another corpse. She recalled the rapid succession in which she had thrust it into the brigand, and then turned and thrown her axe at another rushing towards her.

The last of the brigands had even grinned as he moved in with his spear, thinking far too much of his position versus her unarmed state. He had learned a bitter lessen moments later, when he jabbed towards Rayden with the long-hafted weapon. Moving with cat-like speed, she darted in, disarming him, and executing a hard, debilitating kick to his groin. Without pausing, she unleashed a barrage of heavy punches straight into his pain-contorted face.

Collapsing to the ground and thoroughly bloodied, the brigand was in no condition to continue fighting. He did not resist when his own spear had been placed at his neck a moment later.

Having regained her weapons, she moved to the side of the young woman and crouched to her eye level. In a gentle voice, Rayden said, "It's over. They're all dead. They have paid with their blood. They cannot hurt you any longer."

The young woman stared back at her. It was a hollow gaze, one that conveyed the enormity and horror of what had so recently happened to her.

"I'll get you safely to the city. I have friends there, and you will not be alone. They will help you," Rayden promised in a soothing voice.

"My mother … my father, " the young woman said in a whisper, after a few heartbeats.

The bodies of an older man and woman lay a little farther beyond the site of the fighting, closer to the pathway the family had been traveling when ambushed. Rayden felt a stab of sorrow watching the tears streaming down the young woman's face. She could see that the initial shock was giving way to what would surely be an abyss of lamentation.

Desperation had pushed the young woman's family into the jaws of peril. Like so many in the current age, the privations of war had driven them to seek out the walled city of Careth Athes. While filled with its own dangers, most wanted to take their chances in the city, rather than remain in isolated villages and farmsteads being ravaged by raiders, brigands, and things far darker in nature.

"Valkyrie," the woman uttered, as Rayden helped her carefully to her feet. "You are like the Valkyries … like the stories I once heard as a child. Thank you."

The name of the mythic Shield Maidens sired by the supreme northern god had been applied to Rayden many times before, enough that it was used as a moniker by many that knew her. To hear it spoken in a spirit of gratitude by the young woman was deeply moving, but Rayden was not a goddess.

"I'm a woman, just like you," Rayden said, as they moved away from the tree together. "And we will go to Careth Athes side by side, after I see to the honor of your parents."

While leaving the brigands for the scavengers of the wilds, Rayden labored to create a makeshift pyre for the bodies of the young woman's parents. It was one of the few things she could do to provide any degree of consolation for the grief-stricken woman.

While gathering wood, Rayden took a few moments to discreetly search the corpses of the brigands. As she suspected, they had small pouches laden with coins. Combined, the silver and gold gleaned from the fallen rogues represented a sum that would be very beneficial in a city environment. When she walked back to light the pyre, the newly-acquired pouches hung from the belt around her own knee-length tunic.

After the flames died down, and the bodies of the woman's parents were reduced to ash, Rayden guided her away from the site of the grievous tragedy. A long walk lay ahead to Careth Athes, and the two traveled in silence, each of them left to their own thoughts and reflections.

* * *

"A northerner. Haven't seen one of your kind in a long time," one of the guards at the gate commented, showing some curiosity when Rayden and the young woman finally reached the towering entryway, set within the city's thick stone walls.

"It has been some time since I have been to this city," she replied, with a hint of impatience, eager to continue onward. "I hope it is more hospitable than the lands surrounding it."

"We live in ill-times," the guard said, with a grim expression.

"We do indeed," she responded dourly, as he motioned the two woman onward through the gateway.

The streets beyond were thick with the traffic of pedestrians and animal-pulled carts. Rayden heard the accents of several lands as she led the young woman through the dense multitudes.

The pungent scents of animal dung and bodily odors mingled with those of smoke and meat cooking on fires. The cries of sellers heralding their wares, the laughter of children running through the crowds and the curses of the adults they bumped into, and the low, sustained murmur from a great many people engaged in conversations filled the air.

Careth Athes was no different than most cities throughout the region. It had its markets, dwellings, taverns, temples, palaces and other sites typically found behind protective outer walls. Rayden could find her way around most cities without much difficulty due to the general similarities in their layouts, but Careth Athes was no worry at all, as she had visited there many times before.

In the temple dedicated to the Father God, she found the old friend she needed first.

"Rayden Valkyrie," the middle-aged, paunchy man greeted, smiling as he walked across the open sanctuary chamber towards her.

"Gnaeus, well-met," she responded, nodding to him.

He eyed the young woman, and the smile on his face faded as he drew closer, now able to see her bruises, tear-stained face, and rough state of condition. Gnaeus looked to Rayden, and she knew he understood what she wanted.

"I'm trusting her to you," Rayden announced to him. "My life is not one that is good for her to share."

He nodded. "I shall look after her."

She handed over a couple small pouches filled with coins. "This should cover any expenses for her, with plenty to spare."

"It was not necessary, Rayden, but thank you," Gnaeus replied, accepting the coins.

Rayden looked to the young woman. "Gnaeus is a good and trusted friend. You will be safe with the priests here."

"I wish I could find a way to thank you," the young woman stated, mustering slightly more composure.

"You owe me no thanks. I only did what anyone should have done," Rayden said firmly. Her voice lowered, taking on a compassionate lilt as she continued. "You have a great strength within you. After what you suffered and have been through, to walk with me to this city was proof of that. Allow Gnaeus and the others here to help you in the time to come. I know that you walk in a great darkness now, but do not turn away from seeking the return of light into your life. That is all I ask."

The young woman nodded, swollen, reddish eyes welling up with tears once again. Rayden placed her hand on the woman's shoulder and squeezed lightly, in a gesture of condolence and encouragement. She glanced towards Gnaeus one more time, and nodded.

Turning without another word, Rayden walked away from the priest and the young woman, the soles of her leather boots scuffing against the stone flooring of the temple. In her heart, she knew it would be a long, hard road ahead for the young woman, but Rayden held confidence she would find her way back to a sense of life again, and resolved to return to the temple and see how she was doing before too much time had passed.

For now there were mundane needs to attend, and options to consider. Dusk spread across the city, and Rayden's stomach ached from a lack of sustenance.

It would take a lengthy walk, but she knew of one place

that she trusted to fix that dilemma. Picking up her stride, she set out for the other side of Careth Athes.

* * *

Stepping out of the young night, Rayden felt a host of eyes upon her the moment she entered the tavern. It almost made her smirk, as it echoed nearly every visit she made to such an establishment.

The sight of a tall female northerner, especially one so well-armed, was anything but a common encounter for the men of the tavern. That she was attractive only added to the attention given to her by male patrons whose inhibitions had been loosened considerably with ale.

Rayden ignored their attentions as she worked her way through the common room. Finding a seat along a back wall with an angle that afforded her a fair view of the entrance, she finally allowed herself to rest. One of the tavern's young serving women approached her a few moments later.

"Welcome," the tavern maid greeted. Clad in a long tunic of an earthen hue, she had long brown hair, rather plain features, and a lean figure. "We have boar tonight, if you'll be eating. Just hunted."

"That sounds good to my ears," Rayden replied. "Ale

and a plate of the boar it will be."

The young woman nodded, and began to turn, then hesitated abruptly. She looked back, and Rayden could see the nervousness in her face.

"Are you … a warrior?" the tavern maid asked.

"Yes," Rayden answered, matter-of-factly. She then added, with a hint of bemusement. "Surely you've seen a warrior or two within the city walls before."

"What land are you from? Your skin is so pale," she asked. Before Rayden had a chance to reply, the serving maid shook her head, looking suddenly embarrassed, "I'm sorry, I'm bothering you too much. I was just curious."

"It is okay," Rayden reassured the anxious woman. "I am from lands far to the north, a place of great fjords, majestic mountains, and very cold winters."

She chuckled amiably, thinking of how far away she was from the lands of her birth. The smile faded; as it seemed impossibly far at the present.

"I have never met a northerner, before now," the tavern maid replied.

"Then it is my pleasure and honor to be the first," Rayden responded, with a resurgent grin.

The young woman smiled warmly, her expression showing a trace of relief, as if she had expected a less friendly response. "Thank you … I'd best get you some fresh ale and your meal. The meat is truly excellent."

"I'm looking forward to it," Rayden replied, watching the young woman head away through the congested throng.

For the most part, the crowd in the tavern was of the normal variety. Most were locals, mixed with some travelers like Rayden.

Some of the patrons interacted in small groups, and others were loners like herself. The air was filled with bawdy jests, bouts of singing lacking sorely of any sense of harmony, loud belches, and all of the usual sounds that accompanied a spirited tavern crowd.

It was not long before Rayden's meal and ale arrived, the scents wafting off the former causing her mouth to water. The tavern maid proved to be accurate in her assessment of the boar meat, which was undeniably succulent.

The meat was accompanied with some type of vegetables, and Rayden wasted no time in filling her belly. After the leanness of an extended journey overland, it was good to get a respite from hunting and foraging.

As she ate, her attention was drawn increasingly towards a burly, foul-mouthed man nearby as he harassed the tavern maids, groping at them and making lewd remarks. She'd seen his type before and they always rendered her temper dangerously short.

The current instance was no exception.

He reached out and grabbed the young woman who had served Rayden, snaking his arm about her waist. The serving maid had a full cup of ale in one hand, and some of the contents went splashing down into the man's face, soaking his beard and the front of his dirt-stained tunic as he pulled her into him.

"You filthy slut, you poured ale on me!" he snapped angrily, frothy beer dripping from his beard as he held onto her forcefully.

"I … I'm sorry! I … it was an accident," she protested meekly, with a look of panic as she struggled futilely to get out of his grasp.

"You dirty, ugly wench!" he roared, standing up and smacking her across the face with his open palm. The blow landed hard enough that her nose was bloodied instantly. The drinking vessel flew from her hands to shatter into pieces on the hard-packed dirt floor. "It's what happens when you pour ale on me, you wench!"

He sat back down and took a drink of his ale as the young woman began crying. Tears ran down her cheeks as she bent to start picking up the pieces of the shattered drinking vessel.

The girl flinched when Rayden's hands entered her field sight, the northern warrior joining the tavern maid in the cleanup effort. Seeing Rayden at her side, the tavern maid's startled expression eased.

"Are you going to be alright?" Rayden asked her gently.

Looking up, blood trickling from her nose and eyes brimming with tears, the young woman nodded. "Yes. I'll be fine. This happens at times, but it always hurts to go through it."

"This shouldn't happen. Ever." Rayden responded firmly.

She ignored the boorish man behind her, as he interrupted, "Don't help that wench! She needs to learn her lesson! Let her clean it up alone!"

"Lessons," Rayden murmured, a familiar feeling building inside. She handed all the pieces of the broken pottery she'd collected over to the tavern maiden. Her tone grew harder and the compassionate look in her eyes cooled. "Do not thank me yet. I am not finished here."

Rising to her feet, Rayden turned slowly to face the half-drunk man seated behind her.

"So, you like to hit women?" Rayden asked in a low voice, blue eyes glittering with the energy she felt building within. Blood surged in her veins, raising the alertness of her senses, anger coiled within her heart.

"What of it? The scrawny bitch spilled ale on me," the thick-bearded man replied with a toothy, cocksure smile. "Why do you ask? Do you want a smack too? So what are you goin' to do about it, girlie? Tell me!"

"Well, for one thing, let's see what you think when a woman hits you," Rayden hissed.

Drunk, he was in no condition to even try evading the fist that hammered flush into his jaw. Further, if he were sober, her cat-like quickness was like nothing he had ever experienced.

Teeth went flying as his head jerked violently to the right. Blood oozed from his mouth as his head slumped, chin coming to rest on his ale-damp chest.

Rayden calmly left the unconscious brute behind and walked back over to her plate. Sitting down, she resumed her meal.

The number of lascivious stares cast her way dropped precipitously. Not one man near her showed any inclination to meet her icy gaze. She also noticed a sharp improvement in the way the tavern maids were treated when they came through again.

Lessons had been learned.

When Rayden finished, she slipped the tavern maid an

extra silver coin as the young woman came to collect the empty plate. "This is for the trouble."

She nodded towards the man she had knocked out, who looked to be fast asleep. He would not be getting up anytime soon, and would probably have to be dragged out of the common room.

At first the woman began to protest, but one look from Rayden stilled the objection on her lips. "I pay for any mess I create, and I know he'll be a headache to handle when he awakes. Do not attend to him yourself."

"I won't," the young woman replied. A smile came to her face a moment later "And thank you. Thank you for what you did there."

"No need to thank me, I *enjoy* giving such lessons," Rayden said, her lips turning up in a grin. There was no denying it felt good meting out well-deserved consequences.

Very good.

Having had enough of the tavern, Rayden got to her feet and made her way through the crowded room towards the front door. It had grown more congested inside since she'd arrived. She had to elbow and shoulder her way through.

Rayden paused as she felt a firm squeeze on her butt. Not all lessons had been learned, evidently. Turning, she smiled at the heavily drunk, skinny transgressor with a long nose and narrow face, occupying a spot on a bench she was edging past.

"Warmmmm my beddd tonnnnight," he slurred, swaying where he sat.

"Many would say you have great courage, to do what you just did," she said, keeping the smile fixed upon her face.

A slack-jawed grin spread on his face in response. He replied, "I goooo affftter … wwhat I waantt. Warmmm myyyy beddd."

"No, I rather think I'll warm your face instead," she said, leveling a hard fist to his jaw that toppled him from his seat. He remained inert for a long moment before showing signs of movement.

She looked at his companions, who all looked stunned, and grinned amiably. "Your friend will be fine. Looks like he kept all his teeth unlike the other one. Did you think a woman like me would just give him a slap?" They stared at her wordlessly. "That should help him with his manners. Anyone else need a lesson here? I would be glad to help."

The man's companions shook their heads with dumbfounded expressions. Without another word, she continued on her way out of the common room.

A few people lingered outside the tavern entrance.

Rayden inhaled a long, deep draught of the cool night. The taste of the air was exquisite after breathing the thick, musky air inside the tavern.

While she enjoyed ale, food, and good company, she suspected she would have been giving more lessons had she stayed any longer. As the patrons drank more, and their bravado increased, a few would have sought to make her a companion for the night.

A man would have been an enjoyable diversion, but none were worth her attention in the entire place. So few could measure up to what she wanted that unless she was fairly certain of the man a dalliance wasn't anything she was inclined to pursue. Only a very few could evoke the storm of heat and consummate release of tension that made a night's affair satisfactory.

Starting down the shadow-draped street, she decided to forego getting space at an inn, as the food and lessons she'd meted out had her wide awake. There was one individual in the city who she could count on to not be asleep and have some answers for her. Rayden turned her mind from physical needs and wants towards matters of the near future.

Looking up, she espied the tall structures of the King's quarters looming ahead. Quickening her step, she started for the cluster of palace buildings.

ALL THE LANDS, NOWHERE A HOME

* * *

"Here you are with your beloved scrolls," she said, with the trace of a grin. "In all of this blighted land, you are one of the few who is still happy with his circumstances."

The slender man in the long brown tunic smiled, dark, alert eyes perched above his long nose. "I serve a less-powerful king, but a king nonetheless," Archimenes replied. "So what brings you to our fine city, Rayden? The last time we spoke you said you were heading back north."

"Plans changed," Rayden said, the edge of a frown emerging. Memories of deafening howling filled her mind for a few heartbeats, and though the chamber was warm her skin recalled the icy touch of a night she wished she could forget. "I will go back north when it is time."

"And now? What will you be doing here?" Archimenes said quickly, clearly sensing her rapid change in mood.

"I've been a mercenary before, I've been a guardian, and I've been a pirate when I had to be," she replied, the hint of a smile returning. "I suppose I adapt well enough."

"Indeed you do," he replied, with a tone of admiration.

"The only thing I never desire to be is a queen," Rayden stated. "The open road and an unbound will are all that I need."

"There are none who could bind your will," Archimenes said.

"Dark sorceries are spreading in this age," Rayden said grimly.

"A plight most unfortunate."

He paused for a few moments, slightly protruding eyes looking upon her quietly. She did not miss the hint of pity within his gaze.

"Rayden Valkyrie travels all the lands and calls none of them home," he said gently, a glint of sorrow in his eyes. "How can her friend Archimenes be of help, as she passes through this kingdom?"

The sagely man truly cared about her. Though he would struggle to lift a sword, he touched her heart more profoundly than many brave men who'd battled at her side. Rayden called precious few individuals in the world friends. Archimenes was one of that select number.

"I thought you might know of something where my abilities could be put to good use," she said. "You know me well enough, and you know how I despise being idle."

He opened his mouth, and then closed it. It was as if he had a thought, and then another had stopped him from speaking the first aloud.

"What were you going to say, Archimenes?" Rayden

said coyly. "Don't try to fool me. I know you very well, and have snatched you from harm more than a few times."

He nodded rapidly. "Yes, yes you have, and you will always have my appreciation, affection, and friendship. It is just that … "

A pensive look crossed his face as he hesitated. He looked away, obviously bothered deeply by something.

"Archimenes?" she said, with a light chuckle. "Will I have to hold you over a cliff edge by your ankles, or will we just be friends?"

Of course, she would never have done such a thing, and she knew Archimenes was aware of that. Yet it was disturbing to see her friend so plainly agitated.

"The king is sending warriors to confront a matter to the north and east," Archimenes stated. "It is important enough he brought back his greatest warrior, Briatus, from warding the northern borders."

"What is this matter?" she asked. She'd heard of Briatus, and no idle matter would involve the summoning of such a renowned warrior.

"I believe it is part of something much greater," Archimenes replied, frowning and shaking his head ruefully. "The last war has left so many voids, and darkness is swiftly creeping into them. Word comes of a cult, led by one steeped in mysteries of the netherworld."

"The last war left so many lands in ruin, it is not much of a surprise," Rayden said.

It had been a titanic clash of empires, with no real victor. An ocean of blood had been spilled, such that entire cities had been abandoned and left to ruin in the aftermath.

The remnants of the empires were still picking up whatever pieces they could as unprecedented, new dangers sprouted everywhere one looked. Rayden did not doubt that the cult Archimenes spoke of was yet another manifestation of the demonic elements taking root in the fertile soil of strife, disease, and famine. Yet as long as iron could bite into it and draw blood, she had no aversions to confronting anything out there.

"This cult is worrisome," Archimenes said. "It is a blood cult, there is no doubt about that. Many have been taken from outlying villages in lands the King still tries to protect."

"I am always agreeable to giving such a cult all the blood they want, provided it is their own," Rayden replied, an iron-hard edge in her voice.

"It is not the cult that worries me, Rayden," Archimenes said. "The lands to the north of us are treacherous. No sane person treads there. It is steeped in shadow and already claws at our own borders."

"Is this group sent by the king to go into that land?" Rayden asked.

"No, Briatus and the others will pass by it," Archimenes said.

"Then what are you worried about?" Rayden asked.

"I have long suspected that there is something with its eyes upon us," Archimenes said. "I cannot prove it yet, but my instincts are right far more often than not. Briatus is a golden prize to anything with designs upon the remaining kingdom. Best if that prize does not grow in value with the addition of another who could defend the kingdom."

Archimenes held her gaze for an extended moment. Rayden could see where he was going with his logic, and why he'd been so hesitant to tell her about the mission.

She looked over the parchments with all of their words that appeared like so many strange marking to her eyes. Rayden had never been taught to read, but it did not mean she could not appreciate the gift humans possessed in being able to store their words in such a way.

Archimenes was a warrior of the mind, and the massive collection of writings were one of his weapons. His knowledge girded the insights he held regarding the things happening in the world. His instincts were not blind. Rather, they were well-informed.

Rayden knew that both kinds of warriors, of the mind and of iron, were important in resisting the new rising crop of adversaries in the world. Yet just as Archimenes had to heed his instincts, so did she.

"This darkness can grow only if those willing to fight it restrain their actions," Rayden stated.

"I know what your choice is going to be," Archimenes sighed. The look he gave her was one of resignation. "And I know I cannot sway your mind. I will see to it that you have a place on the galley."

* * *

The salty taste of the air and the breezes whipping in from the sea always invigorated her spirit. Gazing out towards the sun-brushed waves as they rolled towards the land, her eyes drank in the magnificence of the ocean.

The galley was just underway on its journey to the north. A contingent of warriors had arrived at the very last moment, before departure, and Rayden kept to herself as they settled in.

She looked away from the open waters and appraised the newcomers. The men had a tough, hardened look about them, and she did not doubt they were all warriors of considerable skill. Yet they were wolves compared to the bear her eyes quickly fixed upon.

She stood quietly in place as an impressive figure walked the length of the galley towards her. At over six feet in height, she was tall, but the man striding along the deck towered over her.

"Rayden Valkyrie, well-met," the huge man greeted amiably, extending his forearm to her without hesitation. "I am called Briatus. Word came to me that you would be joining us for this voyage. You are most welcome with us."

She clasped his forearm with a firm grip, looking him straight in the eyes as she replied, "Well-met, Briatus. And yes, I chose to join you in your task."

A few light scars ornamented his face, and his nose had signs of being broken before. A broad forehead was made a little larger by the receding line of brown hair, flecked with a few strands of gray. His dark eyes were set deep, and carried the piercing, hard gaze of a man well-inured to combat and strife.

If the tales of him were true, he was not a man given to cruelties or excessive arrogance. He was said to be the kind of man well-loved by those he led into battle.

"I am honored that you would join us," he said. "Word of your deeds travel far in our lands."

"We both live in this world, and our enemies are the same," she replied.

Briatus nodded. "This is true, but I cannot tell you the nature of the enemies we now go to confront."

"Then we will discover it together, and make them taste sharp iron," Rayden responded.

Briatus grinned. "We are going to get along very well, Rayden Valkyrie."

"That is my intention," Rayden said.

"Good … as it is mine … later, we shall speak further," Briatus said. "I must beg leave of you now, to go see the captain of this galley about a few matters."

"I look forward to speaking again with you soon," Rayden said.

"As do I with you," Briatus said, before turning and starting back down the decking of the galley.

* * *

There were a few lustful glances and desirous stares cast her way during the ensuing hours, but the men on the ship were wise enough to go no farther than that. Most were amiable enough, and a few, like Briatus, had heard of her exploits before. None of the latter showed any desire to provoke her.

ALL THE LANDS, NOWHERE A HOME

Banks of oars dipped into the sea and pulled through the water in a strong, rhythmic unison. The creaking of timber and ropes accompanied the voices of men laboring on the vessel as it plied the waters just off the coastline.

Rayden took up a place at the bow of the galley, which lifted and fell with the movements of the water. No sickness came over her, as it sometimes did for those who did not often travel often by sea.

Her balance was acclimating quickly enough. Her body remembered the days she had journeyed and fought aboard galleys enduring much rougher waters.

She rested her hands on the edge of the rail, staring out towards the unbound sea. The horizon appeared endless, and some said that if one traveled far enough they would fall right off the edge of the world.

A part of her wanted to explore the farther reaches of the ocean, to see for herself what the truth of it all was. Death came to everyone, but life could only be grasped by those who dared.

"What is on your mind, Rayden Valkyrie?" the voice of Briatus interrupted. The huge warrior settled at her right side, leaning his muscular forearms on the top strake.

"Taking in the endless sea," she replied, glancing at him for a moment.

"Better than the view from the other side," Briatus replied with a grin.

A barren landscape stretched into the distance from the shoreline. It was the territory Archimenes had shown deep concern about, when she had spoken with him.

"It is good we are passing it," Briatus commented, after a few more moments transpired.

"You'll find no argument from me," Rayden said.

"Something awakens there … something even the likes of you and I want no part of," Briatus stated, in a somber tone.

Rayden turned her head and eyed the coast. The sight of it evoked a grim expression on her face. Whatever human souls still occupied that land were the hardiest of her own kind, or were in league with abominations.

There was no denying the harsh reality spread before her. It was a vision of unfettered corruption, engulfed in ruin and decay as deepening shadows filled the countryside.

"What awakens?" Rayden asked. "I would know what you think."

"You and I both know that unspeakable things haunt the ruins of the lost cities, and prey upon the unwary and the foolish," Briatus said. His eyes lowered to meet her own. "We have both faced our share of the wicked things stalking this world. This is something much more. Something I fear will sweep towards our kingdom soon."

"A sorcerer? A demon?" she queried.

"I do not yet know, but my time along the borders, before I was summoned to take this vessel, was enough to instill wariness," Briatus said. "Entire outposts slaughtered, messengers and scouting parties vanishing. Something reaches forth from the darkness, and it is purpose driven."

"No sign of the nature of the attacker?" Rayden questioned him, her brow furrowing.

"The warriors had been torn apart ... and worse," Briatus said, his voice lowering, and countenance darkening.

"And this cult we go to confront, you think it is related?" Rayden asked, sensing a similar vibe in Briatus to the one she had perceived in Archimenes.

The big man nodded. "I fear it is ... in some way we have not fathomed yet."

"Perhaps we will gain answers on this voyage," Rayden said.

"That is my hope," Briatus replied evenly. "Enough good men have been lost along the border."

Rayden nodded, and said nothing. The look she conveyed in her eyes to Briatus extended the solidarity she intended as the two warriors shared the silence.

* * *

Late in the day, shouts filled the air as chilly winds whipped about the lengthy vessel. Rayden stared in wonderment towards the east as dark clouds pulsing with lightning rolled steadily towards the galley.

Rayden could hear the panic and urgency in the galley captain's voice, as he announced at the top of his lungs, "It is far too dangerous to land here. We have to press north! With all haste! Put all your strength into the oars! We must keep ahead of that stormfront!"

Her stomach churned as surging waves rocked the vessel, reminding her and all aboard of their ultimate futility against the raw power of the sea. The drum of the oar master beat faster, as every shred of strength and stamina left in the rowers was applied to the oars.

Howling winds sounded hungry for human prey, and Rayden's unease deepened as the waves grew further in size and strength. The situation was one she loathed, where she could do nothing to affect her plight. At the mercy of the seas, winds, durability of the vessel, and skill of its crew, she could only wait it out, and hope to survive the ordeal.

At last, the bow of the vessel turned towards the shoreline. It was not much longer before the cry went out for all who could to assist to help with the landing.

Rayden, Briatus, and the other warriors joined the galley's crew as they struggled to beach the vessel. Thunder cracked violently overhead, as rivulets of lightning flashed against the evening sky.

The rain lashed their faces as they strained to move the vessel ashore. After considerable effort, the galley was finally lodged onto the sands.

Though the smell was anything but pleasant, the rower's area of the vessel proved to be the best place to take shelter and wait out the pounding storm. Biding the time, Rayden pulled her cloak tighter, and peered out one of the oar ports. In a haphazard fashion, flashes of lightning brilliantly illuminated the land to the west.

From what she could tell, they had put in to shore near the edge of a forest. The trees looked blackened and bereft of foliage, victims of a greater corruption.

"We will be out of here, as soon as this storm passes," Briatus said, sitting down next to her.

"This is no natural storm," Rayden said, looking to Briatus.

In the shadowy hold, she could see the big man nod his head in agreement. "No dark art can keep a storm going forever."

"The galley seems in good enough condition," Rayden said.

"It has taken no significant damage," Briatus said. "When morning comes we will set out again, if the skies are cleared. Best if all of us get some rest while we can."

"I will heed your advice," Rayden replied. "We will need our strength tomorrow."

"At least we will stay dry," Briatus replied. He nodded to her "Till the sun rises, Rayden." He moved a few paces away, to find enough space for his large body to stretch out fully.

Rayden watched him for a moment, before curling up on the hard wood. Inured to the kinds of discomfort that would bother most individuals, she soon fell asleep.

* * *

A motley chorus of grunting, squealing, and snorting awoke Rayden from her slumber. Instantly she was alert, her instincts attuned to the unmistakable sounds of boars.

She had many encounters with such creatures in her past. Rayden knew them to be formidable beasts, no matter what their size. She'd contended with some true giants of their kind in the north, but a modest-sized sow protecting her young or a provoked herd was nothing to take lightly.

Hurrying to the upper deck and looking over the side, her eyes widened in amazement. A swarm of four-legged brutes surrounded the vessel, digging into the wood of the galley with their tusks.

In the daylight, she could see they were creatures who belonged in the dismal forest sprawling just beyond. Their skin was mottled, devoid of fur, and riddled with strange, lumpy growths. The hideous creatures were nothing like the boars she had hunted and come across during her years traveling a great many lands.

Their forms carried a skeletal aspect, mottled skin pulled tight against their bones so they had a starved, emaciated appearance. More than one of the beasts peered up at her, their narrowing snouts adorned with the vicious-looking tusks they used to tear apart the galley. The sight of a human above them spurred a frenzied response from those immediately below. They pressed against the side and tore vigorously at the timber.

Rayden and the others aboard the vessel realized the relentless creatures would soon collapse the galley. Sooner or later, whether in the galley or on the land, the herd of boars would have to be fought through.

Everyone who had hunted or encountered boars voiced

their views on what should be done. The consensus was that if the warriors and galley crew could keep together, it was not likely that boars would assault a large group.

Rayden had misgivings about the idea, as there was something very different about the boars surrounding the vessel. Boars could be aggressive, but the creatures below were behaving in a highly unusual manner.

All considerations were rendered moot as the galley lurched violently to one side. Some of the lower strakes were gouged and weakened enough to collapse. Shouts, grunts, and squeals filled the air, with several men thrown into the mass of boars while a few of the latter were crushed under the toppled galley.

A few precious moments were gained as a large number of the boars scattered from the galley as it pitched over. Rayden, Briatus, and many of the crew and warriors jumped to the sand, weapons in hand.

Rayden's suspicions about the beasts were realized as the mass of boars surged forward, despite a wall of humans standing shoulder to shoulder brandishing weapons. If anything, a frenzied state came over the boars, now that their quarry was within reach.

"Fight them, and press forward!" Briatus shouted above the din.

Screams abounded as tusks capable of digging through wood tore through flesh and sinew. Iron began drawing blood from the attackers, and casualties mounted on both sides.

Hearing squeals behind her, Rayden cast a quick glance and saw that several boars now flanked the human warriors, and were curling around to come at their backs.

"Behind! Watch your backs!" she shouted.

The line splintered as the boars attacked from the front and rear. Men fell to the sand screaming as sharp tusks crippled them, ripping through their lower legs. Once on the ground, they were swarmed, enduring gruesome deaths as they were gored and eviscerated.

"Forward!" Briatus shouted again, exhorting the warriors and crewmen.

"Cut through them up front, I'll ward the back!" Rayden shouted, splitting the skull of a boar with her short-hafted axe.

Rayden slashed and hacked, moving away from the ship with a condensed group of warriors, fending off any creature that tried charging at them from behind. Briatus carved a path in front with his sword, loosing war cries and eliciting sharp squeals where his iron cleaved boar flesh.

The other warriors stabbed and slashed with their own

weapons, some aiding Rayden and others Briatus. Bolstered by the two living furies warding their front and back, they fought much harder than the other clusters of men left on the beach.

The boars exacted a grisly toll, as the remaining pockets of humans were worn down and overwhelmed; save for one. Five of the men from the galley, Briatus, and Rayden finally made it to the end of the beach, and entered the trees together.

"The bastards have more than enough to occupy them," Briatus stated grimly, casting a glance over his shoulder.

With both of her weapons covered thickly with blood and grime, Rayden looked back but kept moving. The mass of boars had been whittled down considerably in the fighting. Perhaps a dozen of the sickly creatures were left, and Rayden was confident her group of survivors could resist the boars if they pursued.

"So where do we go now?" one of the other men asked.

"There," Briatus stated.

Rayden turned her head and looked forward. Briatus was pointing a little to the right, and upward.

Through the barren limbs of the trees was an unexpected sight. In the distance, atop a large hill, a walled temple structure beckoned with the promise of shelter.

"Let us make haste," she said.

The group picked up their pace, heading towards the hill at a brisk stride. The absence of foliage enabled the warriors to see for a fair distance through the trees, but it also meant that anything lurking within the grim environment could see them. Nevertheless, Rayden preferred to see a threat coming over a close ambush made possible by dense underbrush.

The forest had the sickly-sweet scent of death and decay all through it. Slimy, fungal growths crept up the trunks of the trees.

The only signs of life were occasional things that skittered or slithered along the forest floor, deftly evading Rayden's eyes as they took refuge in the layer of moldy debris carpeting much of the ground. The soft loam made for treacherous footing, something of concern to Rayden if the group came under a new attack.

It was a dead place, and Rayden did not want to be in it a moment longer than she had to. Once or twice, she had the feeling of being watched, but never detected a source for the sensations.

Shortly, they reached the base of the hill. The front gates were wide open, and there was no sign of anyone around. Like Briatus, she kept her weapons out and in her hands as they started up the long slope. Once at the top, the group entered the gateway cautiously.

The outer walls still seemed strong enough, though, like the main structure inside, they showed signs of decay. Rayden guessed the place had already been quite old when it had been abandoned.

The ravages of weather and time had begun to take their toll on the place, cracking stone and leaving openings for wisps of grass to fill. A series of wide steps led to a large temple structure, whose roof was supported by a series of broad columns.

Inside the sanctum, they discovered that part of the roof had caved in, but most of the interior was still intact. A giant statue of an austere-looking woman rose up at the far end of the chamber, a spear was gripped in her right hand, and a scroll in her left. Strength was emphasized in the statue's form, reflected in the firm jaw line and shapely muscle tone of the religious sculpture.

"Ariathan," Rayden whispered reverently.

She did not believe that such a goddess actually existed, but she embraced the qualities of the noble deity. A warrior whose martial fervor was matched with a sagely wisdom, Ariathan was seen as a protector and councilor among the pantheon of gods followed in the region.

There were moments when Rayden wished the goddess did walk the world. In a time of plague and suffering, a divine benefactor would be most welcome.

"Her cult was once strong," Briatus remarked, eyeing the statue. "When our kingdom was an empire, at the height of its power."

"Perhaps more should embrace her once again," Rayden said, still gazing upon the image of the goddess.

"If Ariathan had daughters, like some of the gods did, I can see you being one of them," Briatus said with a grin.

She smiled. "Believe me, if I were the daughter of a goddess I would have done something to get us out of this cursed land long ago."

"And made a feast of those pigs," Briatus responded, with a chuckle. He shook his head. "I must not think of that, as our bellies will go empty tonight."

"Not sure I would want to eat the flesh of one of those decrepit things," Rayden said, thinking of the diseased appearance of the savage beasts.

"No, they did not look appetizing," Briatus agreed. "But we will have to forage or hunt soon, and we cannot go long without water."

"I would caution against drinking anything from a stream or pool in this land," Rayden said. "We can hope for rain, perhaps."

"I fear you are right there as well," Briatus said. "The forest had a fell look about it."

"This whole land is corrupted," Rayden said. "Deeply corrupted."

"We will not stay in it any longer than we have to," Briatus said. "But one night's rest should do us well, and this looks as good a place as any."

The group proceeded to search the temple and grounds within the walls, to make sure they were indeed alone. There was no sign of any inhabitants whatsoever, even wild beasts. Briatus and Rayden alike deemed the place suitable for the night.

It was decided that everyone in the group keep to the temple sanctum, and especially keep clear of the open gateway. It was not worth risking unfriendly eyes seeing signs of them from a distance.

Following the search, the watches were decided for the night. Three of the men took the first watch, Briatus and Rayden had the second, and the last two men in the party would take the third.

Conversation was minimal during the last hours of daylight, each member of the warriors left to their own thoughts. Shadows spread and filled the temple site as the light dimmed with the setting sun. A chill rose in the air, and gusts of wind howled outside, but there were no disturbances to cause concern among Rayden and the other warriors. Even if a storm came, like the one that had driven them ashore, they were well-sheltered within the stone-built temple.

* * *

Eyeing Briatus as he settled down for the night a few paces away, Rayden felt a brief tug of temptation. A deeper, more primal element within called to her in the dark silence. Without a doubt Briatus was the sort of man she deemed worthy of laying with, and if they were not lost in the middle of an ill-fated land she would have allowed the warm tingles of attraction to take further root.

As it was, every last bit of strength had to be reserved for survival. There was no telling what they would face in this hostile land. Even so, a smile graced her lips as she gazed upon his muscular form. If they made it back safely, perhaps Rayden would see if his lovemaking skills measured up to the rest of his attributes. She suspected the brawny man was capable of unleashing an inferno from within her.

With three of the men taking the first watch, she let

herself drift into slumber with pleasant thoughts gliding through her mind. It was a necessary relief to take a few moments to think of things other than blood and death.

Rayden had barely gotten to sleep and into the realm of dreams when an inhuman cry pierced the stillness.

Quickly on her feet with weapons in hand, she looked towards Briatus, who stood with his blade at the ready.

The grating cry sounded again, this time from a little closer. It had a strange quality, the like of which she'd never heard before.

Her gut clenched at the shredded cry that broke out a few moments later. Terror interwoven with a delirious level of pain was conveyed in the shrill, choppy, human outcry that went abruptly silent as Briatus and Rayden reached the entrance to the temple's main sanctuary.

The two warriors peered carefully around the edge of the opening. Behind them, the remaining two men from the galley, who had not been on the first watch, gripped their spears nervously.

Outside, Rayden could see no sign of the three men who had been on watch. The area before the temple building held no traces of movement, so still that the flicker of a shadow, from something approaching from the right, drew her attention immediately.

The moonlight cast the long shadow of a thing that did not belong in the world of men and women.

Rayden's breath stilled in her chest as a creature out of some diabolical nightmare stepped into the open ground.

The thing was long of limb, with shaggy, grayish fur hanging from its legs and arms. The latter extended significantly in a way that, in comparison to the body of a human, was extremely disproportionate. Lengthy talons curved from the six digits adorning the end of each arm and leg.

The face of the creature protruded slightly, with a huge maw situated beneath two holes that took the place of a nose. Its eyes were broad pools of darkness, and at first glance Rayden had difficulty telling if they were hollow or not. To each side of its head stout, upward curving horns narrowed to sharp points.

A rattling growl erupted from its throat as its lips pulled back, unsheathing wicked fangs that glistened in the moonlight. Crouching and bracing elongated forelimbs upon its knuckles, its attention snapped forward, reacting to something ahead of it.

With a burst of speed that astonished Rayden in its sheer swiftness, the creature sprang and raced towards the open gate. Disappearing from sight, the intent of the creature was revealed moments later as another outbreak of terrified screams shattered the night.

A series of movements on the peripheral edge of her vision brought Rayden's eyes around to see one of their companions running from cover. His face was a mask of fright, and no sooner had he started for the temple than the beast reappeared in the gateway.

The man never reached the bottom step.

The beast sprinted across the ground and overtook the hapless man in a few heartbeats, engulfing its victim in a frenzy of slashing talons and flesh-stripping fangs.

The beast's head jerked up, its eyes fixed upon the entryway. Blood and gory bits of flesh dripped from its demonic visage as it stared towards the place where Rayden and the others crouched.

Launching itself up the steps, the creature was inside the temple quickly. It turned, hurling itself at the four humans with a screeching cry.

It drove a set of claws deep into the stomach of one of the remaining warriors under Briatus. Pierced with the equivalent of six daggers at once, the warrior gasped and gurgled as the beast ripped its claws upward with incredible strength.

The second warrior tried to run out of the way, but

was fatally mauled from behind as the creature lunged from where it gutted his comrade. The dying man went down to his knees and pitched forward, leaving Rayden and Briatus facing the creature by themselves.

Up close, Rayden could fully appreciate the creature's staggering height. It was well over a head taller than Briatus, easily seven and a half feet tall.

Larger, stronger, and faster than its two remaining opponents, the creature held almost every conceivable advantage. Yet, as Rayden had learned a long time ago, battles were not always decided on the physical attributes of the combatants.

Seeking to put it on the defensive, Rayden attacked high and low using both axe and sword blade. The creature's reflexes measured up to its speed and strength and only her blade nicked its leathery hide.

Her strikes enabled Briatus to unleash his own attack before the creature could counter hers. His blade sliced the air, wielded with great speed, skill, and power. Only the best of human warriors could have weathered the iron storm the big warrior loosed, but this was no ordinary opponent.

The beast dodged the sharp iron blade and brought its right claws rushing in under the attack. Briatus tried jumping back, but the tips raked his left side, tearing through his tunic with ease and drawing blood from six newly-inflicted wounds.

Rayden launched into a flurry of blows with her axe and sword. Evading one strike from the beast as its claws whooshed by the skin of her right cheek, she did not anticipate the thing instantly whipping the back of its claws through the same arcing path.

She caught the flat, heavy impact from the backside of the thing's claws flush against the side of her face. Spun from the tremendous power behind the blow, she hit the temple wall hard and went down.

"Hey! Come on, big boy! Let's see what you have!" Briatus' voice thundered within the sanctum. "Over here! Just you and me! Come and get me!"

The creature, poised to fall upon its dazed quarry, paused at the brazen interruption. It whirled, showing no concern for Rayden, who had trouble regaining her feet from the lingering grogginess.

The beast's roar filled the chamber as it started towards Briatus. It took slower, purposeful strides, and gazed upon the human like it savored the thoughts of what it intended to do to the defiant man.

Drawing the beast farther from Rayden, Briatus backed slowly towards the statue of Ariathan. The talons of the beast scraped against the stone surface, as if whetting blades for the carving of human flesh.

Shaking her head and blinking her eyes, Rayden struggled to clear the fog from her mind. With nothing blocking the path to the entrance, a golden chance to escape the temple beckoned from nearby; but that was not the kind of woman or warrior that Rayden was.

"Come on, you ugly bastard," Briatus grinned, a wild, fiery look dancing in his eyes. It was the expression of a warrior embracing his end, facing an insurmountable foe without wavering. His next words carried a sense of urgency, and were intended for the ears of his fellow warrior. "Get out of here Rayden! The king needs to know about this ugly bastard! Go! I'll keep it busy!"

His words found no acceptance with Rayden. There was no way she was abandoning a comrade in such peril, even if he was right about the need to alert the king.

Finding her balance and gaining better clarity, she gripped the hafts of her weapons with a stronger command of her faculties. Before her, the creature screeched as it looked down into Briatus' face, exposing a jagged arsenal of blood-soaked teeth.

Her instincts told her it was finished toying with Briatus, and that its final assault on him was imminent. She had to act immediately or leave Briatus to a gruesome fate.

Her footfalls made no sound as she nimbly crossed the stone surface. When she was halfway to the beast and Briatus, she attacked.

Rearing back, she put all of her strength into the throw of the axe in her right hand. Releasing the weapon with the kind of precision honed through years of training and battles, Rayden sent it racing end over end towards the beast. The axe head gleamed coldly in the moonlight as it crossed the space left open to the sky.

The blade buried solidly into the midpoint of the dense black mane running from the creature's head and down the length of its spine. The beast threw its head back, arching its body and loosing a hideous shriek.

Rayden's attack gave Briatus the slim opening he desperately needed. Pouncing on the disruption, he drove his blade deep into the gut of the thing. Enraged, the creature lashed out, grabbing Briatus' arms, lifting him off the ground with the warrior's sword still stuck far within its belly.

Rayden had resumed her approach following the axe throw, and she reached the combatants just as Briatus' feet were dangling in the air. Sword in her right hand, she slashed with all her might at the back of the monstrosity's right knee. The blow struck true, cutting through ligaments, muscle, and bone to sever its leg completely.

Instantly off balance, the beast lurched awkwardly to the right, releasing its grip upon Briatus and toppling to the ground. Grunting with the impact, the big man went sprawling after falling heavily upon the temple's unforgiving surface.

The creature clawed and scrabbled furiously to turn and face the last of the humans. It gnashed its teeth and filled the sanctum with a grating, shrill cry of raw fury infused with agony. In a balanced fighting stance, she looked for an opening to strike at the maimed beast.

A jagged chunk of rock smashed into the face of the creature, eliciting a breathy grunt and spraying some of the thing's blood outward. A quick glance told Rayden that Briatus had taken up a piece of rubble from the part of the roof that had collapsed, and launched the fist-sized projectile at the beast.

A groan accompanied Briatus as he staggered forward with another chunk, the second one large enough that even his exceptional strength barely sufficed to handle it. The veins on his neck ran taut and his face reddened as he took one step after another, drawing closer to the beast. With a loud shout, he heaved the wide segment of rock in a short arc that sent it falling atop the thing's back.

The creature flailed and erupted with all manner of hideous sounds. Teeth gnashing amid its bloodied face, sorely hampered in its movements, the rock temporarily pinned it down.

Rayden saw her chance and rushed in, swinging her blade powerfully. A long set of talons attached to nearly half an arm went flying free in the aftermath.

Unable to defend itself effectively, and losing blood fast, the beast could not ward off the torrent of blows Rayden then levied. Again and again she hacked with her blade into the head of the beast. Not willing to take any chances with a monster that could endure axes to the middle of the back, blades in the gut, and severed limbs, she did not stop until its cranium was rendered into an unrecognizable mess.

Backing up, she breathed heavily and kept her eyes on the pulped front of the beast for any sign of survival. "Do you think that is enough?"

Briatus looked at her and smiled, wincing a little and favoring his wounded side. "Almost. May I borrow your blade? I'm not quite ready to take mine back."

Rayden nodded, and extended him the hilt of her weapon. He grasped it firmly, and walked over to the body of the beast.

Briatus set about cutting the creature's head off entirely. Its thick neck, giving the beast the appearance that it had no neck to begin with, proved difficult, requiring several hard blows to completely work through.

At last, Briatus cut it free. Stooping, he grabbed it by one of the horns, and turned towards Rayden.

"A little proof to take back," he stated, breathing heavily. "We both earned it."

She could hear the sincerity underlying his words, which evoked a grin from her. "I have to say that we do fight well together."

He chuckled and nodded. "Yes, we do. I'm just glad I have an answer to the mystery of what has been happening along the northern borders."

"You have?" she asked.

He nodded. "More than once I have come across marks left by six claws, though no creature of the wild living along the border areas leaves such. I kept that to myself. But *this* answers the question." He raised the head of the slain beast in emphasis.

"Then we will need to get back, and warn the king," Rayden said.

"We do have to get back," Briatus agreed, his expression growing somber.

"How about a few breaths of fresher air?" Rayden suggested. "We can take a look around."

"I hope there are no more of those things in this place," Briatus said.

"Best to have our weapons in hand, just in case," she replied, with a rueful smirk.

Rayden walked over to the headless corpse and pulled her axe free, greatly relieved that the rock had fallen a little higher up the creature's body. She then retrieved Briatus' blade, returning it to him and taking her own sword back.

The two battered warriors walked slowly together out of the temple, heading towards the gateway in the outer wall. A few moments later, they looked out from the high summit, which afforded them a spectacular view of the lands beyond.

Dread crawled up her spine as she took in the swift, dark movements among the trees below. Her ears received the faint, inhuman cries carried along the icy winds, of a distinctive kind that had sounded so recently within the temple sanctum behind her.

Spread across a large swathe of land, a veritable horde of the creatures swept through the lifeless trees.

The multitude of beasts flowed with purpose, not a single one of them tarrying as they streamed from the north.

ALL THE LANDS, NOWHERE A HOME

"Let us hope no more of them come to the temple," Briatus whispered.

Rayden nodded in response, continuing to watch the dismaying scene. It appeared the creatures were moving directly southward, and as her gaze moved from the left to the right, she estimated that many hundreds more moved through the land before the hill.

The two kept their uneasy vigil from the hilltop as the moon continued its trek across the night sky. After awhile, the waves of beasts slowed down to a trickle, and then no more could be seen anywhere the pair of warriors looked.

When the sun's light showered upon the land again, there had no sign of the macabre creatures for quite some time, much to Rayden's relief. Afforded the bounty of daylight, both she and Briatus took an extended period of time watching from the high vantage, just to be sure, before deciding to depart the temple grounds.

Just as they were about to walk away from the gateway and prepare to leave the walled compound, Rayden espied something to the east, out on the glittering ocean. "A galley! No ... two galleys!"

Two vessels were indeed out on the waters of the sea, and they were turning towards the shoreline. The galleys were heading right for the area of land where the heavily damaged vessel Rayden and Briatus arrived on had been beached and then abandoned.

Rayden could not see any movements around the inert galley. Perhaps the remaining few boars had moved onward after gorging themselves on the corpses of the fallen warriors and galley crew.

"Two galleys? Coming from the south, they should be ours," Briatus said, coming over to stand at her side.

"No sign of the herd of boars," Rayden said, keeping her gaze fixed towards the shore.

"They are coming to see what happened, or maybe look for survivors," Briatus said.

"Then let us show them that two did indeed survive this accursed land," Rayden said.

"Let me take up our treasure, and we'll go to them without delay," Briatus said. He turned back to where he had set the bulky head of the monster on the last temple step on his way out to the gateway with Rayden, where they had taken up the extended nocturnal surveillance of a land brimming with peril.

"Rayden!" he called, a moment later.

Hearing the alarm in his voice, she jogged over to Briatus and stared in amazement. There was no form left to the creature's remains. The very skin and bone of the thing was crumbling slowly in the morning light, as if being consumed by some invisible flame.

Looking to Briatus, she saw that his jaws were clenched tight. She would feel the frustration emanating from the brawny warrior.

"We have only our word to take back," he said heavily. "I had hoped to bring more proof."

"They will not doubt us," Rayden said evenly.

"This is no creature of this world," Briatus said. He then added curtly, as a breeze carried off more ash that had been part of the creature moments before, "Let us tarry not a moment more in this accursed place."

Though the night had been anything but restful, it was no time to conserve strength, and the two warriors set off at a brisk gait for the shoreline. Nothing interrupted their return, and by the time they stepped from the trees the beach was swarming with warriors.

Many recognized Briatus immediately as they emerged, and a cry went up among the men. Wasting no time, Briatus and Rayden searched out the galley captains and informed them of all that had happened.

Both captains were weathered, seasoned veterans of a great many voyages. Yet they could not hide the fear that shone in their eyes as Briatus described what he and Rayden had faced in the temple not long before.

The captains had been coming up the coast in order to bring additional warriors to Briatus, at the original destination intended by the king. It was swiftly agreed that the galleys needed to break away from that journey, and return with all haste to the kingdom. The importance of the mission they had been assigned was rendered miniscule in comparison to the warning they now had to conduct.

Before long the galleys were off the beach and rowing south, and Rayden once again found herself gazing out to sea. She did not want to look towards the land, knowing what was moving in the same direction as the galley.

The kingdom they had set out from was laboring to heal after many years of war, and it was about to find itself facing something far, far worse than the warriors of a foreign land. If the massive throng of horned monstrosities kept on their southward trek, it would only be a few days before they reached the northern borders of the Kingdom.

Rayden pushed the troublesome thoughts from her mind. There was little use in worrying about the inevitable. She had survived a hellish ordeal and had not suffered any significant wounds or injuries.

She looked away from the horizon and eyed Briatus at the far end of the galley talking with the captain. He caught

ALL THE LANDS, NOWHERE A HOME

her gaze and held it for several heartbeats before giving her a slow nod. It was the kind of look that conveyed respect and the acknowledgement of a profound, shared experience.

Rayden nodded in return, before looking back out to sea. There was no way of knowing what tomorrow would bring. The past day had been proof enough of that.

Left to her thoughts, a smile came to her lips as the winds caressed her face, buffeting her long blond tresses about. Her spirit was as strong as ever, and she had taken another successful step on a much greater journey.

At the end of each day, in a world where death could snatch the living away at any given moment, to know that she would be able to keep fighting onward was cause enough to celebrate. It meant that Rayden would have yet another chance to find that elusive place she could call her home; and bring a journey of many long, wearisome years to an end at last.

Stephen Zimmer is an award-winning author and filmmaker, whose literary works include the epic-scale urban fantasy series The Rising Dawn Saga, *the epic fantasy* Fires in Eden Series, *and the Harvey and Solomon steampunk tales.*

The Exodus Gate, *Book One of the Rising Dawn Saga,*

was Stephen's debut novel. It was released in the spring of 2009, with The Storm Guardians following in 2010, and The Seventh Throne in August of 2011.

Crown of Vengeance, Book One of the Fires in Eden Series, was released in the fall of 2009, with Book Two, Dream of Legends, following in December of 2010, and Spirit of Fire in June of 2012. Crown of Vengeance received a 2010 Pluto Award for Best Novel in Small Press.

Stephen's short fiction includes the Harvey and Solomon steampunk stories included in the Dreams of Steam and Dreams of Steam II: Bolts and Brass anthologies from Kerlak Publishing.

As a filmmaker, Stephen's film credits include the supernatural thriller feature Shadows Light, the horror short film The Sirens, and the recent Swordbearer, a medieval fantasy short film based upon the H. David Blalock novel Ascendant.

THE WITCH OF RYMAL PASS

J.S. VETER

Roderick sat on a stone with his naked cutlass across his knees. It was a far cry from when she'd last seen him. Then, he'd been naked and she'd been the one with the sword.

It wasn't easy from her current position, but she made careful eye contact with him. It couldn't hurt, she reasoned, for her to remind him just who had had the upper hand the last time they'd met.

Or perhaps it could. Roddy jerked his head and the soldier holding her pushed her face even further into the mud. This was not a normal position for her -- face-down and ass-up -- but she liked to think of herself as adaptable, so she grunted and concentrated on bleeding as quietly as possible.

"Where did you find it?" Roddy asked the captain who'd brought her in. He removed his red-plumed helm and handed it to a subaltern.

"Sniffing around the perimeter," the captain answered. "Said she was one of Sally's girls, but I know all the whores and she ain't one of them."

Roddy used his cutlass to push the hair from her face. She risked another look at him. He was angry, right enough, but she caught a glimmer of unease, too.

Good.

The blade's tip slid slowly past her ear to the heartbeat pulsing in her neck. It rested there, twisting casually

"Hello, Themis," Roddy said. The pressure against her neck increased ever so slightly.

"Hey, Roddy," she said hoarsely. Blood trickled from her mouth. "What a pleasant surprise." She gasped as the skin of her throat parted beneath the edge of the cutlass.

"Wish I could say the same," Roddy said.

She had been in tight situations before and this had a similar feel. Blood dripped off Themis' chin into the mud. At least, she thought, Roddy's sword was properly sharp. Him being such a powerful big man, he should be able to remove her head without much trouble at all. She could *feel* him considering it, another link in a chain that bound them. The blade twisted again and then, thank the bastard gods, the sword was removed.

"Get her up." The soldier hauled her upright and stood

THE WITCH OF RYMAL PASS

her on legs reluctant to hold her. Her sight darkened and she sagged pathetically. Roddy back-handed her, snapping her head back to hit the armoured chest of the soldier. "You pass out I'll kill you right here," Roddy promised.

"Okay," she agreed thickly and tried to keep her head at an appropriately alert angle.

"You searched her?" Roddy demanded. His face was dark with anger. It was that chain again, the first link forged the gods knew how long ago, the heaviest links forged when Alain was killed and Roddy had chosen rebellion over revenge.

"Aye, sir," the captain said. He had scratch marks on his face, three deep and bloody gashes. He was lucky. She had wanted to be captured. Roddy knew it and the fear of it clouded his thinking.

"Hold her. I said hold her!" The soldier grabbed Themis' hair, the captain her bound hands, one boot trapping the chains that bound her feet. Roddy plunged his hand down her blouse and fished around. It didn't take long. She took after her mother's side of the family, unfortunately, but the captain had already found the small knife she hid there. Then Roddy pulled up her skirt.

"We got the rondel," the captain said, but it was not her legs Roddy was interested in. He jammed his hand up none to gently and probed her with his fingers.

"Spread them," he said. She did as she was told. Roddy pushed two fingers inside her and pulled out the metal vial. He opened it and dumped the small switchblade into his hand. "Pussy's got teeth," he said. The soldier hissed in what Themis decided was surprised admiration. Roddy displayed neither. His gold had paid for that blade, after all. A wedding gift, he'd called it.

Bastard gods, he thought. Beneath the blood, bruises and mud Themis looked exactly the same.

"Where the hell have you been?" Roddy demanded. The fire behind him popped. The captain's hand spasmed on the grip of his sword but Roddy doubted any of them could stop her if Themis chose to move. The first time Roddy'd set eyes on her she'd been a ten-year-old slip of a girl gone berserk. She'd killed four of his men and wounded three others before he'd gotten through to her, and the only wound she bore was the one she'd inflicted upon herself.

"Doldarran," Themis muttered. "Across the sands to al Mancuu. Assassination is legal there, did you know? Made a fortune. You should have come." Her eyes were losing focus, her voice growing distant. The soldier shook her awake. "Good times," she said.

"I should have you executed for desertion."

THE WITCH OF RYMAL PASS

Themis actually laughed, though it was a shadow of the one he remembered. "From what?" she said. "An army of corpses? That's not desertion, Roddy. That's just common sense."

"So why come back at all? One last battle for old times' sake? You looking for a reward?"

Themis snorted. "I already told him why I was here," she said, meaning the captain. Her left eye had swollen completely shut and her breath came in short bursts as if it pained her. "The Prince wants a parlay."

"Gods, Themis," Roddy said. "You're no monarchist, and you're sure as hell no messenger. You expect me to believe that?"

She shrugged. "No," she said. "But your men slaughter anyone who approaches your lines. You're within a week of the city walls and His Excremence is piddling on his throne." She drew in another shaky breath. "It was thought I might get through, and I needed the gold."

Roddy looked at her as if, for a moment, she was no one he knew. "Emiliano bought you? He hung your father from the walls, Themis, or are you so far gone you can't remember the sound of his screams?" Her expression didn't change, though the red puddle at her feet continued to grow. Roddy frowned, then stepped back, decision made. "Get her out of my sight," he said. "Lock her up under guard but leave her shackled. No one is to go near her. If any one of the men so much as touches her he'll be executed a traitor."

The soldier seized her bound wrists in one hand, her neck in the other. "Move," he grunted, and hauled her away.

"A lot of history there, sir," the captain observed. "Is she being honest about the parlay, do you think?"

"Possibly," Roddy answered, "but there will be no parlay and she knows it. The Prince is outnumbered, the city is weak and he's lost the support of the Wise. Tomorrow is just a formality."

"So she did it just for the gold, then?"

Roddy hesitated, shook his head. "No, but she'd not turn it down. She's here for a reason. She wants something."

"You make it sound like she meant to be caught."

"She did," Roddy said.

"Sir, are you joking? She fought like a crazed cat. Have you seen what she did to my face?"

Roddy looked closely at the captain. "You're lucky," he said. "You know who that is? That's the Witch of Rymal Pass."

The captain's mouth fell open. "You're sure? How do you know?"

"Because I married her," Roddy said. "I promise you,

she's here for a reason, and we'll have to hope she tells us what it is before my men start dying."

He returned to his tent and his maps, leaving the captain to thank the gods that he had drawn steel on the Witch, and survived.

Themis did her best to hold herself upright. It was tricky given that her eyesight had the unsettling desire to want some down-time right when it would have been useful. Her ears were working perfectly, however, though all they told her was that these soldiers had imaginations no more varied or innovative than any others.

"Promises, promises, boys," she called out.

The soldier released his hold on her neck long enough to cuff her sharply across the head. "Shut it," he said, "or I'll give you something to keep your mouth real busy." He probably wasn't kidding, she thought, and as Roddy trusted him to be alone with her, she guessed his idea of busy would be different from the enlisted men's.

"Smiley!" a voice said. "You brought me a gift!" The new voice sounded Tevalyan, though his accent had levelled. Career soldier, Themis thought, well-travelled. Perhaps even educated.

"Not this one, Garion" the soldier said. "Commander

wants her kept secure and untouched. A traitor's death is the price."

"Then I've the perfect place for her." The Tevalyan swung open the heavy iron door of one of the prisoner wagons, which had been empty since Roddy had ransomed Duchess Taintor. The soldier shoved Themis forward and she fell blindly toward the waggon. "In you go," the Tevalyan said and gave her a push, hand up under her skirt, fingers squeezing the muscled flesh of her ass.

Themis rolled onto her side. The Tevalyan's hand grazed the wound on her leg, making her gasp. It got truly dark for a moment and she missed most of his appreciation. When her vision cleared, she pulled her feet up, panting with pain, and realized she'd lost a boot somewhere. The door swung shut. There was the black hiss of iron sliding against iron, the deep strike on the lock, the slip and kiss of the key. She listened to the men's discussion: details of her capture, the Commander's reaction and her switchblade, which caused much excitement and would probably be the star of many a wet dream by dawn.

"There's a lot of blood," the Tevalyan said. "We should wake the surgeon."

Bastard gods, no, Themis prayed.

"Commander said no one touches her," the soldier

THE WITCH OF RYMAL PASS

said. "He meant no one."

"That wound's going to bleed out," the Tevalyan said. "What will he do when she dies on us?"

"By the looks of him when he set eyes on her, sir," the soldier responded, "he'll probably pin a medal on us."

Themis gave silent thanks to all who follow orders to the letter. She was the last person to slander an educated man, but give her an herb woman or midwife any day over the tender mercies of an army surgeon.

Her struggle with the captain (though she wouldn't have called it that, she'd practically given herself to him) and Roddy's attention had left her with some lovely new souvenirs. The healing had yet to begin, but it was building slowly, like heat in a kiln. It had been a long time since she'd been hurt this badly so it would take a while for the flames to get hot. There had been a time in her life when she could hardly tell the difference between the one kind of pain and the other. She had a feeling it was going to be like that again soon, but tried not to get excited.

Disappointment was such a bitch.

She managed to get to her knees, and from there to a sitting position her governess, had she ever had one, would have been proud of. Her left eye was gummed shut with blood and gods knew what else. Roddy's cutlass had added a new scar to her collection. One rib was broken and her woman's parts were sore, but that's what you got for angering a man in front of his army. Her left thigh missed the strap of her rondel, but the right was a real mess. The captain's knife had dug deep, and while a girl could count on a man to keep his sword pristine, she could never be too sure where his dagger had been.

It was the thigh wound that was going to kill her, and soon, too.

"Anytime, now," Themis muttered. She felt distant, numb, separated from the world. It was the best she'd felt in years.

But it began: a flower of pain blossoming in her skull. She bit down on her tongue to hold the scream in, but even as the blood flowed fresh from her mouth, her tongue was healed. Again and again she bit down, but the flames of healing could not be damped once they started. In her chest, the broken rib knit in an instant, the rough edges scraping lung tissue which tore and healed instantly. The parted muscles of her thigh reached out, caught hold and pulled themselves together again. Skin, new and pink and raw, bubbled over the wound and sealed it shut. She blinked. Scabs and tears poured from her left eye, the bruising absorbed and erased. Her sight cleared and the healing wave

THE WITCH OF RYMAL PASS

subsided. She was lying on her side with nothing but the memory of the pain.

After a long moment, that too was taken from her.

"Leave me that," Themis hissed, but the goddess, as usual, only ever listened when it suited her.

Themis wiggled through her arms so her bound hands were in front of her and removed the second metal vial (the men of the south were such prudes that it never occurred to them that a woman has more than one hole. Themis would *never* have gotten away with it in Doldarran or al Mancuu). She slid the small metal pick from the vial and within seconds, the heavy iron fetters were off.

A moth, silvered by the newly risen moon, flapped through the bars of the door and landed on her bare foot. She shooed it off, but it remained. Themis reached for it and froze. Something had stirred, something fraught and weighted. The pale rectangle of light on the bare oak boards echoed a pattern she had seen somewhere recently.

Next there was going to be a sound, a cough or perhaps a laugh. Its ambiguity would strike her as odd, and she would mark it. She heard it then, coming from the depths of the camp as she knew she would.

The moth lazed past. Themis' fingers shot out and she crushed it in her fingers, the meaning of whatever it was she'd felt evaporating as it died.

This was not the first time she'd felt like she knew what was going to come next. If this was the goddess' hand on her, then it was bloody useless. What Themis really needed to know was when Red's patrol would be returning. Roddy might almost believe Themis had come to request parlay, but Red wouldn't. Red would know exactly why she'd returned after all this time and have her head separated from her shoulders the instant he saw she was shackled, a pretty impressive show of strength for a man who'd been dead for seven years.

Themis found herself rocking on her knees, repeating over and over her prayer to the goddess. She was massaging moth guts between her fingers and didn't know why. In her head, a wheel spun ponderously. Close. So close. The goddess' hand was sure and steady, had practically burned with eagerness when Themis was shoved into the mud at Roddy's feet. It had taken a real effort not to kill him, but Themis had learned nothing if not patience since Rymal Pass.

Tonight.

Tonight Alain's shade would stop its howling

* * *

THE WITCH OF RYMAL PASS

"You." The Tevalyan was back and he'd brought a soldier with a crossbow. The soldier had acrossbow armed and pointed at Themis. "Away from the door."

Themis shuffled back, remembering where she was, remembering that she was a woman and injured. Crossbow eyed her warily; rumours were obviously on the move. His fingers tightened on the trigger as the Tevalyan approached the door and shoved a water bladder through the bars. Themis didn't move. Crossbow looked way too twitchy.

Water safely delivered, the Tevalyan relaxed. Themis could see it in the angle of his shoulders under the boiled-leather armour. The Tevalyan must have been following Roddy for a few years. He wore his hair in untidy locks, Lat-fashion. He also smelled better than men usually do. This was also Lat-fashion, and one which Themis hoped fervently would catch on further south.

"Is it true, what they're saying about you?" the Tevalyan said.

Themis shrugged, "What are they saying?"

Crossbow hissed at the Tevalyan to be silent, but Roddy had only said no touching so the Tevalyan ignored him.

"That it was you did Rymal Pass."

"That was a long time ago," Themis said quietly. She glanced at Crossbow and picked up the bladder. The water was clean and cold, and a kindness. She'd remember that, when it was time.

"So it was you, then?" The Tevalyan had a gleam about him now, as if he was about to learn some great truth.

Themis nodded.

"Holy mother," the Tevalyan hissed through his teeth. Then he punched Crossbow in the arm, a move which made Themis flinch and duck. The weapon wavered only slightly. "It *is* her, see? I told you! She did Rymal Pass!" Then, he saw the fetters on the floor of the wagon. His eyes widened and he backed up a step. Two. Three. "Holy mother," he said again, and Themis saw in him a man who thought this might be his last night on earth.

Crossbow backed up too, weapon still locked and loaded though he was wondering if he could react quickly enough if he needed to. Themis raised the bladder and saluted them with it.

Cowards.

***

Rymal Pass.

No great army followed Roddy in those days. There was only Themis, Red, Alain and a handful of mercenaries who'd

THE WITCH OF RYMAL PASS

burned more bridges than they owned. Some unwashed robbers had taken to attacking the post train between Brekka and Great Sky, and for a while His Lardness -- Jinh Massa, Earl Rotdam by the grace of His Majesty Prince Emiliano Suram Magnificat Tevalya -- had tolerated the attacks as little more than an annoyance. But with the drought the previous summer and the long, cold winter that followed it, the attacks had become more audacious. When the very person of Lady Ellena was assaulted, the Earl was compelled to do more. Late that winter, three different platoons were sent to Rymal Pass, and when news came that the soldiers had been killed, or (worse) had turned coat and joined the damned thieves, the Earl had turned to Tevalya for help. From the capital, the order had trickled down to Roddy, who was kicking his heels in Somersgate due to a protracted case of nerves on the part of His Magnificence the Prince.

There's nothing a prince wants more than a talented general.

There's nothing that scares him more, either.

Roddy was told a small group of bandits occupied Rymal Pass, a pass too narrow for more than one coach to travel at a time. The Pass was an insignificant piece of property as using the main road only added a day's travel between the Earl's lands in Brekkia and the Skyan lowlands.

However, Rymal Pass had paid its tithe two centuries ago when the Earl's ancestor had used it to quell the Pineaen invasions from the north. It was the Earl's proud family history being held for ransom and he wanted it sorted. So Roddy, Themis, Red, Alain and a platoon of boys in royal green found themselves on horseback in the high Brekkian hills at the tag end of a disappointing spring, arrows cocked and ready. For dinner, mind. Not robbers.

Roddy said they attacked at nightfall, but in Themis' memory it was red dawn chasing the soldiers down onto them. Red dawn and a tide of blood as their arrows found the unprotected joints of two of Roddy's men. The attackers were fast, already in place as if Roddy's approach had been known in advance. Themis let her arrow fly into the treed banks above the pass, banks which the Prince's man had said were too steep to be any use for hiding men. Themis sent another arrow into the trees, which were suddenly alive with soldiers.

Soldiers, Themis noted with a thread of dismay, not unwashed herdsmen starving in the barren hills, but soldiers trained and armed. Her third arrow sprang from the eye socket of a man only paces from her horse. Themis threw down her bow and grabbed the first thing that came to her hand, and just as she shaped the thought that they'd

THE WITCH OF RYMAL PASS

ridden into a trap, she was fighting for her life against a man wielding a double-edged sword weighing as much as she did.

Themis was brutally fast. As the blade came down she rolled off her horse. The blade took the horse in the flank, the poor beast screaming as it fell, thrashing in panic and blood. Then Themis was on her feet, finding that the weapon she'd grabbed was her dagger, damn the gods. The soldier actually grinned when he saw its puny length, but he had no idea what he was up against. The truth was, he never stood a chance.

Themis didn't understand why she could do what she did. She'd stopped trying to understand. When the gods mark you for something, Alain had said once, it's best not to question.

As the man's blade came at her again, time slowed. His moves became so greatly exaggerated it was as if Themis could read his intentions before he knew them himself. It was like an embrace, the way she fell into him, dagger coming up to lick him across the throat. His blood burned her and she danced away, drawing her sword now, hamstringing the soldier who besieged Alain, thrusting her dagger left-handed into the surprised face of a soldier too young to be breeched, and then flinging herself into the mass of men surrounding the Roddy, Red and the rest of their vastly inexperienced militia.

Dawn or dusk, when it was over three of the militia were dead, two by arrows and one by blade at the beginning of the attack.

"Bastard gods, Themis!" Roddy bellowed, "You've left us not a one to question!" He began snapping orders at the militia, sending two of them back down the road with messages for the Earl and the Prince's man at Brekk Castle.

Themis sank to one knee, feeling the goddess' flames. Alain had called the flames a gift, said Themis was blessed, but he'd never known the exquisite pain of flesh forced to heal with such speed.

Blessing or not, Themis kept it hidden from Roddy and Red. Only Alain knew of it, from the day Themis, six-years-old, had cut herself with one of their father's throwing knives. The wound had been deep and nasty, mysteriously exposing what ought to be secret. The flames had come quick and hot. Alain had held onto her throughout the healing; his eyes took on the quest for the divine.

Alain attended the wounded in Rymal Pass and Themis, flames ebbing, turned to the bloodied corpses of the men she had killed. She burrowed into their patched and mismatched uniforms, but coins told her little except

THE WITCH OF RYMAL PASS

that the men were paid. Traders and soldiers carried bits from all over the Known and she found nothing to tell her whose men these were. Their weapons were worn with use but of good quality and well-cared-for. Kits held whetstones and cups and spoons, but nothing of note. A few scraps of vellum, much scraped and of poor quality, and then this: a square of new parchment covered with a slanted hand and bearing a half-scored mark she could not read.

The soldier she had taken it from bore a plain insignia over his shoulder the others did not. His face told her little, except that he was a southerner. He wore an expression of surprise, as if he still could not believe he was dead. Themis took the parchment to Alain so he could interpret the scribbling. Red was on the other side of the killing field. His sword was drawn, but one look at Themis was enough to tell her they were all dead. All of them. Again. Red gave her that shrug of his and went up into the trees, looking for clues. Roddy was drawing his horse farther from the carnage, a huge beast of a stallion he loved more than his own life. He snapped at another of the militia: gather the horses, prepare to mount up.

"Here," Themis told Alain, handing him the parchment on her way to Roddy.

"Help Alain," Roddy told her, "while Red and I track

back to their camp. If anyone else jumps you, keep your damned blade in its scabbard. I need someone to question."

"It was a trap," Themis said.

"I don't know that?" Roddy said. "Trained soldiers, no insignia, good steel? Of course it was a trap."

"The Earl or the Prince?"

"Rotdam's not got the guts." Roddy spat blood, rubbed his jaw. "The Prince, of course, but I have nothing to prove it. You've made a fucking mess of this, woman."

"I know."

Roddy reached out for her, touched the line of her jaw then let his hand drop. "Mind you, I do love how you dance." But he was looking past her, as if he'd seen something.

Themis looked back at Alain. His Wise's robes were speckled with darkening blood and the parchment was falling from his hand. He was staring past Themis, at Roddy. He opened his mouth to say something, but Themis never heard his last words.

There was a punch, as if all the breath had been sucked from the world and then the sorcery flared. Bright, bright it was, as if the sky itself were aflame. Then, an impact sent Themis flying, tumbling head over heels and over the side of the road, down thirty feet through scrub and rocks until she landed in a heap at the bottom of the scree.

THE WITCH OF RYMAL PASS

Broken leg, broken collarbone, but for once the goddess got it right and Themis pulled herself back towards the road, where Roddy was dangling from the roots of a tree protruding from the embankment. He was out cold. He wouldn't remember Themis heaving him back to the road where she found that the horses and all the men had been torn apart in the blast.

Red.

Alain.

His Wise's robes were shredded and scattered over most of the road. There was nothing left of him. With the flames of the goddess still supporting her limbs, Themis knelt in the midst of the gore, searching for anything, anything at all, that she might recognize as her brother. The blood on the ground was cooling quickly, congealing against the skin of her palms. It was as if every life she had taken had been paid for in one sorcerous blast. The wound which opened in her now was going to take a lot more than flames to heal.

"Sorcery," Themis muttered. Why? But the answer was in her own flesh, in the hand of the goddess which lay cold and unforgiving on her soul. Roddy had not been the Prince's target.

Themis had been.

Alain.

Themis closed her eyes, lips shaping a prayer.

I'll do it, you bitch. I'll serve you, do whatever you ask, so long as you put Alain's murderer on the tip of my sword.

When Roddy came to all he found in the tide of blood was Themis' footprints. Her path of revenge took her straight to the Prince's man at castle Brekk, then spiralled outward, an ever-increasing wake of death that finally petered out with Alain's death unanswered. Then Themis was gone from report, and, at last, from rumour.

Alain would have said that the gods work in mysterious ways. Themis would have told him he was full of it. But she'd been at her vengeance for seven years, and the end of it had been within her grasp that very first day.

* * *

Themis listened as midnight watch was called, a low whistle picked up and passed along the picket. The rumours running through the provinces these days weren't worth shit. Roddy's boys were no longer a rag-rag group of mercenaries out for a seasonal rape-and-pillage. Roddy had whipped them into impressive shape since leaving the prince's employ, turning them from soldiers of fortune into warriors. He'd even played tame to the Latland king , waiting until southern politics lined things up for him nice and neat. Roddy's departure from Latland, when it had come, had been so sudden that the king still thought his hired swords were out on manoeuvre.

Roddy marched into Ettenwolde eight weeks ago and Duke Taintor didn't know what had hit him. His hastily assembled men barely had time to buckle on their swords when Roddy's army swept through.. The rumours that the duke had locked himself in Gerent's Tower when the gates of the castle had given way were entirely false. The whey-faced duke had locked himself in his own privy rather than face Roderick, and that was exactly where Themis found him after Roddy's army pulled out.

Forcing the lock had been too easy, leaving Themis to think Roddy had liked the idea of leaving Taintor there. Themis had shown the duke the notice she'd pulled off the gate when she'd arrived, "Not the entire thing, just this mark *here."*

He'd been more than happy to read it for her, certain she would spare his life. He had been so certain, in fact, that Themis had time to recite all of Rutger's Ode to him before he understood he was not going to survive the damage her blade had done. Men like Taintor got her goat: lads ten-years-old had died defending his reeking carcass, and he had the nerve to call *her* unnatural? The privy was too good for him. Roddy had not changed at all, Themis thought as she listened to the watch change. The rhythms of this army were the same as every group of soldiers he'd commanded since he'd sworn for her father. Alain had been dead for a while now, but his advice was still good: it was time to move. The Tevalyan, piddling his britches in the presence of the Witch of Rymal Pass, had yet to ask himself how she had gotten herself free of her shackles, but he would soon. Themis picked the lock of the wagon and let herself out.

Her feet hit the ground and the guard opened his mouth to shout out a warning. Themis' hand flew forward, stiffened fingers catching him in the throat. He choked, stumbled and impaled himself on his own weapon. He died, eyes wide, wondering how his sword had jumped from his hand to hers. Themis had no explanation, but as she hoisted his carcass into the wagon and closed the door, she suggested he take it up with the goddess when she welcomed him.

"Then come back and illuminate me," she whispered, kicking off her remaining boot. She took up his swordand aimed herself straight as a drunken whore for the centre of the camp, where five tents marked the centre of command.

Themis had been following Roddy's army for a few weeks as they fought their way through Taintor's lands. The

THE WITCH OF RYMAL PASS

Duke had thrown everything he had at them, but Roddy's hits were hard and merciless. If the Prince had ever had any doubts about his former general's plans, they were long gone. Roddy would settle for nothing less than the full republic. The Prince's sons were already dead, and his nephews had not been heard from since they took ship out of Randmouth. The Prince knew he would be next. Roddy and his army were going straight for the capital and there was enough support for Roddy in the Council of the Wise that the Prince had no choice but to ride out and meet him.

Tomorrow. Tomorrow. The word went unsaid throughout the entire camp.

It had been Roddy's dream. Revolution, he'd called it, not rebellion. Alain had urged a political uprising, but Roddy only understood swords and slaughter. It was the only argument with Alain that Roddy had ever won: Alain had been murdered and the murderer had gone unpunished, and Roddy had promised to cut Themis to bits and post her remains to the nine borders of the Known if she deserted him.

Themis had always loved Roddy's way with words.

The Roddy she'd known despised tents. Roddy had preferred to do his business in the eyes of the gods. That way, he used to say, they couldn't claim to be shocked when it came time for them to ante up. Roddy's piety used to trouble her, but Themis had come to see he had a point. When it came to the gods, it was best to keep all cards on the table.

Themis staggered along, counting on the foolhardiness of men. Strictly speaking, women weren't allowed in the camp, but it was not unknown, especially on the eve of battle. Couplings were hurried and furtive, as if the men knew the eyes of the gods were on them. When Themis passed by they were not far wrong. Her goddess rode her, made her feet sure in the darkness, the sword light in her hands. Themis walked the path to his tent as if she'd walked it many times before, and she couldn't shake the feeling that somehow, sometime, she had.

That was how she knew the Tevalyan would recognize her at once.

Crossbow's bolt leapt at her from the darkness. It whirled as it came, barely missing the raised arm of the soldier who intended a warning. The bolt's trajectory would end right in the middle of her forehead. She admired the accuracy of the shot, even as she grabbed a man who'd just enjoyed groping her tits, thinking her just another camp whore. She thrust the man in front of her with one hand even as she flung her sword at Crossbow catching him in

THE WITCH OF RYMAL PASS

the unprotected hollow of his throat. The soldier never got his warning out. Themis plucked a dagger from the corpse dangling from her left hand and plunged it into the soldier's eye, pulling it back as he fell. Shaking grey matter from the tip, she dropped the corpse and met the short sword of the Tevalyan, pushed his weapon up and placed a knee in his groin. He paled, grunted, and her blade found his heart. A death quick and easy, kindness for kindness. The Tevalyan died with her name on his lips. Four dead. Two heartbeats.

Alain had said the ways of the gods could not be known, and even in her worst moments he had faith enough for them both. He'd been sure the goddess had something wonderful planned for Themis. He'd said that what she could do was a gift.

Themis left the bodies where they lay. She had two minutes left before the body she'd left in the wagon was found.

The next one died when he grabbed Themis' skirt and pulled back a hand sticky with blood. The heel of her hand shoved his palate into his sinuses. The soldier staggered back, hands up over what was left of his face. Themis' dagger silenced him before he could scream. He slumped on a pile of gear and she left him there, just another sack of provisions.

Alain had said the hand of the goddess guided her.

Some few of these men Themis had trained herself. Now their blood dripped from her hands, splattered her bare feet and ragged skirt. She knew what was said of her, what tales were had been tossed from Fellis to Southbridge. *Witch,* they called her, and *abomination* and *oath breaker.* Some cursed her, and that brought a bitter smile to the surface.

Go ahead. Try.

Another soldier gave way, flesh splitting like an overripe fruit. Then the horn sounded. Her guard had been found. There was a stunned silence from the camp and then the men were scrambling, the sound of their weapons a kind of music. Themis walked on. The hand of the goddess was on her; it burned like deep winter. It brought her no peace, but her hands flashed out now and then, killing three more who fell before they knew who she was.

Themis had been marked at birth. She felt the goddess, that impatient slut, pushing her, always pushing. Themis' feet, so certain, stumbled as if losing their way. She veered, shook the goddess off, went on with the curse of her purpose hanging about her neck.

Try!

She wanted to shout it, wanted the red tide to continue, wanted to bathe in blood until the heat of it warmed her

THE WITCH OF RYMAL PASS

through. Seven years she'd been gone, believing that Alain's murderer had died in the very sorcery he'd paid for. Seven years of slaughter and men, but none of the blood, none of the mindless screwing, washed Alain's blood away.

And none of it released her from her deal with the goddess.

The news of Roddy's leaving Latland had reached Themis in Aranople, where she had been negotiating the death price of a wife's lover. Roddy's march might not have moved Themis, but the news of who marched with him did.

Seven years wasted.

Try.

Themis was already cursed. Already lost, and the one person who had loved her in spite of what she was, was dead. *Alain.* Slain by sorcery, slain by a man she'd thought dead, who even now turned as she slit the canvas of his tent. His brigandine, unbuckled, still lay over his shoulders, his mat of red locks reached to his waist. Red's eyes barely flickered as she entered, and though his sword lay on the bed behind him, he did not make a move to pick it up. He'd seen her engage fifty Publican soldiers on the field at Marlbridge and emerge unscathed and laughing, dripping blood and gore. He'd sensed the death-cold hand on her soul. They hadn't set eyes on one another since the sorcerous attack at Rymal Pass and he'd convinced himself he'd imagined things. But seeing Themis standing there, blood-covered and not looking one day older than the last time he'd seen her, his memory was coming back.

Themis knew exactly what he was thinking. He was wondering if he should call for help, calculating how fast she could move, how many men besides him she would kill before sheer numbers -- *maybe* -- took her down. He made the only decision he could. When one of the men scratched at the tent, Red ordered him away.

"Themis," Red said. "How many times do we have to do this?"

Themis snorted uneasily. There was the feeling of slipping into something well-known, like the pantomimes the children put on at Midwinter. She shook it off. "Why, Red?" she asked. "I need to know. I called you my friend."

"It wasn't me."

The sorcery made sense, when Themis had thought about it. The kind of killer she was, no assassin could touch her, and no wound could hurt her. She'd tracked the sorcerer himself all the way to Doldarran. It had taken her over a year. Pathetic wastrel of a man, the sorcerer denied doing the ritual even as he shit out his life, smothered with her own tunic which she'd found in his rooms, stiff with the lamb's

THE WITCH OF RYMAL PASS

blood of the ritual and wrapped in strands of her own hair.

The thought suddenly disturbed her as it hadn't before. Not the dying, but the denying. The memory was on her, *hard,* the smell of blood and excrement and the pathetic struggles of the man, the weak, ugly snivelling of his shrunken little wife and the musical sound of the golden bangles on her wrist. When she came back to herself, Themis found she had her dagger pressed into the gap of Red's brigandine.

"Don't deny it," she hissed. "Your mark was on the parchment." The words echoed forward and back. She swore. Red smelled of horses and sweat. Red always smelled of horses and sweat when she came to him. There was enough pressure on the dagger to prick his skin through his under tunic. Her hand was twisted in his hair. She would not let him look away from her when she killed him. She wanted to see the spark of life fade when he finally died, and when she joined Alain at the end of things, she would pass the memory on to him as a gift.

"Themis, anyone could have put my name down." Red whispered. He had never shown fear before, and he didn't now. Blood blossomed through his tunic.

Truth was, Red was not that kind of killer. He preferred the sword and the intimacy of blood, but it had been Red's mother's wedding bangles that had paid for the spell. "You played dead," she said.

"I played for time," Red answered. "I thought it was the Prince, too. But he knows better than to use sorcery against the Wise."

Themis' hand shook. The feeling was both new and familiar, as if she had done this for the first time before.

"Think, woman," Red said. "Who benefited from that attack on us? From Alain's death?"

Themis had never thought of Alain's death in terms of benefit. That had been her brother's way of dealing with the world. And Red's. All Themis knew was the black hole in her soul and the deal she had made to fill it. It was a weight around her neck: deliver the murderer, and Themis would serve. The service had yet to begin and the goddess was out of patience. Her voice was an angry buzz at the back of Themis' head; Themis couldn't remember when she'd gone a minute without hearing it. One quick motion was all it would take and all would be silence. One thrust and the goddess could take control at last.

Who'd benefited? Not the Prince. He'd lost his children and tomorrow would lose his head. Red? He was exactly where he'd been at Rymal Pass, dogging Roddy on his quest for rebellion and republic.

A Republic – as if. That had been Alain's word, a

THE WITCH OF RYMAL PASS

word Roddy had laughed at and called a rebellion in pretty ribbons.

Themis was no monarchist, and Roddy was no republican.

Roddy.

Roddy.

Roddy had saved her, homed her, armed her, bedded her. In her head, the goddess pushed and pushed: *Get it right this time.*

"Enough," Themis whispered. She slipped the dagger through Red's ribs. It made a soft, sucking sound. His eyes widened only a little, as if the pain was not what he'd expected. She held Red as he staggered, fell with him, eyes never leaving his, legs straddling his torso, her hand holding the dagger in place as if she could hold onto this climax forever.

"Wrong again, Themis." At least that's what she thought he said as he died, but the cutlass erupting from her gut distracted her. She slumped over the blade, watching with fascination as it receded. The goddess was clamouring in her head now. Clearly, she'd annoyed her something awful.

A foot connected, kicked her off Red's corpse. Plain soldier's boots they were, worn and replaced many times.

Roddy had always hidden his ambitions in simple clothing.

He leaned over Themis, foot on her chest, slick cutlass against her throat. "Nicely done," he said, and although he was gloating, there was still the fear in his eyes. There needn't have been, Themis was bleeding out right then and there. The goddess had left her and the silence in her soul was wonderful. It felt like she could float away. "Yet again, your family has given the New Republic the heroes it needs: the martyr for the cause and the one who avenged his death. I'd forgotten how useful your impulses can be."

Themis cared nothing for his cause. She never had. She'd done what she came to do. She was free.

"Look at you," Roddy said. He was wiping his blade on Themis' skirt, "not so scary anymore. Turns out you do bleed like the rest of us."

The hands of the goddess were cold, but death's embrace was warm as blood. He came like a lover, death did. Themis held Alain's gift fresh in her mind. Roddy saw her smile and spat on her.

"You still think Red did it? Alain really did get all the brains, didn't he? He knew exactly who killed him, him *and* his damned revolution." He shouted for the men outside and barked orders. "Dress the general in his armour. We'll burn him at dawn; his pyre will light the birth of this so-called 'Republic'." Roddy picked up his helm and settled it on his head. The red horse-hair plume fell down his back as he left. "The crows can have the witch."

The red one, Duke Taintor said when Themis told him to read the mark she'd shown him. It was the same mark as was on the parchment that killed Alain; she had seen it here and there as Roddy's army moved south. *The red one.* The tent flap fell behind Roddy.

Who'd benefited? Whose cause would have fallen flat if not for an accusation of sorcery used against one of the Wise?

Somewhere, a circle was nearing completion, its arc about to close. Themis had no voice left. Her eyes had shut and her heart fluttered like an infant's born too soon. The soul fights on far longer than the body. Her gift for Alain was meaningless. She was going to him with nothing.

No.

The purpose Themis had been born for waited still; it towered like mountains in darkness. The goddess could not let it end like this, although she probably wished she'd never answered Themis' prayer at Rymal Pass. "**Say the words**", the goddess said, and her voice was like a gale in winter. "**Say the words.**"

Themis' lips moved. That no sound came out mattered not at all to the goddess. Prayer is spoken with the heart, not the lungs, *I'll do it, you bitch. I'll serve you, do whatever you ask, so long as you put Alain's murderer on the tip of my sword.*

"**Very well,**" the goddess said. Themis felt a wrenching dislocation. "**Try to get it right this time, will you?**"

Roderick sat on a stone with his naked cutlass across his knees. It was a far cry from when she'd last seen him. Then, he'd been naked and she'd been the one with the sword.

Jessica Veter graduated from the Centre for Medieval Studies at the University of Toronto before trying Japan and then England on for size. She returned to Canada with some strange vocabulary and an off-kilter accent which she's been hammering back into shape ever since. Weaned on science fiction and fantasy, Jessica writes more of the same in Flamborough, Ontario. You are welcome to visit her at www.jessicaveter.com.

TRANSCEND REALITY WITH SEVENTH STAR PRESS!

On the following pages we would like to introduce you to some of our titles featuring Sword and Sorcery, Post-Apocalyptic Fantasy, Epic Fantasy, YA Fantasy, and more!

To get more information on Seventh Star Press and our titles, please visit:

www.seventhstarpress.com

or connect with us at:
www.twitter.com/7thstarpress
www.facebook.com/seventhstarpress

SEVENTH STAR PRESS

Enter an ancient world of heroes, blood, and steel in the tales of Gorias La Gaul from Steven Shrewsbury! Hard-hitting Sword & Sorcery in the vein of Robert E. Howard.

Softcover ISBN: 9781937929800

eBook ISBN: 9781937929831

Softcover ISBN: 9780983108634

eBook ISBN: 9780983108641

Explore post-apocalyptic fantasy worlds in the Seventh Star Press anthology *The End Was Not the End*, from editor Joshua H. Leet!

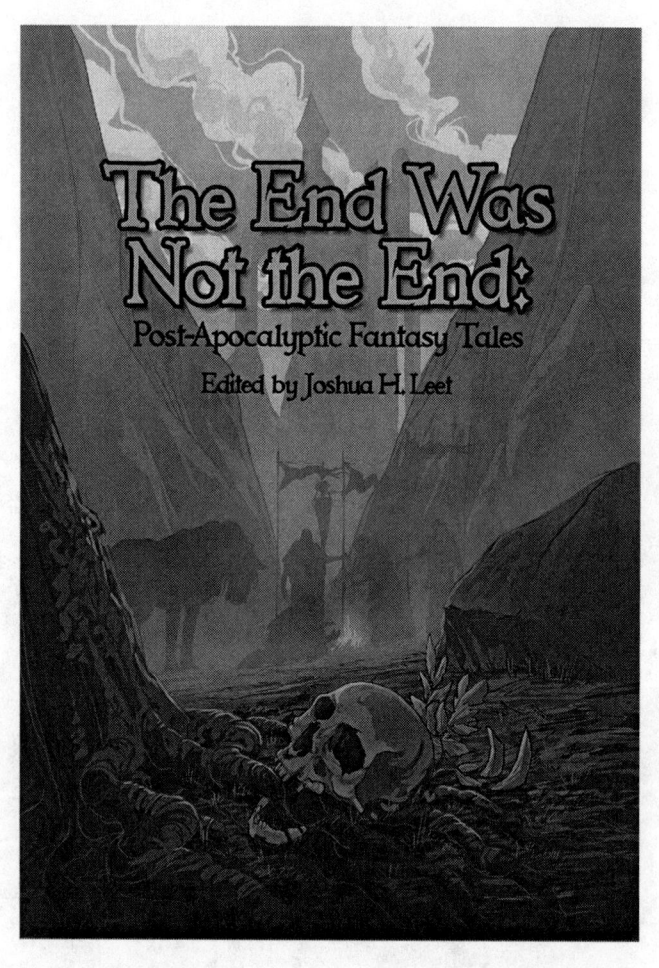

softcover ISBN: 978-1-937929-07-7
eBook ISBN: 978-1-937929-15-2

Explore the world of Ave in the Fires in Eden Series from Stephen Zimmer! Epic Fantasy for those who enjoy authors like George R.R. Martin, Steven Erikson, and Brandon Sanderson.

Softcover ISBN: 9780982565612

eBook ISBN: 9780982565698

Softcover ISBN: 9780983108627

eBook ISBN: 9780983108610

Softcover ISBN 9781937929855

eBook ISBN 9781937929862

Begin your journey into The Brotherhood of Dwarves, the popular YA Fantasy series from D.A. Adams. An action-filled saga where the dwarves are not just sidekicks!

Softcover ISBN: 9781937929916   Softcover ISBN: 9781937929923

eBook ISBN: 9781937929930   eBook ISBN: 9781937929-947

Softcover ISBN: 9780983740254   Softcover ISBN: 9781937929787

eBook ISBN: 9781937929909   eBook ISBN: 9781937929770

The highly-acclaimed Leland Dragon Series from Jackie Gamber! Strong character-driven YA Fantasy for those who enjoy authors such as Christopher Paolini.

Softcover ISBN: 9780983108672

eBook ISBN: 9780983108696

Softcover ISBN: 9781937929893

eBook ISBN: 9781937929817

A pair of single author collections now available from Seventh Star Press!

Explore several hard-hitting sword and sorcery tales of Gorias La Gaul in Steven Shrewsbury's Blood and Steel: Legends of La Gaul, Volume I.

Softcover: 978-1-937929-28-2
eBook: 978-1-937929-29-9

Have many action-driven fantasy adventures in the world of Ave in Stephen Zimmer's Chronicles of Ave, Volume 1.

Softcover: 978-1-937929-30-5
eBook: 978-1-937929-31-2